YAYO 4

Lock Down Publications and
Ca$h
Presents

YAYO 4

A Novel by *S. Allen*

YAYO 4

Lock Down Publications
P.O. Box 944
Stockbridge, Ga 30281

Copyright 2021 by S. Allen
YAYO 4

First Edition January 2021
Printed in the United States of America

Lock Down Publications
Like our page on Facebook: Lock Down Publications @
www.facebook.com/lockdownpublications.ldp
Cover design and layout by: **Dynasty Cover Me**
Book interior design by: **Shawn Walker**
Edited by: **Lashonda Johnson**

Stay Connected with Us!

Text **LOCKDOWN** to 22828 to stay up-to-date with new releases, sneak peaks, contests and more…

Thank you!

Submission Guideline.

Submit the first three chapters of your completed manuscript to ldpsubmissions@gmail.com, subject line: Your book's title. The manuscript must be in a .doc file and sent as an attachment. Document should be in Times New Roman, double spaced and in size 12 font. Also, provide your synopsis and full contact information. If sending multiple submissions, they must each be in a separate email.

Have a story but no way to send it electronically? You can still submit to LDP/Ca$h Presents. Send in the first three chapters, written or typed, of your completed manuscript to:

LDP: Submissions Dept
P.O. Box 944
Stockbridge, Ga 30281

DO NOT send original manuscript. Must be a duplicate.

Provide your synopsis and a cover letter containing your full contact information.

Thanks for considering LDP and Ca$h Presents.

Dedication

I dedicate this book to my beautiful mother, Karen Collins, for remaining loyal, supportive and staying down with the kid when everybody else jumped ship after the judge slammed the gavel, in attempts to destroy my life. I love you with all the air I breathe. By the time this book is published, I will be released from the belly of the beast and back into society to continue on my path of a prosocial, righteousness way of living, and feasting off the profits in the process. As you know, you will definitely be at the table...I love you, Ma.

Acknowledgments

Shout out to Cash and the rest of the Lockdown Publications Family. We at the top of the food chain when it comes to this book game and at the top we will remain.

To my haters, too many to name, keep doing what y'all doing. You only motivating me to keep dropping this gangster shit! In the words of Beanie Siegel...Your handshakes ain't matching y'all smiles...I am him!

Drill
-Street Definition-

Drill- To meet with extreme aggression. To kill or attempt to kill another human being despite consequence, moving with strategic acts of violence, resorting to the fatality of an individual or individuals!

S. ALLEN

Chapter 1

It was 1:35 pm when Yayo's plane landed at O'Hare Airport. It had been a pleasant ride for him. All the other times he had flown on a plane, he was being transferred from a different prison because of a disciplinary infraction. During these plane rides he was shackled from head to toe with a belly chain, making sure he wouldn't slip out of his cuffs as inmates were known to do. Now he sat looking out the window…free as a bird literally. No cuffs, no belly chains, leg irons or my other objects securing his body, he was finally free, and it was the best feeling he felt in a long time.

He had been handed a life sentence by the federal government and sent to serve his time in some of the most vicious prisons in the United States of America and encountered trials and tribulations that most men would have folded and perished under those conditions. Yayo had come in the federal system a wild young goon and now was leaving a grown man, with integrity and dignity, morals and principles.

Allah had blessed him, giving him another chance at life. Meeting Mr. B was that blessing…getting Yayo back in court on the bogus indictment, the government overturned the life sentence and gave him one hundred twenty months, which he only had to serve eight and a half years of and today, his sentence was up.

Yayo had made plans with Shakira to pick him up from the airport, and then drive him to the halfway house on Chicago Avenue and Christiana, on the city's west side. The feds had given him six hours to get to the halfway house. Yayo told Shakira to bring his daughter with her, but Shakira refused. She'd waited eight and a half years for her baby daddy to come home, and she needed some alone time with him. "You can see your daughter the next day," she told him, being selfish.

Yayo couldn't wait to feel the warmth of Shakira's body. He had missed her dearly and needed her body in the worst way. Walking through the tunnel and then into the airport lobby, he scanned the crowded sea of people, searching for Shakira. The only property he had with him was a brown manila envelope that contained his paperwork.

Shakira was on her cellphone talking to his mother Karen, when she spotted Yayo walking out of the tunnel. Her heart began to beat fast as she jumped up and ran toward him, almost screaming his name. Yayo heard his name and looked in that direction, only to see Shakira running toward him. A smile spread across his lips.

"Yaton, baby!" Shakira yelled, jumping into his strong arms. Yayo dropped his paperwork on the ground, now holding the mother of his child. The smell of her perfume was like heaven as he held her for dear life.

"Baby!" Shakira said through her tears, while she planted kisses all over his face, before sticking her tongue in his mouth. Yayo and Shakira kissed passionately in the middle of the airport lobby.

"Damn, what's up, wifey?" Yayo said, finally coming up for air and putting Shakira down, still holding her in his embrace.

"Oh my God, Yaton. I can't believe you are home, baby, this is like a dream."

Yayo pinched Shakira on her butt.

"Ouch, boy!" she said, rubbing her booty.

"Now you know this is not a dream, but very much a reality," Yayo smoothly replied.

"Baby, I'm so happy you are home…I have been waiting so long for this day to come…You just don't know." A tear fell from her eye, this time it wasn't a tear of pain and despair, but a tear of joy. Yayo wiped the tear from her cheek.

"Shakira, so have I…I have longed for you since the day the feds took me away from you and my family. There has not been a day or night my thoughts have not been consumed with you and Shamira. Matter fact, where is my baby at now?"

"She is at your grandmother's house, baby, let me call Honey real quick so you can FaceTime her. Oh shit, hold up! Hello, hold on, man… here he is right here," Shakira said into the phone before she passed it to Yayo…Yayo grabbed the phone.

"Hey, Ma!"

"Hello son, how does it feel to be a free man?"

"It feels great, Mom. When are you coming to the city? You are supposed to be here already," Yayo said, while he and Shakira made their way out the airport.

"I know, Yaton. Darrell had something going on at work and we missed our flight, but we'll will both be there this weekend. Do you need anything, son?" Karen asked.

"No, Mom, I'm good. I just need you here so I can see you."

"Well, don't worry about that, son. We will be there."

"Ok, Ma, listen… me and Shakira are leaving the airport now. I'm going to call you once I get to the halfway house."

"Well ok, son, I will be waiting for your call and Yaton?"

"Yes ma'am?"

"I love you and welcome home."

"I love you too, Mama."

After leaving O'Hare Airport, Yayo and Shakira headed back to Chicago. He sat in the comfort of the passenger seat of Shakira's Audi 8. The leather seat fit him like a glove as Beyoncé's "Cater to My Man" pumped through the speakers. He looked over at his wifey. While she drove singing along to the lyrics, his eyes roamed over her body.

It was the beginning of summer, so Shakira was rocking a short Hermès dress, exposing her toned thighs. The front of the dress was low-cut, putting her cleavage on display, a diamond chain with a heart charm hung between her plump breasts. Her hair was tied in a slick ponytail, hanging to the middle of her back, while Dooney and Burke shades covered her eyes.

Yayo's dick began to swell at the sight of his beautiful woman. He placed his hand on her thick thigh. Shakira put her hand on top of his and guided his hand under her dress, placing it on her fat kitty. Yayo used his middle finger to pull her panties to the side, before inserting his finger in her love canal. She was wet and warm. Shakira let out a slight moan, before squeezing her thighs tightly together to prevent Yayo from fingering her while she was driving.

"Baby, chill out… we about to be at the room in about thirty minutes," Shakira purred to her man. Yayo pulled his finger out of his woman and stuck his finger in his mouth, savoring the taste of

11

her love. He was starting to have a flashback of the day he was released from St. Charles Correctional Facility, where he was serving a juvenile life sentence for being convicted of a homicide. After finishing his time, Shakira was there to pick him up. Just having that flashback let him know that Shakira was that ride or die bitch…she was his queen.

At that moment, he regretted getting another woman pregnant and bringing another child into the world that did not come from Shakira's womb, but what was done was done. Ms. Sanchez had given birth to his seed, but it was Shakira who held the key to his heart, her undying love and loyalty was undisputed, and his loyalty was to her.

"Shakira?"

"What's up, baby?" Shakira asked, turning the music down.

"Remember when you picked me up from St. Charles when I was a shorty?"

"Yes, baby…How could I forget?"

"I'm just saying, it looks like we going back in time," Yayo said.

"But it's a big difference this time, Yaton."

"What's the difference?" Yayo asked, trying to see where Shakira was taking the conversation. Shakira took off her shades.

"The difference is then you came home on some bullshit, you ran to the streets. Now, you are on a different path, I just hope and pray that you stay on that path, because I need you…Shamira needs you…baby, the whole family needs you. You are the glue that bonds this family together." A tear fell from Shakira's eye. Her words stung his soul but at the same time brought him to the reality that he had a major responsibility. His family was depending on him and there was no way he could let them down.

"Shakira, I'm home now and I'm not going anywhere. You can believe that," Yayo vowed, meaning every word he spoke. Shakira felt the sincerity in his words, but at the same time, she could never forget the life her baby daddy lived before he went to prison, and she knew at any time the streets could come calling.

"Yayo, I believe you with all my heart. I never want to lose you again, it would break me mentally, physically and spiritually…I would be lost."

"Baby, I already told you, I'm here to stay." Yayo said, taking Shakira's right hand from the steering wheel and kissing the back of it.

"Thank you, love… I love you so much," Shakira replied, letting Yayo's words wash away her worries.

"I love you too, baby." Shakira looked at her watch.

"Boo, you want to go somewhere to eat before we go to the room?" Shakira asked.

"Wow, baby, I'm cool. I'm too excited to eat, my appetite ain't on nothing, but listen. I need you to go out south real quick…on 79th and Green."

"What's on 79th and Green?"

"You sure ask a lot of questions, woman," Yayo joked.

An hour later, Shakira slid her whip down Halstead Street on the south side of the city. The streets looked a lot different since Yayo had seen them last. The same streets that he and his squad, the G.B.C., had dominated and soaked with blood. Since he had been gone, he stayed in tune through newspapers and knew the streets were more violent and hostile as the murder rate was extensive. Shakira stopped at a red light on 79th and Vinciness.

Yayo looked at a group of men posted on the corner, all or most of them sported dreadlocks and white T-shirts. He was a street nigga and knew they were gang members as one of the men threw up a sign with his right hand…a pitchfork, letting their alliance to the GD's be known. Yayo knew the area was on heavy rotation with the gangbanging. The light turned green and Shakira pulled off from the crowd of young goons. A few moments later, she was making a right at Green Street.

"Yayo, where am I going?" she questioned.

"Pull up and park in front of this building." Shakira did as her man instructed and parked in front of a large red brick building with a statue of a large crescent moon and five-point star on the top of it. It was a mosque, a temple for the Islamic.

"Baby, I will be right back…I'm going to go in here and pray."

"Oh…okay," Shakira said, a little confused at seeing this part of Yayo. Yayo had told her that he had taken his Shahada, but she knew nothing about the Muslim religion and knew it was going to take some time getting used to. But Yayo was her man and no matter what religion he chose she was with him. Yayo had made a complete one-eighty. No more dreads, it was now a crispy bald head and beard. Shakira noticed Yayo was now more positive and prosocial about life…his words were more powerful, and his gained intellect had her infatuated…she was definitely turned on.

Yayo got out the Audi and made his way inside the temple. He had driven past this building a hundred times. Had even shot one of his enemies on the next block on Emerald Street but had never known it to be an Islamic temple.

Walking inside the mosque, Yayo found the bathroom, washed his hands as well as face, took off his New Balances and socks and washed his feet. Placing his right hand over his left above his navel, he began to recite the following. "Oh Allah, glorified, praiseworthy, and blessed thy name and exalted thy majesty…and there is no deity worth of worship except thee…I seek refuge in Allah from the rejected shaitan…in the name of Allah, the beneficent, the merciful… Al-fatihah, Praise to Allah, lord of the worlds… the beneficent, the merciful. World… Master of day of judgement…thee alone we worship and to thee alone we turn for help. Guide us in a straight path. The path of those when you favored… and who did not deserve thy anger or went astray… In the name of Allah, the beneficent, the merciful." Yayo finished cleansing his soul, then kissed the pavement, pouring his soul to Allah.

While in Pollock Penitentiary, Yayo knew that as a man he needed some kind of religion to balance out his life, and after attending a Juma service with Mr. B., he noticed the peace and tranquility that the Muslims had about themselves. He had been through so much pain, violence and destruction he needed something to humble his being, so he figured he would give Islam a try. After taking his Shahada, he felt an inner peace which he had never felt. So, all his praises went to Allah.

After making prayer, Yayo put back on his socks and shoes and left out the temple.

"You good, baby?" Shakira asked as Yayo got back in the car. He answered her question by kissing her softly on the lips.

"Let's get up outta here, I got plans for your body and I only have a few hours before I have to be at the halfway house." Shakira pulled away from the curb and thirty minutes, later they arrived at the Holiday Inn downtown Chicago. Shakira wanted to take Yayo home to the condo, but she lived on the north side and they were a little pressed for time. She had already paid for the room online, so after going to the front desk to get the key card, they made their way to the second floor to the suite.

Once in the room, they wasted no time. Yayo grabbed Shakira by her thin waist, passionately kissing her while she tugged at his joggers. Just feeling Shakira's body pressed against his had his monstrous meat on swole. Yayo pulled Shakira's dress over her head and tossed it to the side and stepped back to admire her flawless body as she stood in her Victoria's Secret thong and matching laced black bra. He pulled off his fitted white V-neck T-shirt and wife beater. Shakira was speechless as her eyes roamed over his chiseled tattooed chest and his six-pack identical to a washboard. His sexy, but yet thuggish appearance had her pussy sopping wet. Yayo laid her on her back on the bed gently and pulled her thong off, her pussy was trimmed to perfection. Just the sight of her thick body made him want to shoot his load all over her, but he wasn't having that.

Shakira unsnapped her bra, freeing her 38-C titties. Yayo planted kisses all over her, starting at her shoulders, he knew her shoulders was her spot. Then he took one of her hard nipples in his mouth, sucking then savagely biting down gently in between. Shakira moaned out of pleasure and pain. Yayo made his way south until he found what he was looking for, Shakira's swollen love button. He feasted on her clit like it was his last meal, while she palmed his bald head.

"Baby... Baby... I'm cumming, baby," Shakira screamed as she squirted all over her man's face. Yayo swallowed her juices like it was a double shot of Ciróc, savoring the flavor. Shakira could take no more, she pushed Yayo off her pussy, now it was her turn to do the pleasing.

Crawling to the foot of the bed where Yayo stood, she pulled his joggers all the way down, boxer briefs as well. His ten inches sprung from his boxers, tapping Shakira under her chin. She grabbed his shaft with both hands and gently stroked it, at the same time staring him in his eyes before putting him in her mouth. Yayo moaned from the feeling of her warm tongue. Shakira tried her best to deep throat him, which she knew was impossible. Yayo grabbed the back of her head, pushing it down on him, the head of his dick hitting the back of her throat caused her to gag and a tear to escape from her eye. She took his dick out her mouth and ran her tongue down the sides of his hard cock and then sucked on his balls. Yayo was in lustful bliss as she gave him head.

"Baby, I need you in me… now," Shakira commanded, standing up then getting on the bed in the doggy style position. The last time Yayo had sex was with Ms. Sanchez. Even though that fifteen minutes was a thrill it was nothing like what he was experiencing now with the love of his life. He climbed on the bed and positioned himself behind his queen. Grabbing her voluptuous and meaty ass cheeks, he entered her from the back. Her tight wet walls fit him like a glove.

Shakira moaned in ecstasy as Yayo filled her to capacity. He started with slow deep strokes, not wanting to nut so soon, but he knew that he wouldn't last too long. Shakira's pussy was just too good, not to mention, he had been waiting to feel her insides for over eight years now. "Ahh baby, you feel so good," Shakira purred, feeling Yayo all in her stomach. Yayo sped up his pace, digging into Shakira. Her juices flowed, drenching Yayo's stomach and thighs, she was as wet as a waterfall.

The only sounds inside the massive hotel suite were the sounds of wet flesh slapping against each other. Yayo pounded Shakira until he felt his volcano about to erupt. Shakira buried her face in the pillow as her king punished her, she had come four times already and she felt like she was about to have a heart attack.

"Aw shit, Shakira," Yayo almost screamed, shooting his hot load inside of her in three long, strong spurts. Pulling his now semi-erect dick from her pussy, cum leaked out of her and down her thighs. Yayo collapsed on top of her.

"Damn girl, I missed you so much," Yayo said, planting kisses on the back of her sweaty neck and shoulders. He rolled off of her, now laying on his back.

Shakira snuggled up next to him, laying her head on his heaving chest.

"I missed you too, Yaton. Why you just kill my kitty cat like that?" Shakira asked him, rubbing his chest with her manicured nails.

"Because it belongs to me," he replied, kissing her on the lips.

"It definitely does. I hate you have to go to this goofy ass half-way house. Why they just don't let you come home?"

"That's just how the feds do it, baby. Don't worry, I won't be there long. My mans supposed to help me get a job. All I gotta do is show these people I can maintain steady employment, then they will let me go," Yayo replied.

"Who is your mans?" Shakira probed...being nosy.

"One of my Muslim brothers."

"Oh, yes... baby, before I forget." Shakira got up and went to get her handbag.

"Here you go." She handed Yayo a new iPhone 11. He looked at the hi-tech phone, confused. Last time he was on the street, he had a Boost Mobile.

"How you turn this on, Shakira?" he asked. Shakira laughed at him then grabbed the phone back. For the next thirty minutes, she showed him how to work the new phone, set up his Facebook account, and how to use the new apps the phone offered so he could listen to music and download videos.

"So, when will they let you come home for visits?"

"I should get my first one this weekend."

"That's good, baby, because I can't wait to get some more of this," Shakira said, squeezing his sticky, deflated dick.

"You ain't gotta wait till the weekend to get this…you gotta come pick me up tomorrow anyway to take me to my new job. We gotta get it how we can get it."

"I know that's right," Shakira replied.

"But let's get up outta here so I can make it to the halfway house on time. Mess around and be late they a be trying to send me back to the penitentiary on a violation, and we definitely can't have that," Yayo said.

Forty-five minutes later, Yayo was pulling up to the halfway house on Chicago Avenue and Christiana on the city's west side. A few dudes sat on the porch smoking cigarettes and kicking the bobo. Shakira parked in front of the brown brick building.

"What time you want me to pick you up tomorrow, Yaton?"

"I don't know, let me see how they running this place…what the rules are and all that shit, then I'm a call you."

"Ok, baby…Yaton?"

"What's good?"

"I'm so glad you are home. Shamira is going to be so happy to see her daddy, so make sure you call tonight so you can FaceTime with her."

"I will." Yayo gave Shakira a passionate kiss before she popped the trunk and they got out the whip. Shakira had gone shopping for Yayo to get him some new gear, shoes and his hygiene items. She already knew Yayo was going to be straight because Quavon had already told her he was going to bless his brother and for her not to spend her money, but Shakira was hearing none of that. She wanted him to be comfortable while he was at the halfway house, so he wouldn't have to ask anybody for anything. Shakira helped Yayo carry his bags to the door.

"Alright baby, I'm a see you tomorrow."

"Ok, baby…Don't forget to call me tonight so you can talk to Shamira."

"I wouldn't forget to make that call if my life depended on it," he replied, before he kissed her and made his way in the halfway house.

Yayo walked inside the halfway house and to the officer's station, where two female staff members sat at the desk playing cards, until he walked up. One of the females was light-skinned, with a short bob hairdo, resembling the actress Nia Long. The other one was heavyset, looking like Nell from the old black TV show *Give Me a Break*... They stopped what they were doing eyeing him down.

"My name's Yaton Anderson, 07505-424," Yayo informed them, giving his name and registration number.

"Damn girl... You can tell he been gone for a long time, sounding like a damn robot, like he been saying that shit twenty years," Nia Long joked before both women gave each other hi-fives and burst into laughter. Yayo kept his facial expression stone faced.

"Ok, Mr. Anderson... go down that hallway and go to the first door on the left, that's the case manager's office, her name is Mrs. Childs. When she get done with you, come back and we'll will get you settled in," Nia Long said. Yayo shook his head before he turned and made his way to the case manager's office. When he got to the door, he knocked three times before he heard a female voice telling him to enter. Walking inside the small office, Yayo looked around, only to see an older black woman who looked to be in her late fifties.

"Close the door behind you please." Yayo did as he was told. "You must be Yaton Anderson?" she asked, opening up a brown folder with Yayo's picture on it.

"Yes ma'am."

"State your registration number."

"It's 07505-424." Mrs. Childs opened the folder, looking over 's file.

"Alright, Mr. Anderson, I see you have just been released from U.S.P. Beaumont. You have three years of supervised release, and your probation and parole have given you a six-month release date from the halfway house. Your home detention date is set for six months from today, in which you will be released from our custody. Now, if you happen to get and maintain a job, you can be released sooner than your original home detention date and you will be able to go home on home confinement. Keep in mind, Mr. Anderson, that you are still in custody of the B.O.P.

"That means if you violate any of these rules in this handbook you are about to receive, your disciplinary infraction will be processed the same way as if you were still on the compound you just came from. So, my advice to you is to keep your nose clean and don't violate any of these rules." Mrs. Childs handed Yayo a handbook with all the rules he was to abide by. Yayo took it and thumbed through the thin booklet.

"Sign right here, saying you received a copy of these rules." Mrs. Childs handed Yayo a pen and pushed a clipboard in front of him. He signed his John Hancock, saying he received the rules.

"Do you have any questions, Mr. Anderson?"

"When can I get my first home visit?"

"Tomorrow, you will be able to go out and look for employment... if you stay out of trouble, you will be forwarded the opportunity to get a pass this weekend," Mrs. Childs informed Yayo, which was music to his ears. He couldn't wait to see his family. He had no plans on getting in trouble or doing anything that would jeopardize his home passes. After Yayo finished with Mrs. Childs, he made his way back to the office where Nia Long and Nell awaited him.

"Are these your belongings?" Nell asked, pertaining to the bags Yayo left in front of the office...his clothes that Shakira had bought him.

"Yeah...why, what's up?" he asked.

"Well, we are going to have to go through it to make sure you not bringing no contraband up in here," Nell said, picking up some of the bags and putting them in the office.

"While she doing that, come with me and I will show you where you will be sleeping. Follow me, Mr. Anderson." Yayo followed Nia Long up some stairs, he noticed how she was putting a certain switch in her hips.

"This is your room right here, Anderson," she said, stepping in front of a door. "You will get your property later on tonight when we get finish inventorying it... And Mr. Anderson, I googled you

20

when they said you were on the way. I see you was a boss when you was out here…well, just know I'm a boss bitch and I find you very attractive. You have been gone a long time, so whenever you ready to get your nuts out the sand, please let me give you some assistance," Nia Long stated with a lustful tone in her voice before she turned and left, leaving Yayo standing there. Yayo was not impressed with her whorish flirting. He could still smell Shakira's scent on his body and was wondering how Nia Long didn't.

Yayo walked inside the small, single-man room and looked out the window. Looking out, he could see Christiana Street. A group of men stood on the corner serving fiends. It was crazy how the government released inmates coming back to Chicago smack dead in the middle of the hood, straight to a violent war zone… Chi-Raq. Yayo pulled his cellphone out the pocket of his joggers. Going in the manila envelope containing his paperwork, he fished out a piece of paper he was looking for that had all his contact phone numbers on it. After finding the one he was looking for, he dialed the number. The phone rang three times before somebody picked up.

"As-salamu alaykum."

"Salaikum Salaam. My name is Yaton and Mr. B. gave me this number and told me to call once I landed," Yayo informed.

"Yaton, how are you, brother? I was anticipating your call. Are you good?"

"Yeah. I'm peaceful, just ready to get to the business," Yayo replied, pertaining to the business he promised Mr. B. he would handle, doing all he could to make a difference in the streets of Chicago. The youth had no guidance because most of their fathers were either in jail, dead, or addicted to some kind of substance, forcing them to be raised in single parent homes or worse…finding love from one of the many gangs in the deadly city. Yayo had influence in the streets and Mr. B. wanted him to exploit his leadership qualities to at least try to save as many young lives as he could, and that's exactly what he planned to do.

"Listen brother, you have just come home, take time to relax…spend time with your family. We want your head clear when you enter this. By the way, my name is Kewann, is this the number I can reach you at?"

"Yeah family, you can hit me on this line," Yayo said.

"Very well, Ock, we will be contacting you soon…Welcome home," Kewann said before he hung up the phone. Yayo tossed his phone on the bed and got to looking back out the window. It was a hot sunny day in the middle of summer. He had finally made it home after going through the dark times that came with federal prison. He stood on his principles as a man and as a gangsta, in some of the most tiring conditions, and returned home untouched…He had conquered the beast. Looking out the window at the grim city of the Chi, he just hoped and prayed he could leave his deadly past behind him and start a righteous prosocial life for himself, as well as his family.

Chapter 2

Omega sat on his grandmother's front porch, serving fiends. In his hand was a fifth of Hennessy. Since the death of his homie Ace, he had become an avid drinker. He went from being on top as chief of the Homicide Crew, to ducking in and out of Chicago selling cocaine. He lost Ace and K.I. to the vicious gunplay in the Chi. Not to mention, Marcus was serving a fifty-year sentence in Statesville Penitentiary for murder and had another thirty-ball waiting on him in Tennessee for a body, when he robbed and murdered the owner of a gun store. Goon was nowhere to be found or heard from, so the Homicide Crew was dismantled to the core.

It hurt Omega's heart that K.I. had been killed in retaliation for when they whacked Roy, a west side heroin dealer. He loved K.I. and had grown up with her from the sandbox, so he tattooed her name over his right eye and Ace over his left. Revenge was carved in his heart, but he didn't have the money or guns to go to work with Quavon and the Get it Boy Clique, who he dreamed responsible for his dead homies. For all he knew it could be a murder contract on his head and for that reason alone he had to be cautious and stay on the move and get his money at the same time.

Omega had met a white chick named Jenny at a club in Milwaukee. she lived in a small town in Wisconsin called Evansville. They had been messing around for about a year now. To say Jenny was sprung would be an understatement. Omega would dip to the Chi, cop work from a Latin King named Rico, post up on 59th and Bishop to hustle on the south side, where he would serve crack cocaine. After he was done hustling, he would call and have Jenny come scoop him and take him back to Wisconsin.

Omega felt his life was spinning out of control, but one thing he was adamant about and that was killing any and everything associated with the G.B.C....and when time presented itself, he was going to do just that. Omega took a swig from the bottle of Hen as a crack head walked up.

"What's up, youngster, let me get two for this eighteen I got?" the crack head stuttered nervously, knowing how Omega didn't take kindly to short money on his block. Omega sat the bottle on the steps and went to the sidewalk where the fiend stood. He looked up and down the street suspiciously before he spit two dime bags of crack into his palms. The crack head stared at the two stones of the devil's love. "Come on, youngblood. You ain't got no bigger ones than that? Them look a lil short," the crack head said, looking at the two stones. A mean mug plastered across Omega's face before he snatched the crumpled bills from him and threw the two bags of crack at the fiend.

"You better take these bags and get the fuck on...fuck you gone come short, then got an opinion? Get you stupid ass on." Omega sneered, raising his shirt, showing the crack head the handle of his strap. The crack head bent down to pick up the bags and took off running down the street to get away from the violent Omega.

Omega walked back up on his grandmother's front porch and continued where he left off...with the bottle. While getting his drink on, an unmarked cruiser cruised down the block slowly. When they passed Omega, the officer in the passenger seat gave him a smirk and pointed his finger at him, signaling a gun. After the car passed, Omega knew it was time to bounce as this was the third time the detectives had rolled through the hood. He grabbed his phone and called Jenny to come pick him up. A couple hours later, Jenny pulled up on 59th in her tinted Dodge Intrepid. Omega hopped in the passenger seat.

"Hey boo," Jenny greeted, pulling away from the curbside.

"Ain't shit...what's up with you?" Omega laid the seat back and tilted his Chicago Bulls snapback low over his eyes and put his gun on his lap. Even though the Intrepid was tinted out, he was taking no chances moving through the city...the same city where his adversaries lurked.

"Nothing, you want to stop and get something to eat before we get on the highway?" Jenny asked.

"Naw, I'm cool...but what the smoke sack look like? We got something to smoke?"

"I got about a quarter ounce left, you want to stop and get something to smoke?"

"Ain't no question, go west...we can slide through K-Town, they got that Gorilla Glue, they ounces five hundred."

About forty-five minutes later, they was pulling in the K-Town section of the city on the west side, the block was Keystone and Washington, a hood governed by the Gangster Disciples.

"Pull up right here, shorty," Omega told Jenny, pointing to the middle of the block where a group of men was posted up...One of them approached the car, Omega rolled the window down.

"What's good, Joe? We got them black twenty-dollar bags of that gas," he said, pulling out a Ziploc freezer bag full of the twenty-dollar bags "Three for the fifty," he continued, letting Omega know he was giving out deals for the day.

"Naw, I'm cool on the bags, my nigga...I'm trying to cop an ounce of that shit."

"An ounce, huh? That's gone run you five hundred, playa." Omega pulled out the knot of money out his pocket and peeled off five hundred-dollar bills and passed them to the guy through the window.

"Be cool, my nigga, I'll be right back," the man said, before he went to go get the weed.

"Mega, don't you think you shoulda waited till he came back before you gave him all that money? What if he don't come back on some crud ball shit?" Jenny asked as she had been got like that before.

"If he don't come back with my product or my money, I'm a get out and shoot one of these bitch ass niggas in the face." Omega's tone was calm but at the same time sinister, causing a chill to run down Jenny's spine. Since messing with Omega, she knew he was truly about that life.

Two minutes later, the same guy emerged from the gangway and walked up to the car and passed Omega the ounce through the window. He could smell the exotic marijuana as soon as it came through the window, now filling the car with its funky aroma.

"Good looking, fam."

"Don't trip...Next time you come through, just ask for Fonzo, 'G.' Matter fact, put my number in your phone." Omega got his cellphone as Fonzo proceeded to give him his contact info.

"That's a bet, my nigga, I'm a get at you."

"Say less," Fonzo replied and walked over to where his guys stood.

Jenny was at a stoplight on Kedzie Avenue when Omega told her to pull into the Shell gas station so they could gas up and get some blunts. She stopped on the side of the pump and parked. Omega put his Glock .22 on his waist and got out to pump the gas, then walked into the gas station to pay. After paying for his items, he was about to walk out the gas station until he bumped into some-body from his past. Both men froze like two deer caught in head-lights. Omega didn't know if he should hug the individual or pull the Glock off his waist and put two in his face, while the individual looked as if he was having similar thoughts. Omega and Goon were now face-to-face, both from the same hood, both strapped and both trained to go. It had been two years since they'd last seen each other.

It was like Goon had disappeared from the face of the earth after the night he was with Marcus, and they were set up by Stacy and her roommate, for Choppa and the G.B.C. to kill them. Marcus had got knocked a few months after the incident, but nobody had heard any news on Goon's whereabouts, which had the Homicide Crew on edge. Goon was affiliated with them and was in the trenches putting in work with the crew. For all Omega knew, Goon could've gotten knocked and was out on the streets working for the feds. Why else would he just get ghost without notifying the squad about his motives or actions? It wasn't in his character, whatever the reason Omega was about to find out, and if Goon's story didn't add up, he was going to leave his brains leaking, that he was sure of.

"Long time no see, how you been, family?" Omega said, keep-ing his demeanor in check, caging the demon that was praying to be unleashed.

"Yeah, it's been a minute, bro...I been cool, just trying to stay afloat, how you been?"

"You know fam I'm a be blunt and assertive with you, I think you got a lot of explaining to do." Goon cocked his head to the side, thinking about pulling the 9mm Taurus off his waist, deciphering if he should take Omega's statement as a genuine concern or threat.

"Yes, my nigga, I do, but I don't think this is the time or place," Goon retorted.

"You right…You mobile…what you on?"

"Yeah, my car outside. You can hop in and we can bend a few blocks, or we can meet up somewhere. It's up to you, my nigga." Omega thought on it for a quick second. It would make more sense for him to jump in the whip with Goon, than to meet up with him. He didn't want to let Goon out of his sight. He knew Goon was a strategic killer, anytime was too much time for him to think and put together a plan to kill him or worse, set him up with the police. Omega knew he had to seize and capitalize off the moment.

"Look bro, I got this broad in the car waiting on me, I'm a tell her I'm a get up with her later and hop in with you. We can bend a few blocks and smoke."

"Sounds like a plan, let me grab some squares and some Back-woods. I'm a meet you outside," Goon said.

Omega walked outside and got in the car with Jenny.

"Ah, shorty… take this and dip to the mall and spend it. I got to holler at this nigga real quick. I'm a call you when I get ready for him to bring me to you," he told her, peeling off four hundred off his knot and giving it to Jenny.

"Omega, you not about to do nothing crazy, are you…Please baby, let's just go home," Jenny pleaded, accepting the money from him.

"Don't trip, ma…I ain't gone do nothing crazy unless he say something crazy."

Omega watched Goon come out the gas station, scanning the parking lot like he was in search for him. He walked over to where Goon was standing by a clean, tinted Ford Focus.

"What's good, my nigga…You ready?" Goon asked, taking a sip from his Lipton Iced Tea as Omega approached.

"Yeah, let's bounce." Goon jumped in the driver's seat as Omega took the passenger seat. Goon pulled out of the gas station parking lot as Money Bagg Yo blasted through the custom speakers. Omega started splitting a Backwood down the middle, Goon hit the Alt button on the Sony Xplod Console.

"So, what's really good, Omega?"

"That's what I want to know...You was gang, then you just took off for two years. Niggas thought you was dead or locked up. Bitch ass nigga nailed Ace and K.I. and you were nowhere to be found," Omega stated, looking at Goon through his peripheral vision as he laced the middle of the blunt with gas. If Goon reacted any type of weird way, he was going to bust his head at the next stoplight...Period.

"Omega...I had to get ghost, fam. I was with the nigga Marcus, he plugged me with these bitches, we was crushing them hoes one night at they condo. I went outside to get some more blunts and it was some niggas sitting in a black Porsche truck all incognito and shit. I called fam phone and to come outside with the pole because I left mine in my jacket that was up there with him. Marcus came out and them niggas hopped out and started clapping.

"Fam bust a few times and got to the whip and pulled off. I ain't gone lie, Omega, I was ducking behind a house during the shootout...I was unarmed," Goon said, replaying the story. Omega finished pearling the blunt, lit the tip of it and took a strong pull from the exotic...He was listening attentively.

"Then what?" Omega asked, exhaling the smoke through his nostrils then passed the blunt to Goon. He accepted it and took a pull before he went back to telling the story.

"I ended up losing my phone, so that's why I couldn't get at Marcus. I didn't know who them niggas was, you already know we in the streets doing what we do, putting niggas down and shit. So, I went to Indiana to lay low for a minute. About a month later, I find out this nigga Marcus got booked for the demonstration we did in Tennessee.

"You already know he was spooked to death when we did that...Even though he been putting in work, it be a different story

28

when them people got you in that small room talking bodies. A nigga who known to be a stomp down gangster a turn into Patti La-Belle at a concert singing his heart out. I didn't trust that nigga like that…Straight up, my nigga."

"So why you didn't get up with the rest of us? Me, Ace and K.I.?"

"My nigga…I ain't know if them people was watching y'all or what. I was just being safe." Omega took another pull before he responded.

"You had plenty of time to get up with us before Marcus got knocked. You should've got up with the guys after them niggas tried to wet y'all up at shorty crib. You just left us in the dark. We could've come to the table and put this shit together, before these hoe ass niggas killed our people." A tear rolled down Omega's cheek at the thought of Ace and K.I. laid to rest at Burr Oaks Cemetery, and his heart started to beat fast. Omega didn't know if Goon was telling the truth. There was nobody to vouch for his story, which didn't make sense to him.

Goon was gang, if his intentions were good and what he was saying was true, he would be getting killed for nothing. Omega had already made up his mind. Goon's actions had gotten Ace and K.I. murdered. He loved Ace with all his heart, and he had insatiable thirst for blood for anybody who was the cause of his demise…directly or indirectly. He knew he had to rock Goon to sleep if he wanted to accomplish what he was about to do, as Goon was a thoroughbred killer. But the fact of the matter was, Goon had to go.

"Man, that's fucked up about Ace and K.I. Death to the niggas who did that," Goon vowed as he got on the Dan Ryan Expressway, his eyes watery as he thought about the Homicide Crew.

"Where we going, Goon?" Omega asked, rolling another blunt of loud.

"I'm just riding, my nigga, you trying to go somewhere specific?"

"The word on the street is the Get It Boy Clique was the ones who put Ace down, you know they stronghold is on 69th and Wolcott. What's good, you trying to slide on them niggas?" Omega sneered. Goon thought about it for a minute, he hadn't seen Omega in two years and could tell by the request that Omega was testing his gangster. He'd told Omega everything except the truth, which was he knew it was Quavon and the G.B.C. that sent the hot ones at Marcus and he was scared... Scared to die.

Goon looked at this as an opportunity to gain back Omega's respect and restore his street credibility, and what better way to do it than dropping one of the opps? Goon looked at Omega through bloodshot eyes before he said, "Let's slide."

Omega smiled wickedly at Goon. "Let's slide, scud," was his only reply, then turned back up the volume on the radio. Lil Durk and Only the Family's new track, "Green Light" blasted through the speakers, getting them both turnt up and putting them both in a murderous state of mind, ready to lay a bloody drill down.

It was late night in the city of Chicago. It was a hot summer night as the heat index was a hundred degrees. Lil Von was at the counter ordering his gyro and French fries as his potna Mud stood outside the establishment on security with a 30-shot Glock on his waist. The restaurant they were at was called Fat Albert's, located on 69th and Ashland Street, not far from their hood in the Englewood area, on the south side. The restaurant was considered a death trap because it was located smack in the middle of two warring rival gangs, the Get It Boy Clique whose territory was on 69th and Wolcott, all the way to Damon Street. Their rivals were the Goon Squad, whose hood ran from Winchester Street to Justine. Going to Fat Albert's in the daytime was ok, due to the open flow of traffic, but it was at night that the danger loomed.

It was only the beginning of the summer and already ten people had gotten shot at Fat Albert's with four of the shooting resulting in homicide. Most of the young gangsters paid crack heads to go to the restaurant to get their food but tonight, Lil Von and Mud had violated this protocol and strapped up and went to Fat Albert's themselves. Lil Von and Mud were G.B.C. gangsters employed by Choppa...the G.B.C. general. Lil Von and Mud sold crack and heroin for the Get It Boy Clique and was subordinate to anything Quavon or the G.B.C. laid down, and in return for their loyalty to

30

the gang they drove foreign whips, kept pockets full of colored money, and the recognition in the streets as being a part of the Get It Boy Clique.

Goon pulled inside the Food For Less gas station on 69th and Ashland and parked on the side of the pump. He noticed he had less than a quarter tank of gas, and since he and Omega was out lurking for opposition, he wanted to gas up as "proper preparation prevents poor performance."

"You need anything out of here, scud?" Goon asked Omega.

"Just grab two packs of woods." Goon got out to pump the gas while Omega's phone vibrated on the clip of his Hermès belt. Grabbing his phone, he saw it was Jenny calling. Jenny was mad as hell because Omega had made her get a hotel room after she finished shopping at Evergreen Plaza. She was heated because she was supposed to be back in Wisconsin tonight, so she could be at work in the morning. She was a bank manager at the Bank of America in Evansville, Wisconsin. She was going to have to call in and it was a strong possibility they would give her, her walking papers. Omega ignored her, sending her straight to voicemail.

Omega was looking around, checking his surroundings when he looked east, catty corner of Ashland and saw a dark blue Aston Martin Vantage, the car was parked at the curb in front of Fat Albert's. A dude with shoulder-length dreads posted up on the side of a vehicle in front of the restaurant. Omega didn't know the individual but recognized the Aston Martin and knew it was associated with the Get It Boy Clique, he was sure of it. He had seen the vehicle on Wolcott numerous times. He couldn't believe his luck, catching the opps at the wrong place at the right time. Omega pulled the Glock .22 off his waist and pulled the slide back, putting one up top just as Goon was getting back in the driver's seat.

"Check out buddy." Omega pointed across the street at Fat Albert's. Goon didn't even respond he just pulled the .9 off his waist.

"It's two of them niggas, one of them in the restaurant," Omega informed. Goon was about to put the car in drive until Omega grabbed his arm.

"Nah fam, we ain't gone pull up…we gone walk up. Come on, my nigga, I'm about to blow these niggas down…On Ace grave," Omega said through clenched teeth and got out the car, Goon followed suit, leaving the car running, the two of them now en route making their way across Ashland to go drill something.

Lil Von paid for his food and made his way out the restaurant, he still had five G-packs of heroin to hustle off, so he was amped to get back to the block to grind. Mud got in the passenger seat as Lil Von jumped in the driver's seat and hit the push button *start*, bringing the Ashton's engine to life.

"Hold up real quick, shorty, let me dump this out," Mud said, opening the door so he could dump the tobacco out the blunt. Neither one of them were on point, not noticing the two men walking briskly across Ashland until it was too late. Omega reached the SUV, Glock extended in front of him. Lil Von looked to the left and was now looking down the dark barrel of a .40.

"G.B.C. killer pussy," Omega hissed before he pulled the trigger in four rapid sessions *Boc, Boc, Boc, Boc.* The first two slugs hit Lil Von in his cranium, blowing his brains out in a pinkish, mushy mist. His brains and skull fragments soiled the side of Mud's face, making him get active and reach for his gun as he staggered out the truck, still in shock from seeing Lil Von get punished. Goon rushed him, pointing his pole at him. *Moc, Moc, Moc, Moc, Moc.*

Shooting Mud in his chest and stomach, the 9mm slugs ripped through him like butter, dropping him on his back. A few bystanders stood in front of the liquor store on the corner and watched as murder was being committed. Goon stood over a dying Mud, pointed the gun at his face and emptied the clip, putting his brains on the pavement.

Omega and Goon darted back across Ashland, hopped into the whip and pulled away from the murder scene, leaving two of their opps deceased, adding them to the already high murder rate. Little did they know, they had just ignited a war in the streets, with the undisputed Get It Boy Clique.

Chapter 3

Yayo stood on the corner of Chicago Avenue and Pulaski, in front of Popeye's Chicken. It was a week since he had gained his freedom and today was Friday, the day he was able to go home for his pass. He had only been home a week and still had not adjusted to being back in the free world, even though Shakira had picked him up every day from the halfway house to job hunt.

He went out every day to fill out applications for employment, going to restaurants and department stores seeking employment, and the rest of the time was spent at a hotel where he and Shakira would get reacquainted with each other's bodies. Two days out the week, Shakira brought Shamira. Seeing his daughter was the best feeling of his life. When Shakira pulled up to the halfway house with Shamira in the car, Yayo almost broke his neck jumping off the front porch to get to her.

"Daddy!" Shamira yelled, wrapping her arms around his neck as he scooped her up in his arms. Yayo held her for dear life while the tears fell from his eyes. It was a very emotional moment.

"Hey, baby girl! Daddy missed you so much," Yayo said, planting kisses all over her face. She was eight years old and had grown, but to Yayo, she was still his baby. That day was all about them. They went downtown to Mrs. Field's Cookies and then walked to the Buckingham Fountain, where they sat and ate ice cream. Shamira told her father all about her friends at school and how she was about to start gymnastics next month. Yayo listened to his daughter give him the rundown of her young life without interrupting her, not once. He was intrigued by how smart she was and how assertive her communication skills where. When he was snatched up by the feds, she was just a baby, and now he was in the presence of a beautiful young lady.

Shamira was a replica of her mother, with her smooth caramel skin and long shiny black hair that was in a neat ponytail…her hair rested to the center of her back. Shamira also held some of Yayo's features, but it was evident she bore his bloodline. She was sweet as pie but in a blink of an eye, her behavior could be impulsive just as her father, could be diplomatic or if the situation granted… become murderous.

Looking at how much his baby had grown caused him to reflect on how much of her life he had missed. His guilt began to set in, thinking about how he missed her first words, her first steps, her first day at school, how he left his baby mama out in the world to raise their daughter alone made him tear up. Shamira noticed it.

"What's wrong, Daddy?" she asked, getting off the bench they were sitting on and walking up to her father. Yayo pulled her into his embrace, looking in her pretty brown eyes.

"Shamira, baby…I'm sorry for leaving you and Mommy and I swear as Allah is my witness, I will never leave you again, that's on my soul," Yayo vowed.

Shamira wiped the tear that threatened to roll off her father's cheek before she said, "Daddy, don't worry… Everybody makes mistakes. I will always love you, Daddy." Shamira's angelic voice melted his heart. Yayo knew the most important thing in his life was his family, and he would do nothing to jeopardize his freedom.

Yayo looked at his watch and saw that Shakira was running late. It was hot as the Sahara Desert and the busy mid-day traffic on Chicago Avenue had him a little nervous, a few times cars had stopped at the light on Chicago Avenue and the occupants of the vehicle flashed him gang signs out the window. Yayo was definitely back at home…Chicago, the murder capital. A few moments later, Yayo heard what sounded like a marching band coming up the street. A cocaine white Bentley truck, followed by a Maserati Levante, and a black Porsche truck swerved into the parking lot of Popeye's. The ground beneath him shook as if it was about to be a small earthquake, the bass from the Lil Baby track rattled the pavement as the foreign whips parked and the doors swung open.

"What's good with it, big bro?" Quavon yelled to Yayo over the music, jumping out the Bentley truck. Yayo smiled at his brother and started walking toward the vehicle. Crusha, Reggie G and Choppa got out the Maserati and two individuals got out the Porsche truck and stood posted. Yayo walked up and hugged his brother.

"What up, shorty?" Yayo said. Still smiling, he stepped back to look at his lil brother. Quavon had a lit blunt of Sour Diesel Kush in his hand. He was dressed in an all-white linen short set made by Ferragamo. His shirt was unbuttoned, showcasing his custom-made diamond G.B.C. chain, diamond-studded Cartier frames covered his eyes as while Mauri sandals adorned his feet.

"Man, what the fuck is up?" Quavon shouted, geeked up that his brother was free and back on land. He'd waited years for this moment and now the time had arrived. Crusha, Reggie G and Choppa walked over to pay homage and respect to the co-founder of the Get It Boy Clique

"Man, what up, baldie?" Choppa joked, embracing Yayo.

"Choppa...what's up, brother, how have you been?"

"You already know, big homie, getting to the bag and doing what I do," Choppa replied. Yayo already knew what was up with Choppa. He could smell the death on him, he knew Choppa was an assassin when it came to murder, it was why he employed him into the C.B.C.

"Yayo...family, you just don't know how much I missed you. It's a blessing to have you back on deck, my nigga." Reggie G walked up and hugged his chief.

"I missed you as well, Reggie, I been hearing a lot about you brother."

"I hope all good things," Reggie G retorted.

"No doubt, brother. No doubt." Crusha walked over with his hands clasped behind his back and stared him in his eyes before he spoke.

"It's been many moons and many nights, Yayo."

"Yes, it has, Crusha...tell me something I don't know, OG," Yayo said, not breaking eye contact with Crusha.

"Yayo, a lot has been going on since you have been away, the times have changed dramatically. You left us a foundation to stand on and that foundation has made it through these times, and we remained at the top of the food chain, and the G.B.C. is still a force to be reckon with, as you left it," Crusha said before he embraced Yayo.

"Crusha, my brother, your loyalty has never been in question. As you said about times changing…it's time for those times to change again. When the time is right, I will tell you all…how 'we' the G.B.C., will change them. I love you, brother," Yayo whispered in Crusha's ear before he let him go from his embrace. Crusha was a little confused from the words Yayo had just spoken, but whatever he was talking about, if it came from Yayo then he was with it.

"Yayo, let's bounce. Shakira sent me to scoop you up, she told me to bring you to the condo up north," Quavon said, taking a pull from the blunt. Yayo looked over at the three individuals posted by the Porsche trucks, with their hands under their shirts.

"Quavon, who is your company?" Yayo asked, pointing to the men he didn't recognize.

Quavon looked over to where Yayo was pointing.

"Oh them? They my shooters. You always said to protect what I love, and I love me, so that's what they get paid to do…shoot. Nothing more, nothing less. Let's bounce, bro, you got some people waiting to see you. Y'all follow me," Quavon said to his men. Yayo was about to get into the Bentley truck, but stopped.

"Quavon…Aye bro, you gone have to put that out. I can't afford to catch no contact. I might get a dirty UA," Yayo said, pertaining to the blunt Quavon was smoking on.

"Oh, my bad, big bro," was Quavon's only reply before he tossed the blunt to the side.

Yayo sat on the passenger side of the expensive SUV as Quavon glided the whip down Lake Shore Drive. Looking over at his brother, he could see the rumors he had heard throughout the prison system about his brother was definitely true. His phone rang non-stop and the personal armed security that tailed him was an indicator that he was in the streets something serious. Quavon turned the music down so he could speak to his brother, his mentor, his friend.

"So, big bro, how does it feel to be free?" he asked, starting the conversation he had waited many years to have. Yayo was leaned back in the comfortable leather seat.

"I can't lie, Quavon, it feels real good."

"Yaton, things are not the same in the city like when you was out here. A lot has changed, it's basically the same game, different playas and the stakes are a lot higher."

"Oh yeah?" Yayo said, half-interested.

"Yeah, bro. Only thing that hasn't changed from the time you got snatched up is that the Get It Boy Clique is still in supreme control over the city. We own Chicago, hell, the Midwest for that matter...my nigga, we even got strongholds in the south. Like I told you when I came to see you, some hoe ass nigga had the audacity to kidnap me...Me, Quavon! Some millionaire nigga name Top Cat, then had the nerve to offer me a slot in his organization. Dumb nigga there.

"You know, Yaton, when we used to talk, you used to drop deep jewels on me bro, and I soaked that shit up like a sponge. I learned from your mistakes. You used to tell me that life was chess, not checkers. I finessed these weak-minded niggas out here and put myself in a position of power.

"Don't get me wrong, Yaton, it wasn't easy, you left some loyal niggas in the camp...Choppa, Crusha, Reggie G, I love them niggas to death and the G.B.C. wouldn't be where we are today without them or their blind loyalty...Not to me, but to you. You also had some snakes, fake cornball ass niggas that was laying in the cut...disloyal maggots like T.B. But guess what, Yayo? Them niggas is all dead. You hear me...dead!"

Yayo just shook his head at his younger brother. He had told Quavon when he came to see him in Pollock to leave the game alone, but Quavon was adamant about being the hood star he set out to be. Only thing he could do was try to get Quavon to listen, but Quavon was a grown man and would make his own decisions.

"Quavon, how many people have died?" Yayo asked him.

"Shit, a lot...and a lot more gone die if niggas decide to go against the grain," Quavon retorted.

"Brother, I can see you have learned nothing from my situation. Quavon, they sentenced me to life in prison. I shouldn't have to tell you that, because you had front row seats to my demise. If Allah hadn't blessed me and put a certain individual in my life, I wouldn't be here talking to you right now, Quavon. All of this," Yayo waved his hand around pertaining to the two-hundred-fifty-thousand-dollar truck they were riding around in. "means nothing when you walking the yard with a life sentence. Do you know what my out date said, Quavon?" Quavon glanced over at his brother as he drove.

"Nah bro, what it say?"

"My out date read *deceased*, Quavon, that's what the government put on my paperwork. I had to see that shit every time they issued me some kind of paperwork. This material shit is not worth it, lil bro." Yayo pleaded with his brother. He was trying to get Quavon to see the bigger picture and that it was only two ways out the game, and that was jail or the graveyard.

"Yayo, I understand you have been through a lot, but you need to understand that it's no getting out for me, it is what it is. I love the nigga I have come to be. I'm content with being able to fuck any bitch I choose, ride in these fly ass cars and with a head nod, get one of these hoe ass nigga's brains knocked out they shit. I own three dispensaries in Cali and I got a plug across the border with unlimited coke and heroin, My nigga, you ain't even seen the movie, *Chi-Town Beast*. I produced that," Quavon boasted.

"That's what I'm saying, Quavon, leave the thuggin alone and stick to the legit. You smarter than that. Get out while you still can, fam."

Quavon was digesting what Yayo was speaking when his iPhone sprang to life. "Speak on it," he answered as he got off Lake Shore Drive, entering the Rogers Park area of the north side.

"What…when, hoe ass niggas… Y'all already know what to do. Send the Blackout Squad over there, I want that shit on the news tonight," Quavon ordered before he ended the call.

"What's up, lil bro? Everything all well?" Yayo asked, seeing the agitation on his brother's face.

"That was Choppa, he just found out two of the lil homies got nailed last night in front of Fat Albert's. Lil Von and Mud was both G.B.C. I told him to send some hitters to them hoe ass niggas' hood to handle that Nation Bizness."

"That's what I'm talking about, Quavon. When is the killing gone stop? All this shit is senseless," Yayo vented. Quavon looked over at his brother as he stopped at a red light on Clark Street.

"Listen, fam. I was willing to hand all this over to you, the plug, the blocks, and everything I have built since you have been gone. I'm willing to give you my seat at the throne, but I see we not on the same page and I'm cool with that, but you can save all that preaching shit for the choir. You just do you and best believe I'm a continue to do me. But I'm a tell you this, bro. Crusha, Reggie G and Choppa are going to be highly disappointed in the decision you making. They gone feel exactly how I feel."

"And how you feel, Quavon?"

"Like you abandoning the struggle," Quavon answered.

Yayo thought about what his brother was saying. He knew Quavon and the Get It Boy Clique would feel some type of way about him getting out the game because he was the one that started the gang. But he was a changed man, and he was on a mission to restore life and positivity to the streets. He had promised Mr. B and given him his word. And his word was his bond.

Money motivated a lot of people and he knew Quavon was loaded with it, so he knew his brother was ten toes down, he just prayed that he opened his eyes before it was too late. Yayo figured he would leave the conversation alone, it was no sense continuing to talk about it, it was like beating a dead horse. He grabbed his phone and place a call. The phone rang a few times before somebody answered.

"Hello?" she answered.

"What's good, how are you?"

"Yaton?"

"Yeah, it's me."

"I see you waited a whole week to call me," Ms. Sanchez replied. She had been checking the Bureau of Prisons' website and saw that Yayo had been released from federal custody a week ago. Each day that went by, she got more agitated that he had not attempted to call her and Jamarie.

Now that he had finally called and she heard his voice, it felt as if the weight of the world had been lifted off her shoulders. Even though she had stayed in contact with him through letters, it was a strong thought in her mind that he would just come home and forget about her and her son, so the phone call was somewhat of a relief.

"My bad, Amanda, I had a lot going on this week. I had to go job hunting and plus they have me going to this re-entry program," Yayo said, telling half the truth.

"Oh, I see… So now what? Do I have to fly to Chicago so we can get this blood test done, or are you going to come this way?" she asked, getting straight to the point.

"I have to be in this halfway house for six months, but it's a possibility they can let me out early. I can't leave the state of Illinois until then."

"Six months is a long time, Yaton."

"Six months is nothing, shorty. We have waited this long," Yayo retorted. He wanted to take a blood test on Jamarie just as bad as she wanted it done. He had a strong feeling Jamarie was his, but it was nothing like knowing for sure.

"Listen, Yaton. We did what we did and like I told you, I wish we wouldn't have done it, but it happened and Jamarie is here and that I don't regret. But please, Yaton, get this blood test done so my son can at least have a father, because I know for a fact you are his father."

"And like I told you, once we get this test done and it comes out Jamarie is mine, make no mistake about it, I'm going to step up to the plate. I will love him as he is my son, I will be in his life as a father is supposed to be in his son's life, and he would never want for anything…I know what it's like to not have my father in my life and Jamarie will never go through that…Period. But Amanda, I got some buisness to take care of. I'm a call you later on, is that cool?"

"Ok, Yaton, that's cool. Make sure you stay safe and welcome home, baby daddy," Ms. Sanchez said genuinely, at the same time letting him know of her certainty that he was Jamarie's dad. Yayo ended the call with her and stared out the window, watching the streets go by. He couldn't wait to get out the halfway house so he could shoot to Louisiana to take care of his business.

"Bro, what kind of *Maury* shit you got going on?" Quavon asked jokingly.

"My dude, it's a long story," was Yayo's only reply before he turned the music back up, letting Lil Durk's *Fake Love* blast through the subwoofers.

Twenty minutes later, they pulled into Shakira's driveway. Her condo was located in Evanston, Illinois, a small suburban town far north of Chicago. Yayo was impressed at Shakira's home. Quavon parked behind a two-door, red Mercedes Benz with Florida license plates. The Maserati parked behind them. Quavon hit the push button *start*, killing the engine.

"Welcome home...Chief," Quavon said sarcastically before he got out the truck.

"Get out your feelings, lil nigga," Yayo retorted, his words hit Quavon back. Yayo got out the truck as Crusha, Reggie G and Choppa exited the whip, the two men in the black Porsche truck stayed posted, doing what they got paid to do...Security. Quavon led the way to the front door of Shakira's home. SWV could be heard coming from the other side.

Yayo was about to ring the doorbell until the door swung open. Shakira had seen them pull up. Now she stood in the doorway in a one-piece Balenciaga dress, with Louboutin red bottoms on her feet, the straps from the six-inch pumps laced around her toned calves.

"Took you long enough," she said, putting her arms around his neck and kissing him. Yayo pulled her close by the waist, passionately kissing her back.

They were fixed in a lip lock when Yayo heard, "Daddy!" Yayo pried himself away from Shakira only to see Shamira running toward him. He scooped her up and kissed her on the forehead.

"What's up with Daddy's princess?"

"Daddy, wanna see my room?" Yayo put Shamira down. Shamira was excited her daddy was home.

"Yes baby, you know Daddy wanna see your room."

"Hey, Uncle Quavon!" Shamira said, hugging her uncle.

"What's up, lil bit?" Yayo stood back, watching the exchange between his daughter and his brother. The love was genuine, letting Yayo know his family was tight and the love was there.

"Come on, baby, there are some people that want to see you," Shakira said, grabbing Yayo by the hand, leading him to the patio where the music was coming from. When he got to the patio, all he heard was, "Surprise! Welcome home, Yaton!"

"Surprise, Daddy!" Shamira yelled. Yayo smiled like he was a kid on Christmas morning at the sight of his loved ones. On the patio was his family. His mother Karen, his stepfather Darrell, Davon, his loving grandmother Honey and Shakira's best friend Candy. Karen walked up and hugged her oldest son.

"Hey, Momma...did you drive all the way down here?" Yayo asked, remembering seeing the Benz with the Florida tags.

"Sure did, I would've walked if I had to." Karen gave him a kiss on the cheek. "Welcome home, son."

"Thank you, Ma."

Darrell walked over to Yayo with a bottle of champagne and two glasses, then handed one to Yayo and filled his glass with the expensive Ace of Spades, before he filled his own glass. "Let's make a toast, Yaton."

"A toast to what?" Yayo asked, staring Darrell in his eyes.

"A toast to a new start...A new life," Darrell explained to him. Yayo was in a good mood and didn't want to spoil it by reminiscing on the past. Darrell was right. He had a new life with a new start. He wasn't going to condemn Darrell for the past...but he wasn't going to forget it either. Yayo raised his glass.

"To a new start and a new life," Yayo said.

"To a new start and a new life," Darrell countered as he and Darrell toasted, putting the past in the past. Yayo downed his liquor in one shot. It was against his parole to drink, but tonight was a special night and a couple drinks wasn't going to hurt him.

"Good to see you, big bro," Davon said, coming over to greet his brother. Yayo's heart started to beat fast at the sight of his brother. He hadn't seen him since he got locked up, only in pictures and most of them was with Davon in a wheelchair. He could remember like it was yesterday when he was at U.S.P. Pollock and he received the email saying Davon had gotten shot. It was as if his heart shattered into a million pieces, and then to hear he would never walk again crushed his spirit. But now to see Davon standing before him made him proud.

He wasn't the same little Davon he remembered, now standing in front of him was a grown man, a pillar of the community, with a great job and living a prosocial lifestyle. Davon had elegance about himself. He was dressed in brown Brunello Cucinelli linen shorts, a crème-colored Thom Sweeney short-sleeve button-up, with matching Stacey Adams square toes on his feet, while a Brequet Depuis timepiece surrounded his wrist. His hair was in three-sixty waves and the goatee on his face was trimmed to perfection. Yayo was impressed with his brother's grown man swag as he hugged him.

"What's up, Davon...I missed you, brother."

"I missed you too, Yaton...like a car payment," Davon joked hugging his brother. Even though Davon had been through a traumatic experience, he still held his jolly demeanor.

"Man, look at you." Yayo stepped back, admiring Davon. "Seems like life been treating you good, fam." Davon put his head down.

"Bro, I just do what I'm supposed to do to take care of myself, but I been stressing hard, Yaton."

"Stressing about what, fam?" Yayo asked, seeing his brother's mood swiftly change. Davon looked up at him.

"Stressing about you, bro. Since they took you out that courtroom with them shackles on, it seems like they took a part of me with you. I look up to you, Yaton." Yayo's eyes began to water, hearing his brother speak from the heart. He put his hand on Davon's broad shoulder.

"Davon, I made a lot of bad choices in the past and I'm sorry my situation caused you to be stressed out. I wish you'd never went through that, and if I could turn back the hands of time, I would...believe me. All I can do is move forward to the future and make sure I never put us in that situation again," Yayo said before he hugged his brother again.

"That's all I wanted to hear you say, Yaton," Davon replied.

"God is good. God is good, thank you, Jesus." Yayo pulled away from Davon's embrace to see his grandmother Honey standing with her arms open. It had been eight years since he had last seen her. She was now eighty-seven years old, had lost her vision in one eye and now walked with a cane, but her mind was sharp like she was twenty years old. Yayo hugged his grandmother.

"Hey, Granny. I missed you," Yayo said, squeezing her into his chest.

"Boy, be careful, feel like you gone break my back with your strong self." Yayo bent down and kissed his grandmother on top of her head.

"Granny, it seems like you got shorter since the last time I saw you," Yayo joked.

"Well grandson, if I'm getting shorter, then I need to pray to the Lord and tell him to stop what he doing, because my life is in his hands." Honey laughed. "I missed you, grandson, and I'm glad you are home. Me and your mama made your favorites, fried chicken, baked macaroni and cheese and homemade biscuits," Honey told 'em.

"I can smell it, Granny, it smells great." Honey reached up and ran her hand over his smooth bald head.

"Grandson, all the pictures I saw of you in that jail you had long hair. What happened to it?" Yayo rubbed his head.

"You know, Granny, I just thought it was time for a change, you know." Honey smiled at him.

"Well, I think you look fantastic... it fits you. You remind me of your grandfather Edgar, both of y'all have those peanut heads."

"He sure do have a peanut head." Yayo turned around to see Candy standing there.

"Candy, what up, lil sis? Man, come over here and give me a hug," Yayo said with his arms open. Candy was Shakira's BFF and was definitely a friend of the family. "What up, big head, how you been doing?" he asked her.

"Nothing much, big bro. Just taking care of my lil daughter, Briana," Candy replied.

"Where she at? I want to meet her. You already know I'm going to spoil my lil niece. How old is she?" Yayo asked.

"Three going on twenty-five. She with her daddy right now, but you will meet her soon," Candy said, letting Yayo go. "It's good to have you home, big bro, just make sure you stay out because you have a family that loves you. And please talk some since into that knucklehead brother of yours." Candy walked off to go make herself a drink.

Yayo looked over at Quavon, who was talking to Choppa. He could tell by their body language that they were politicking about some Nation Bizness, and the way Choppa was listening attentively, he knew Quavon was discussing murder.

"Come on, everybody, the food is ready!" Shakira yelled out to the patio, letting everybody know to come eat. For the next hour, Yayo sat at the table surrounded by nothing but family and friends. It was only the blessing of Allah that he was now sitting at the table with his loved ones. This was his inner circle, everyone sitting at the table was his loved one...the ones he would shed blood for. After everybody was done eating, drinking, and reminiscing on the past and planning for the future, Yayo told Quavon, Crusha and Reggie G and Choppa to meet him outside on the patio. The men stood from the table and make their way to the back to holler at Yayo.

Once outside, they all took seats on the lawn chairs...Quavon remained standing with a bottle of Ciróc in his hand as he pulled a freshly rolled Backwood from his front pocket. Yayo wasted no time addressing his family.

"My brothers, I called y'all back here to speak to y'all about something serious."

"What's good, brother, talk we a talk back," Crusha said, while Quavon lit the tip of his blunt and took a strong pull.

"I want to talk to y'all about what's going on in these streets. First and foremost, brothers, as you are aware the feds gave me a life sentence, they sentenced me to die...You all know this."

"That shit was fucked up," Choppa intervened.

Yayo continued. "While I was in the belly of the beast, I met a great man from Memphis, Tennessee, his name was Bernard, we call him Mr. B. It is because of this great man I am a free man today. This great man took the time out his life to help me get my freedom back. He was a beast with the law, Robert Kardashian had nothing on this man. This man has a great vision, and that vision is to bring our people together and to stop the bloodshed in our streets and to bring about peace. I gave this man my word and as you all know, my word is my bond. I have to keep that promise."

Yayo looked in the eyes of his men, everybody was hanging on to his words… All except Quavon, who had his back turned, looking out to the backyard while he smoked his blunt.

Crusha was the first to speak. "Yayo, with all due respect, how do you expect to bring peace to the streets of Chicago? It's been too much animosity and too many bodies. This new generation is fucked up, they don't even want to hustle or get money, all they want to do is drill shit and body niggas. They don't want to listen, it's just the way of the world, you been gone so you don't see it."

"You right, Crusha. I don't see it, but what I do see is a bunch of young black men out here with no father figures or guidance. We can't condemn our youth, it's not their fault they grew up without a father or their mother is addicted to heroin, they missing the love in the household, so they resort to the streets to get the love…the fake love. That's why I turned to the streets, I looked at Jug-Head like a father figure, but the nigga used me and then told on me about a body, getting me sent to prison…that ain't love.

"Then when you go to jail or prison, you are forced to adapt and use violence as a survival tactic. The mental shit we go through in prison… if you not mentally strong, it will only make you worse. With nobody to give us the rules of life, we go astray. I'm a living testimony, fam." While Yayo was speaking, Davon came out to the patio to join them. Yayo continued, noticing his brother had come out.

"My brothers, if we can reach these young brothers and show them another way of life, we can make a change in our communities," Yayo said. Quavon flicked the blunt roach over the balcony before he turned around and said with bloodshot eyes.

"I wish you would've preached this Jesse Jackson bullshit when I was a shorty. Maybe I wouldn't be out here like this. I ain't got time for this hypocritical ass shit. I got some Nation Bizness to stand on. Choppa, let's ride, fam." Choppa was G.B.C.'s undisputed leader and he had to follow the chain of command and follow orders.

"I'm a get up with you, big homie...and welcome home, my nigga," was Choppa's only reply before he stood and followed Quavon back in the house. Yayo just shook his head as he watched them leave. He knew Quavon was too far gone. He also knew Choppa was only being loyal and subordinate. But he could tell Choppa was listening and at this point, that's all he could ask from the Get It Boy Clique. One thing for sure, he was not going to give up on them or the streets...Even if it killed him.

Chapter 4

Later on that night, Choppa was in a basement on 69th and May. He was at an important meeting with the G.B.C. Blackout Squad. The Blackout Squad was a clique inside the G.B.C. that only did one thing, and that was kill. In attendance was Clay and Troy, identical twins from the Princeton Park area of the city. They were twenty-five years old and had been putting in work for the Get It Boy Clique for three years…their gunplay was official.

Then there was Kill-Will, from the west side. He had been rotating with the G.B.C. for two years and had already shot and killed nine people for the gang. He was ruthless with the pistols. Last, but not least, was Vietnam, the elder of the group. He got his name because he had served a deployment in Vietnam back in the day. He returned to society burnt out and addicted to heroin, but Choppa knew better. He knew anybody that served in a ground war in Vietnam had issued their share of death and was a cold-blooded killa.

Choppa had handpicked the Blackout Squad personally. He only summoned them when a deadly message needed to be sent. Normally, he would let the lil homies on the block retaliate against their rivals for Lil Von and Mud's murders. But Quavon was adamant about the Blackout Squad putting in the work, so he was following orders. Choppa sat on the couch with two Glock .40's on his lap.

"Now listen, my niggas, you have been called upon by the Chief himself. He wants a message to be sent to these Goon Squad niggas. As y'all know, them hoe ass niggas murked Lil Von and Mud, so retaliation must be precise and swift. They killed two of ours, so no less than four of them die tonight. Nothing is to step in the way of that…is that understood?" Choppa asked. Vietnam looked up from the pile of heroin he was sniffing out of a piece of aluminum foil.

"Youngsta…You said what needed to be said, so we gone do what need to be done," Vietnam slurred, the heroin in his bloodstream putting him in a mode to murder.

"Say less, my nigga," Kill-Will said, loading 7.62 rounds into the banana clip, belonging to a Draco AK-47. The twins remained silent while loading the drums to their Glocks, ready to slide on their opposition, being loyal to the gang. After receiving the mission from their superior, the Blackout Squad loaded up in a stolen Jeep Cherokee SRT, also known as a striker, en route to enemy territory to run a bloody drill.

Quazo, Dip, G-Red and a few other Goon Squad gang members stood posted on the corner of 71st and Winchester drinking, smoking weed and thugging it. It was late Friday night, and they were out doing what they do. Dip hit the bottle of 1800 Tequila just as three local chicks from the hood walked up.

"Look at these lil thots," G-Red said, sitting on the mailbox, breaking down a Backwood to fill it with Kush.

"Thot? Nigga, you got me fucked up!" Rose said with her hands on her hips. Rose was a redbone, thick in all the right places. She was from the hood and when she saw the Goon Squad on the corner, she knew they were drinking and smoking and wanted to try her hand at getting a free buzz.

"When y'all broke ass gone get off the block... Bag selling ass niggas, get y'all weight up," Lizzett stated, getting on bullshit with her cousin Rose.

"Lizzett, if you don't get your busted ass down the block...Reject MiMi off *Love & Hip Hop* looking ass," Quazo intervened jokingly. This was a normal for the Goon Squad, playing the dozens with the local hood rats. They had all had their way with them sexually at one point or time. They had all attended Englewood high school with them, so the traded insults was nothing personal.

"Work your way up to an ounce, broke ass niggas, Quavon might give it to you for the low," Gi-Gi said. Gi-Gi was the finest of all three girls. She was five-four, and a hundred and thirty pounds with a thick phat ass and big titties. She wore her hair like Amber Rose, she was definitely like that.

"Bitch...shut your bald head ass up, talking that Quavon shit. Bet you won't take your ass on Wolcott, you ain't gone do that because you know them G.B.C. hoes gone beat that ass," Quazo said, getting mad. Gi-Gi was speaking highly about the opps. The men on the corner erupted in laughter at what Quazo had just said. The crowd on the corner thickened, doing plenty of smoking, drinking and shit talking. It was just another night in Englewood, little did they know shit was about to get nasty.

Vietnam turned down 71st and Winchester. Driving down the dark block, he saw the crowd standing on the corner.

"What y'all wanna do, youngster?" he asked the rest of the team occupying the vehicle.

"Spin the block one more time," Kill-Will said from the passenger seat, scanning the faces in the crowd behind the tent. The twins sat silently in the backseat with black ski-masks covering their faces, clutching their Glocks with 50-round drums attached to them, locked and loaded. Vietnam made a left on Winchester and came back down the block. Kill-Will pulled the ski-mask over his face and cocked the AK.

"Y'all listen, I'm a pull up on the corner and call one of them youngsters to the truck like I'm trying to cope some work. y'all get out and do what y'all do. You know it's females out there?" Vietnam stated, reaching under the seat for his .44 Magnum.

"Fuck 'em...they with the opps, clap they ass too," Kill-Will said.

"Man, that's the second time this Cherokee came down this block," G-Red said, getting off the mailbox and pulling his .9 out. On point and noticing the SUV make its second round through the block, he walked to the curb, hammer out, ready to get active if need be. The truck pulled to the corner slowly as the driver's side window rolled down.

G-Red was about to up his pole and bust until he heard the person behind the wheel say, "Ay youngster, who got some work out here?" G-Red squinted his eyes, trying to see the driver in the truck, the driver seemed to look like a crack head, so he tucked the gun back on his waist and walked up to the driver's side of the vehicle to make the sale.

"What you want, old school?" G Red said, spitting a few bags of crack into his palm.

Vietnam raised the large hand cannon, pointing it in G-Red's face before he growled, "Your life, mutherfucka," and squeezed the trigger. *Boom.* The hollow point .44 slug literally blew G-Red's head off, he was dead before his body even hit the concrete. The doors to the Cherokee flew open and the Blackout Squad emerged, hugging the triggers on their poles.

Moc, Moc, Moc, Moc, Moc. One of the twins let the Glock ride, wetting Dip up from head to toe, dropping him on his back. The Goon Squad was taken by surprise as hot slugs flew in their direction.

"Ahhhh!" GiGi screamed at the murderous scene going on in front of her. Her screams were silenced from a 7.62 round that knocked off half her head, painting the concrete with her brains.

Moc, Moc, Moc, Moc, Moc, Moc. The Glock jerked in one of the twins' hands as he aired Quazo out while he tried to flee from the gunfire. He fell face first to the pavement from getting shot in his back. Kill-Will stood in the middle of the street, spraying everything moving, Rose caught a slug in her stomach that knocked out her intestines, killing her instantly.

The shooting lasted for a minute and ten seconds before police sirens could be heard. The hit squad hopped back in the truck. Vietnam was about to pull off from the scene until he saw one of the opps crawling, holding his stomach. He calmly got out the truck.

"Vietnam, let's get up outta here," Kill-Will said, pulling the sweaty ski-mask off his face, hearing the siren getting closer and closer. Vietnam walked up to the wounded individual and put the cold steel to the back of his head. Pulling the trigger and wetting the grass with his brains, he jogged back to the Jeep got in and pulled off, leaving 71st and Winchester soaked in blood and six dead bodies sprawled out on the block.

WGN News

"I'm Vannesa Johnson..."

"And I'm Tom Wolbert and you are tuned in to *WGN News at Nine*. On today's top story, police are looking for the men involved in what authorities are saying is a massacre on the city's south side. Let's go live with Dionte Collins, who is live at the scene of 71st and Winchester on the south side. Dionte, can you tell us what's going on and why the authorities are calling this crime scene a massacre?"

"Thank you, Tom. I'm standing here on the 7100 block of Winchester Street, where this violent shooting has taken place. Witnesses say a dark-colored SUV pulled up to the corner right here and called a man to the vehicle and then shot him. Three men then got out the same vehicle and opened fire on the crowd of individuals, killing six wounding four others in the shooting. Police investigating the shooting seem to believe the shooting to be gang related. Police would like anybody with information on the horrific crime to please call 911 immediately."

"Thank you, Dionte."

"You bet."

"On other news..."

Quavon logged off the news on his iPhone, satisfied with the work his goons had just put in. He was tired of playing with the Goon Squad, which was nothing but a new generation of the Against The Grain clique known as the A.T.G. Quavon had enough money, drugs and killers to have their entire hood demolished, but he didn't want to bring the feds. That's what had gotten the F.B.I. on Yayo's back in the day and he learned from his brother's mistakes. But in order to stay in a position of power, he would have to remain the lion in the jungle if he wanted a chance at survival.

Quavon had even gotten a lion tattooed on his back, representing his animal ambition in the streets. The words under the lion's head read, *A lion...A person with a King mentality. A leader, who has complete confidence in himself, knows what he wants and is going to get it. He makes sure he and his family are straight. Normally, he calls the shots, but he has no problem putting in his own work, aggressive but yet righteous. Only results to violence when necessary. How to deal with a lion like me? Simple, respect me or die.*

Quavon took a strong pull from his blunt and inhaled, letting the exotic strain relax his nerves. Yayo had finally come home from the feds, but he had come home different than he had gone in. He respected Yayo for wanting to change his life for the better, but what he didn't respect was him trying to brainwash the G.B.C. with all that Martin Luther King shit and getting his men off focus.

Even though Yayo was the co-founder of the Get It Boy Clique, he no longer wanted part of that life. Quavon offered his brother a seat at the throne but he didn't want it, and Quavon wasn't going to press him. If Yayo didn't want the empire he started, then so be it, he would remain the undisputed boss of the G.B.C. Yayo was his brother and they had come from the same womb, but Quavon wasn't going to let anything or anybody stop him from remaining at the top of the drug game.

If Yayo isn't on the same battlefield as me, then it would be in Yayo's best interest to stay off the field, period... Quavon thought. Quavon was in a hazy state of mind when his phone rang, bringing him out of his THC-induced trance. Looking at the caller ID, he saw it was Choppa and answered.

"What up?" he answered as he picked up the ounce of loud off the glass table to roll another blunt.

"What up, you catch the news?" Choppa asked.

"No doubt, my nigga. Make sure you reward them niggas righteously," Quavon said, using his shoulder to hold the phone to his ear while he rolled the weed.

"Already did...they got twenty-five geez a piece."

"You get it out the box?" Quavon asked, pertaining to the Nation box. Dues had to be paid monthly, a thousand dollars a month from each member. These funds were put up for guns, stash houses or anything else conducive to the Get It Boy Clique.

"No fam, I paid them out my pocket."

"Paid 'em out your pocket? Damn, my nigga, put me on!" Quavon joked, lighting the blunt.

"Ha, ha, ha...Sounds good. On a serious note, I just got a call from the homie Suge in Memphis."

"What he talking about?" Quavon blew smoke through his nose. Suge was a Blood gangbanger who was getting money with the G.B.C. He moved a lot of bricks for Quavon.

"He said he having some problems with some individuals."

"Oh yeah? Why he ain't take care of it? Why he calling down here? What, he want us to fight his battles for him? He got enough soldiers down there, tell' em to get active."

"The problem ain't with niggas in the streets, it's with them boys," Choppa informed him. Quavon took a pull from the blunt.

"Check it out, shorty. We ain't gone have this conversation on the phone, where you at?"

"I'm on my way back to the city, coming from Aurora," Choppa replied.

"Alright, look... slide on me. I'm at the spot over on Drexel, we can chop it up then."

"Say less," was Choppa's reply before he ended the call. Quavon tossed his phone on the couch and hit the blunt. If Suge called to the Chi for some aid and assist, then the situation must be serious and slowing down money, and Quavon wasn't trying to hear none of that from niggas in the streets or the law.

Two hours later, Quavon and Choppa sat in Quavon's basement, smoking out of a quarter pound of exotic marijuana and drinking on a fifth of Rémy XO.

"Now what's going on, and what the nigga Suge talking about?" Quavon asked.

"He say it's a new officer on the drug and gang task force on the north side of the city. I guess since he new on the force, he trying to make a name for himself and let his presence felt in the streets. Blood even said he jumped out on one of his workers, pistol-whipped him, then planted some dope on him. He say they been sweating all the blocks and projects that he got locked down, where all his money coming from...Our money." Quavon listened intently.

"My nigga say he's fucking up the business something decent with all the undue heat, he says his hands is tied. He don't know what to do," Choppa said. Memphis was a gold mine and Quavon couldn't afford to have his operation in the south shut down. He had a monthly deadline to meet with his Mexican plug, Mr. Castilino. He was responsible for moving a thousand kilos of heroin and two thousand bricks a month, and the state of Tennessee was definitely making sure that quota was met. Suge was a pure hustler and had the state under lock and key.

"Choppa, we can't afford to let these numbers drop in the south. Castilino flooding us with this shit and his money has to be right at the end of the month. If not, we might as well lace our boots and get ready to go to war with the cartel, because ain't no ducking rec. No excuses, that's the oath I took with dude when I killed his worker, Top Cat. Then came back with the money Top Cat owed…it was a blood oath."

"So, what you saying, chief?" Choppa asked, already knowing where the conversation was going.

"What I'm saying shorty, is I need you to personally go down there and handle this Nation Bizness."

"Why can't he have one of his men handle that shit." Choppa asked, he wasn't scared to put a nigga on the pavement, he had an impeccable body count, but killing an officer of the law was a different beast. Something he had never done. Quavon took another pull from the blunt before he passed it to Choppa. The basement was dimly lit as thick smoke hung in the air like fog.

"My nigga, this ain't like running a drill on one of these niggas in the streets. This has to be strategically done and not too many people can even know about what it about to be done. If we leave it up to them niggas down south to put the work in, there's no telling who will know. Cops start getting nailed then they retaliate with vengeance. Niggas start getting popped, the niggas start talking, we don't know dude 'nem like that, feel me?" Choppa inhaled the smoke, acknowledging what his boss was saying.

"I trust you, Choppa, to get this done right. Go down there do your homework on the pig. Then execute and get back to the crib, small shit to a giant," Quavon said, letting his diabolical words give Choppa the morale he needed to go to Memphis to handle his function and perform righteously. There was no way they could lose their strong hold in the south, so Quavon needed Choppa to handle the business, and get away with it.

Growing up in the streets, Quavon had heard that Yayo had a police officer murdered. The entire city knew of the incident as it gave Yayo respect as well as power, even though he was serving a life sentence in a federal penitentiary. Quavon wanted that power and respect. Quavon and Choppa kept smoking, drinking and talking murder. Quavon would reach another level of the game by getting a cop's head bust, but his nerves and conscience was numb, replaced by money, power and respect.

S. ALLEN

Chapter 5

"Jenny, would you please shut the fuck up! You blowing me with all this whining shit. It is what it is."

"It is what it is? Omega, what am I supposed to do now? You don't care because you don't pay these damn bills," Jenny fumed. She was heated because she had just got fired from Bank of America. Fired, because she wasn't able to make it to work on Monday morning, due to her being stuck in Chicago waiting on Omega. She had already had a verbal warning, a write-up and was told she had no more chances.

Jenny was thirty-two years old and had worked at the bank since she was twenty-one. In those eleven years at working for Bank of America, she had worked her way up from teller to a bank manager, and now after all of her hard work she was now a perfect candidate for the unemployment line. All because she fell in love with a street nigga.

Jenny was born Jenny Dorsey to two prosocial parents in Janesville, Wisconsin. Jenny grew up and went to a predominately white school. She was popular at school and was a star cheerleader. she was blonde, thicker than most girls her age as she had toned shapely legs, a nice set of tits and plump ass to match. In her high school years, Jenny was starting to be curious about black men. The town of Beloit was the neighboring town to Janesville. A lot of black families had migrated to Beloit from Rockford and Chicago.

Along with them came the drugs, guns and gangsterism, turning the city of Beloit into a baby Chicago. Jenny went to a house party with her friend, Corene. While at the party, she met a young black thug named Sancho, and after some drinks, ecstasy pills and a few blunts, Jenny found herself in the back room getting pounded by nine inches of black meat. That one night changed her life as she was now only attracted to black men.

At age eighteen, Jenny moved to Evansville with her parents, where she continued high school. Wanting to move out of her parents' home, she applied for a job at Bank of America, the largest bank in Evansville. Jenny worked hard at the bank for six years before she was promoted to manager. She was living a normal life.

That was, until she met Omega at a club in Madison, Wisconsin, called State Street Brats. She was at the bar when he approached her, offering to buy her a drink. Jenny was attracted to the street nigga in front of her. She let her eyes roam over him. His bald head was tattooed, which gave him a goonish appearance, and his black Balenciaga hoodie went well with his dark gray Armani jeans. The diamond cross that hung from his neck was flooded with clear diamonds. She was turned on by the baller in her presence, making her pussy moist.

Jenny didn't want to come off as a hoe and fought the urge to give him the pussy on the first night, but that urge held complete dominance over her mind frame and she gave in. Later that night at a Motel 6, Omega sexed her in every position possible and the words he spoke softly in her ear as he deep stroked her to ecstasy, melted her heart and made her cum at the same time. She fell in love with him the first night.

From that point on, she had been with Omega. She knew he was involved in drug dealing. She would drop him off in Chicago to hustle and when he came home, he would have knots of money on him. At one time she had even caught him cooking crack cocaine on her stove. But lately, he was becoming more careless about what he was doing and about her priorities, which was why she was in the predicament she was in now... out of a job.

"You act like you can't go get another job. You got a good work history, go apply to a job at another bank," Omega said nonchalantly as he pressed on the buttons on the Sony Play Station controller, playing Call of Duty on a large seventy-five-inch. Jenny stood in front of the TV, blocking his view her face flushed red with anger. Omega threw the controller on the couch, aggravated.

"Omega, it's not about just getting another job, I liked my job. You know how long I have been working there? How could they just fire me like that?" The tears start to roll down her cheeks. Omega stood up and walked over to her, grabbing her by her slim waist and pulled her close, her face now buried in his bare tattooed chest. He ran his fingers through her long blonde hair.

"Baby, fuck them at that bank, it's their loss. Don't even trip, you know I'm a take care of you," Omega whispered in her ear, his lips slightly touching hers, causing her to get moist between the legs.

"They bogus as hell, all the nights I worked overtime for them, all the money I counted for them assholes…And they just gone fire me like that," she cried, her warm tears wetting Omega's chest. The thought of money plus Jenny's large breasts pressed against him caused his dick to get hard. Jenny felt his hard tool against her midsection. Omega envisioned Jenny sitting in a room in a bank counting mounds of dead presidents, causing his sick criminal mind to kick in overdrive. He was the best when it came to the game of finesse. Omega lifted Jenny's chin so he could look her in her watery eyes.

"Fuck them, baby. They did you wrong, so we gone do them wrong," he said, softly kissing her on her lips before she could register what he'd said or respond. Omega stuck his tongue in her mouth as she kissed him back. Putting his hands down her shorts, he squeezed her ass checks, spreading them apart before running his middle finger gently across her tight asshole…Jenny moaned in pleasure.

"Come here, baby girl." Omega took Jenny by the hand and led her to their bedroom. Once in the bedroom he laid her on her back and pulled her shorts and panties down slowly while staring in her blue eyes. Jenny began to rub her manicured fingers over her throbbing love button while she watched Omega take off his Champion joggers and then his boxer briefs. His massive hardness stood at attention, causing her mouth to water. Omega climbed on the bed, stalking his prey.

"Baby, take your shirt off," he commanded as he stroked himself. Jenny did as she was told. She wasn't wearing a bra, so the shirt freed her DD's. Her large protruding pink nipples looked like two baby thumbs. Omega started to kiss her on her lips, neck, then made his way to her titties, where he squeezed them together and savagely and equally sucked them. Jenny was going crazy, she loved how Omega sucked her titties. He then eagle-spread her legs. Using his thumbs, he pulled the hood from over her swollen clit and started to French kiss it.

Jenny came from the feeling of his lips and tongue on her pussy and grabbed the back of his head, pushing him on her pussy with more pressure, she was soaking wet as Omega sucked on her clit like a savage beast in heat, giving her back-to-back orgasms. He knew he had her just where he wanted her and slowly put the tip of his dick inside of her, pushing in only a few inches before he pulled out.

"Omega please, baby…Give it to me, I need you," she purred.

"You love me?" Omega asked, pushing inside of her but not all the way in before pulling out again.

"Yes, I love you…I love you." Omega pushed his meat inside of her again, this time all the way in, filling her up to capacity. She could feel him in the pit of her stomach. Omega slow stroked her deeply. Jenny clawed at his back as her thick thighs wrapped around his waist. Omega waited until Jenny was about to have another breathtaking orgasm before he whispered softly in her ear.

"Baby, I love you so much…I would do anything for you. I would kill a muthafucka for you. You my everything, do you believe me?" he asked her.

"Yes, I believe you."

Omega continued to stroke her. "You don't need them at the bank…fuck around come in there and take all that shit…You deserve it, baby."

"Baby, I'm about to cum again," Jenny moaned, digging her nails in his back. Omega sped up his pace on his stroke, knowing he had her where he wanted her.

"Jenny, you gone help me rob that bank. I'm a do it for us. I love you, girl."

"Oh my God, baby, yes. Yes. Oh my God," Jenny shouted as she experienced a ground-shaking orgasm, not knowing what she had just committed to. Omega continued to pound inside of her walls until he exploded inside of her, filling her up with his seeds.

Pulling his semi-erect dick out of her, he collapsed on his back, his chest heaving up and down from the work he just put in. Jenny laid her head on his sweaty chest. She looked up into his eyes.

"Omega?"

"What's good, shorty?"

"Whatever you do, please...don't ever leave me." Omega kissed her on the head.

"Baby girl, I will never leave you, you are my wifey," Omega replied, laying it on extra thick. Jenny kissed him on his lips and laid her head back on his chest. Five minutes later she fell into a deep sleep, spent from the dick game Omega had just laid down. Omega smiled like the cat that swallowed the canary. Not only did he just fuck her pussy, he also fucked her mind as well. He knew the best way to pull off a heist and get away with it, was that it had to be an inside job.

Omega slid from under Jenny and reached on the dresser to grab the half-blunt of Kush in the ashtray and lit it. Taking a strong pull from the loud, the weed entered his bloodstream, relaxing him. Omega began to plot. The only thing stopping him from killing off the G.B.C. and seeking revenge for Ace and K.I.'s murders, was money and soldiers. Quavon had his money up and a small army of shooters that would kill at his beck and call...there was no way he could compete. But with his financial status proper, he could recruit shooters as he knew in these days and time, niggas weren't loyal to other niggas, but the money other niggas used to feed them.

If he robbed the bank and got away with it, he could return to Chicago and start a serious recruiting campaign in the city, and once his numbers were up, he could rage war on the G.B.C. and soak the streets with their blood. Ace and K.I. would look down on him from the heavens above and be proud their lives did not end in vain.

Omega hit the blunt and thought about the murders he did with Goon a couple nights ago. Goon was one of the reasons Ace and K.I. was in the ground, so he wanted to murk Goon as well, but since he did the drill with him a few nights ago, he now saw him as an asset instead of a liability. He would just put Goon's death sentence on the shelf. He would use Goon and his deadly trigger finger to get to the top…and once he achieved his murderous goals, then Goon would be put to rest with the opposition.

Omega got off the bed quietly trying not to awake Jenny, picked up his cell phone and went to call Goon. The phone rang twice before he answered.

"What's good, Joe?" Good answered seeing it was Omega calling from the caller ID.

"You already know what it is…homicide, what's your location, my nigga?"

"I'm laying low, posted, what's the bizness?" Goon asked.

"Aye, look fam, I got a real major play for us, but I can't talk about it on the phone. I'm a work out the details, then I'm a come slide on you and put you on game," Omega said.

"Say less, my nigga, just let me know when you ready."

"That's a bet, stay safe. Homicide."

"Homicide," Goon replied and ended the call. Goon tossed his phone to the side and buried his nose in the pile of cocaine on the glass table in front of him. Since the double murder he committed with Omega, he had been constantly getting high, trying to calm his nerves as well as his demons, as he kept seeing the face of the man he shot in cold blood in his mind. It had been a few years since he caught a body and the nervousness after committing the act of murder seemed to succumb his mental.

Bumping into Omega at the gas station was the last thing he expected. He was trying to move through the city with caution, because he was ducking the law, the Get It Boy Clique, as well as his own team…the Homicide Crew. He knew he was wrong for getting ghost on Marcus the night the cats in the Porsche truck tried to bring them a move, but what was he supposed to do? Step in the line of fire and throw rocks at them? He didn't know how the gang was going to take what he did. He'd called Marcus outside and them niggas started busting, even though he didn't, it would look like Goon set Marcus up to get killed. Even if he told the story how it went, it wouldn't make sense by the way it sounded and it would be a strong chance he would get his life taken for that bad decision he had made.

Then to make matters worse, Marcus got knocked for the murder in Tennessee, how, he didn't know. Marcus had nailed a few dudes with the pole, but you had to be a different type of gangster to hold up in that interrogation room when them crackers start talking football numbers, and on the inside, Goon felt Marcus wasn't cut like that. It hurt Goon's heart that Ace and K.I. had been killed, he cried like a baby when he found out how they found K.I. in a dark alley with her brains blown out, it crushed him. He fucked with K.I. hard. To Goon, even with her being a female, K.I. was the baddest bitch to play the murder game.

With everything going on and Goon having no facts, he felt it was best if he just got low, as he didn't want to move with objectivity and end up getting killed, or worse, locked up for murder. Running into Omega was a surprise, he hadn't seen his mans in a long time and was happy to see him. Omega was family, he was Homicide Crew, and they were the last two left from the gang. When Omega asked him to run a drill on the opps on 69th, he knew Omega was testing his loyalty, as well as trying to read his temperature.

Putting the work in was nothing, it gave him a sense of relief when he blew Mud's brains out in front of Fat Albert's. Killing one of the opps was retribution for Ace and K.I. now, Omega had called and said he wanted to holler at him about a lick. He didn't completely trust Omega as he didn't know his intentions or motives. So, when he did meet up with Omega, whenever that might be, he would make sure his gun accompanied him. They were playing the murder game and at any point and time, friend could easily turn into foe without warning.

The next morning, Omega awakened to the smell of bacon frying. Looking at the clock on the wall, he saw it was 9:45 in the morning. Omega got out of bed and made his way to the bathroom. After taking a shit, he stepped in the shower and turned on the water. The hot water coming from the shower head felt good. Omega was excited because he had come up with the plan to rob Bank of America. But what excited him more was what he was going to do with the funds from the robbery. If everything went right, he was going to knock Quavon off his throne, and the Get It Boy Clique would be extinct in Chi-Raq.

Omega let the water run over his body, hoping Jenny hadn't changed her mind about giving him the information he needed to successfully pull off the heist. He knew she was vulnerable, and this would be the best time to exploit her weakness. After showering, Omega got out and got dressed, putting on a tight V-neck Polo shirt, stone washed Rockstar jeans and a pair of red and white *Space Jam* Jordans and made his way downstairs. Following his nose, he went to the kitchen. Jenny had her back to him, flipping a pancake. She had on a pink pair of Victoria's Secret boy shorts, a Van Dutch tight T and a pair of Gucci flip-flops. Omega stood there admiring her flawless body, resembling the white model, CoCo. He cleared his throat, almost scaring her half to death. She turned around.

"Hey, baby…how long you been standing there?"

"Long enough," Omega replied smoothly, taking a seat at the head of the table where two rolled blunts of Sour Diesel sat next to an empty plate.

"Hope you hungry, daddy," Jenny said, before she came over and loaded his plate with pancakes, turkey bacon and cheese eggs.

"Damn, baby. All this for me?"

"Only the best for my king," Jenny retorted. Omega liked the mood Jenny was in, which only boosted his morale to lay his lick down. After Jenny made her plate, she sat at the table with her man.

"Damn, shorty. This shit fire," Omega said, chewing a forkful of the buttery pancakes.

"Thank you, baby." After demolishing his breakfast, Omega grabbed one of the pre-rolled blunts, sparked it and took a strong pull, and held the smoke in his lungs before blowing the smoke out.

"What you got going on today?" Omega asked.

"Nothing really, I have to go to the bank to clear out my desk. Uhh, I hate I have to even go back there and look these people in the face," Jenny vented with frustration in her tone, eating a piece of turkey bacon. Omega, like a cobra full of venom, went for the strike.

"So, you still on what I asked you last night?" He took another pull from the blunt.

"Hell yeah, why wouldn't I be? Fuck them. Baby, I just don't want you to get in trouble. It would fuck me up if something happened to you," Jenny said, genuinely concerned about him. Omega wasn't worried about getting caught, he was just happy she was still with the demonstration.

"Listen, baby. Long as you give me the right information, everything will go smooth. What's the best way to hit the safe?" Omega questioned.

"Well baby, it's four tellers, the assistant manager and the bank manager. The bank manager has the key to the safe, but baby, the safe only opens electronically at certain times throughout the day. So, your timing has to be right." Jenny ate a fork full of cheese eggs.

"Ok...Continue, I'm listening. Is there any security in the bank?"

"No, we don't have security."

"When is the most money in the safe?" Omega probed, taking another hit from the blunt.

"Well, the Brinks truck drops off between five hundred thousand to eight hundred thousand on Monday for the payroll checks. They put the money in a room, where it sits until Wednesday. Then we take it to the vault, break the bands and fill the teller station and cash cows," Jenny informed him. Omega started to choke from the smoke caught in his lungs and the numbers Jenny had just spoken.

"Shorty...you mean to tell me it be a half-mil sitting in one room? Who got the key? Or is the room just open or what?"

"The room is always locked, and the bank manager has the room key and the vault key."

"Who is he?"

"His name is Michael Barnes. He's an older white man, about sixty-five years old, he lives here in the town of Evansville. He took my place as bank manager."

"Damn shorty, you had access to all that paper like that and you didn't let me know? We could have been rich." Omega sneered, screwing his face up at her. Jenny came over and sat on his lap and took the blunt out his hand.

"Mega, don't be mad at me. I never thought I would be in this predicament and involved in something like this, and at the same time, I still feel like I shouldn't be letting you do this," Jenny said, pulling on the weed.

Omega sneered. *Bitch, you ain't letting me do shit. I got the information I need, you expendable as fuck now*, Omega thought. He didn't love Jenny. She was a good piece of ass, but he wasn't trying to play house. He was trying to take over the murderous streets of the Chi, and put Quavon and his crew of flunkies in the Burr Oaks Cemetery.

"Nah, baby girl, we making the right decision. After we do this, our future will be set. Then we can move to Cali, get married, start a family and live our lives and never have to worry about money. Or anything, for that matter. Now this what I want you to do. When you clear your desk out, I need you to take pictures with your phone. Take pictures of the vault, the teller's station, the money room and the back door. Once you do that, send it to my phone, erase the pics off your phone and go to the phone store and get another SIM card and destroy the other one. Ok?"

"Ok baby," Jenny said. All she was stuck on was the word married. With Omega putting a ring on her finger, she would be willing to do anything for him.

Omega patted her on her thick bottom, signaling for her to get off his lap.

"Shorty, you can take my car, I'm a take yours…I need to run to Chicago real quick to get up with somebody. I will be back later tonight."

"Mega, just let me go handle this business at the bank. It won't take long, then I can drive you," Jenny pleaded, wanting to go with him.

"No, baby. I will be back, and when I come back, it's going to be all about us. A nigga gone try to put a baby in your fine ass." Jenny started to blush. She went in her purse and gave Omega the keys to the Dodge Intrepid. He kissed her on the lips before he went to get his Glock .357 and dipped out the crib, en route to Chi-Raq.

Three hours later, Omega and Goon sat in a bar on the north side of the city, called Al's, located on Loyola Street. They were discussing the robbery of Bank of America over shots of 1800 Tequila. Jenny had sent Omega the pictures he requested. He now had the layout of the inside of the bank in his iPhone 11. He had also done some light homework on the outside of the bank before he got on the highway headed to the Chi.

From what he saw, the bank was located in a residential neighborhood. The back of the bank was in a parking lot that was connected to a one-way street, that led to a main street. *It would be a sweet getaway*, Omega thought. Goon never thought in a million years that Omega would ask for him to aid and assist in robbing a bank. When Omega mentioned he had a move for them, he figured he was talking about a drug dealer.

Goon had robbed and shot plenty of dope boys in the Chi, earning him his name, but he had never run in a bank. To Goon that was nothing, it was just recreation. He was definitely with the lick, putting the steel in the face of some scary ass cracker for that dough would be a piece of cake. Goon downed another shot of tequila as he continued to listen to Omega lay out the plans for the robbery.

"This the inside of the bank, my nigga." Omega slid Goon the iPhone. Goon used his finger to scroll through the images. Omega continued. "This shit sweet, fam, the Brinks truck gone drop off the money on Monday. At least a half-ticket."

"Why we just don't hit the truck? They probably just dropping a small portion of the money to the bank, the motherload probably in the truck," Goon asked, cutting Omega off while looking in the face of an old white bank teller on the phone. Omega thought about what Goon had just proposed for a few seconds. What he had just said made sense, but he quickly dismissed the idea.

"Na fam, if we hit the truck, we might have to blow they ass down, them crackers carry poles. It's a small town and the police station on the next block. We get active, they gone here them shots and you already know how that's gone go."

"Indeed," Goon replied, seeing the logic in what Omega said.

"I got an idea, it's a small police station on the next block. Small like on *The Andy Griffith Show* shit, it's also an elementary school on the same block as the police station. This what I was thinking, fam, we gone use one of those Walgreens TracFone's, get the number to the elementary school and call in a bomb threat. You already know they take that shit serious, every cop, fed and detective in the county gone rush to that school. We gone use the scanner and once the call come across the airwaves, we gone run up in the bank and do what we do! Make sense?" Omega said with a devilish smirk on his face.

"Boy, on homicide... you a genius, that sound official. What we gone do with the bread?" Goon asked, wanting to get more in depth and wanting to know the move. He was taught to always plan from the beginning to the end. Omega let out a slight chuckle, this was the part he was itching to get to.

"Goon, we gone take over the streets."

"How we gone do that? Talk, I'll talk back."

"What are niggas loyal to in them streets?" Omega asked Goon.

"That's a no brainer scud, Niggas loyal to that paper...that's fact."

"My point exactly. We gone buy up all the drugs and whips, go around recruiting these young savages in the city. A nigga a kill his dog, day one nigga for twenty geez and a Range Rover. Feel me?"

"Ain't no question," Goon replied.

"We gone recruit shooters from each side of the city and make them Homicide Crew. Once we get our numbers up, we gone eliminate all them Get It Boy Clique and put that soft ass nigga Quavon in the dirt. We gone finish what we started, we gone make Ace and K.I. proud of us, my nigga," Omega vowed. Goon smiled at the diabolical plan that was just laid down. A lot of blood was about to be spilled in the streets and in the end, the demise of the G.B.C. would be served on a deadly plate. There would be a transfer of power over the gang-infested streets of Chicago.

Chapter 6

It was almost 4:00 when Yayo looked at his watch. He had fifteen minutes until his lunch break, and he couldn't wait. He had secured a job at the Ford Assembly Plant and was making twenty dollars an hour. Kewann had set the job up for him as one of the Muslim brothers was in charge of the hiring at the plant. Twenty dollars an hour was peanuts to the money Yayo was used to seeing, but he wasn't tripping off the money, as far as his financial status, he was straight. Yayo had managed to save up forty-six thousand in prison from hustling on the compound, so he had a comfortable kitty put up.

Yayo had been home only a couple of months and was still trying to get used to being free. The ability to eat, sleep and be around his family was almost unreal, it was if he was living a dream. For eight and a half years he had been confined and living by controlled movement. He had no control over his life whatsoever. His entire life and everything in it was dictated by the Federal Bureau of Prisons but now all of that was over and it was taking some time to get used to.

The buzzer sounded off inside the factory, meaning it was time to take his break. Yayo went to the vending machine, purchased a turkey burger, and put it inside the microwave in the breakroom. Once the microwave beeped, Yayo got his burger and got an orange soda from the pop machine and made his way to the parking lot. He was coming out to meet Kewann for the first time. He had spoken to him a few times on the phone, but never met him face-to-face.

Walking out the building, the bright sun blessed his eyes, causing him to squint them as he scanned the parking lot. Kewann told him on the phone he would be in a Pepsi-blue Lincoln Continental. Yayo noticed the vehicle off to the side of the parking lot and made his way to the whip. He saw a dark-skinned brother sitting behind the wheel, a black kufi covering his bald head. Yayo could hear the locks being unlocked as he approached the car. He walked up to the passenger side of the Lincoln. Kewann signaled for him to hop in. Yayo got in the luxury automobile.

"A salaam alaikum, brother," Kewann greeted in Arabic.

"Walaikum assalam," Yayo greeted back.

"It's finally good to see the face that goes with the voice."

"Likewise, brother," Yayo responded.

"So, how is the job going? I know it's not the best job, but it gets you out the halfway house, Ock."

"I can't complain, all blessings I'm grateful for."

"No doubt…listen, Ock. I want to get straight to business. I'm going to give you a little history on what we are about and where we came from. Like you, I was in federal prison, in the United States Penitentiary. It was in those same prisons that I met Mr. B…I call him Bernard. I took my Shahada at a young age. I came into the system with a fifteen-year sentence for a gun. I was wild, impulsive and had no sense of direction.

"The reason for me not having my direction was for the simple fact I had nobody to steer me in the right direction. My father was murdered when I was only ten years old, my mother was strung out on heroin. So, I did what most black men in the ghetto do, resort to the neighborhood heroes. The drug dealers and the gangsters. I adapted to a life of crime and fell victim to its mishaps…fifteen years in federal prison. Bernard cuffed me, I was wild and untamed. We built a solid friendship. He would always tell me that it was easy to fix the problem with the violence in the streets of our urban ghettos, and I know he told you the same." Yayo nodded his head in the affirmative.

"All we have to do, Ock, is reach the minds of the youth and get in their minds to teach them a better way."

"How do we do that?" Yayo asked.

"By using influence from brothers like yourself. Yayo, if you can influence hardened street criminals to believe in what you believe in, and to live their lives according to your politics, your dreams and ambitions, then you can definitely captivate the minds of the undeveloped juveniles, catch them before the street corrupts them completely. We can do this by marching a campaign on the highest crime areas in the city, the county jails as well as juvenile facilities.

"We have a crew of highly intelligent men like yourself, dedicated to the cause. Chicago is just the starting point…the world will be our ending. Do you understand me, brother?" Yayo took the last bite of his sandwich and balled up the wrapper and took a swig from his orange soda to wash it down.

"I completely understand, Ock. We definitely need to reach the youngsters out there. I been watching the news and it's already been three-hundred-something murders in the city and the summer just started. It's sick out here. I'm just honored to be able to be a part of the movement."

"And it's an honor to have you a part of it, my brother. How much longer do you have to be in that halfway house?" Kewann asked him.

"I have to be there another four months, but my case manager told me it's a strong possibility I can get out as early as next month, as long as I keep doing what I'm doing and keep my nose clean."

"That's great, brother. As soon as you are released from that minor captivity, then we will get right to business…understand?"

"Understood, fam."

"Oh, by the way, I talked to Bernard. He asked about your well-being, I told him everything was all well with you, he sends his love and blessings."

"Tell 'em I send mine as well and I will get at him real soon," Yayo said, looking at his watch. "That's my time, fam. I got to get back on the clock."

"Very well, Ock, we will keep in touch. Make sure you get your mind right, it will be time to jump in the battlefield soon, in hopes to save our race from this pandemic of urban genocide." Kewann shook Yayo's hand before Yayo got out the whip, making his way back inside the plant. Yayo's morale was up. He couldn't wait to get released from the halfway house so he could help secure the lives of the forgotten and lost.

Choppa sat low in the passenger seat of a 2020 Tesla, Suge was behind the wheel gliding the foreign whip through the north side of Memphis. Choppa had touched down in the home of the blues late last night and wasn't going to return to Chicago until he accomplished what he had come to do. And that was to kill the detective on the drug and gang task force that was interrupting the flow of Quavon's money.

Suge was riding Choppa through the land, showing him the most lucrative spots that was bringing in the most numbers. These spots were also hot spots, the ones that was targeted by the new detective. Choppa found out his name was Detective Calvin Holmes, also known in the streets as "Spicey." Spicey was a forty-five-year-old white boy and was originally from Birmingham, Alabama. He worked his way up from traffic cop to detective in a fifteen-year period. Wanting more action and higher wages, he transferred to Memphis to work on the drug and gang task force...also called the Memphis Devils. Spicey saw working with the Memphis Devils as an opportunity to exploit his violent tactics on the local street dealers in Memphis...And was starting to exploit these vicious tactics on Suge's workers. Choppa pulled the photograph of Spicey from the brown manila envelope.

"So, this the pale face cracker that's bringing all the undue heat to your people, huh?"

"Yep, that's the sonovabitch," Suge replied. Choppa stared at the man on the picture, sizing him up.

"Y'all got his routine?" Choppa asked, already knowing the answer. If they'd their homework, then they would've already put the work in.

"Nah Blood, we ain't got his routine but he work at the precinct, North Memphis Precinct," Suge told him. Choppa placed the picture back in the envelope.

"All right, Blood, y'all just shut down all the spots until further notice...That come down from Quavon."

"If we shut down, then how we gone meet the month quota?" Suge asked, making a left on Bill Street.

"Don't worry about the monthly quota, my nigga, things will be back to normal momentarily. We don't need nobody getting knocked and put in no situations, feel me?" Choppa said, making sure Suge understood the orders that were given. Suge and Choppa rode through the trenches of North Memphis before they went to a bar to have a few drinks to kill some time. They continued to converse about the move that was about to be put down, until Choppa called an Uber.

He had gotten the information he needed from Suge…that was a name and a face and place of employment. Now it was time to do the groundwork. Everything was on hold, which he knew couldn't last long, so that meant he had to handle his function properly…as well as swiftly.

Choppa took an Uber to Memphis Airport to Enterprise where he rented a low-key tinted Buick Lucerne. After purchasing the rental with a bogus credit card, Choppa put the Northern Precinct in the GPS system and followed the directions to his destination. Choppa parked a block away from the police station, leaned the seat back and watched the activity through the fifteen-hundred-dollar night vision optic binoculars…stalking his prey like a lion in the jungle.

It was 3:30 in the morning when a black Crown Victoria pulled into the parking lot at the police station and parked. Two men exited the vehicle, one black, one white. Choppa focused his attention on the white officer, zeroing in on the white officer he identified as Spicey.

Detective Calvin Holmes, aka Spicey, went in the precinct to clock out from his twelve-hour shift. After completing some paperwork, he left out the station and walked to his car…a Dodge Challenger, popped the trunk and put his bag in it, closed it and got behind the wheel, and pulled out of the parking lot.

Choppa pulled off, tailing him close, but not close enough to look suspicious. Choppa followed him to Orange Mound Memphis to a low-key neighborhood. The detective turned down a one-way street called Hermes Street. Choppa kept straight, not trying to alert Spicey. Choppa doubled back down the block. Looking to the left, he noticed a X5 BMW truck and lime green Dodge Challenger parked behind it in the driveway, the same Challenger Spicey was driving.

"Bingo!" Choppa said to himself. He had found the residence of the intended target. He now knew Spicey worked from 3:00 pm to 3:00 am, drove a lime green Challenger, and where he stayed, that was all the information he needed to kill him.

The following morning...4:00am

Choppa waited patiently on the side of Spicey's home. It was early 4 am in the morning, the grass had a moist frost covering it as a few birds began to chirp. A couple of the residents had just awakened, getting out of their beds, going to their kitchen to boil water for make a pot of coffee to give them the energy they needed to start their day.

A black hoodie covered Choppa's dreaded head, a black Velcro gator mask covering the lower part of his face, while his gloved hands held a fully automatic, short barrel MAK-90 with no stock. A 30-shot Polygram magazine was loaded with hollow point 7.62 caliber rounds, also known as cop killers. He had been lying in wait for two hours for Spicey to pull up. His patience had finally paid off as he saw a car pull up at the beginning of the street and put the left turn signal on and make a left on Hermes Street...it was a lime green Dodge Challenger.

Click Clack...Choppa pulled the slide back on the MAK-90, chambering a round. Spicey pulled into the driveway, parked and killed the engine to the Challenger. Choppa stood from his position as Spicey got out the vehicle and went to the trunk. After popping the trunk, he grabbed his bag as Choppa stealthily approached him with the assault rifle extended in front of him.

Spicey closed the trunk and when he turned around, a hooded individual stood before him holding a rifle, the clip longer than a federal prison sentence. Spicey dropped his bag and went for his holstered service weapon, a .40 caliber Taurus Millenium...his attempt was futile, all he saw was the bright flash from the rifle.

Cha, Cha The first two slugs hit him in the chest, almost blowing his heart out his back. *Cha, Cha, Cha* Choppa let the MAK-90 bark, the rifle jerked in his hand from the slight recoil. The powerful slugs knocked Spicey to the side of the Challenger, the 7.62 rounds punished him...He slid down to the concrete but yet still breathing.

Walking up and pointing the hot tip off the barrel to his head, Choppa pulled the trigger once more, *Cha* blowing Spicey's head off, shutting his lights out forever...ending his life on earth.

Choppa jogged back to his car and pulled away from the scene. Quavon was adamant about the flourish of his money eleva-tion...Nobody was to stop him and his ambition and if they tried, they would be laid to rest. Nobody was exempt, not even the law.

S. ALLEN

Chapter 7

Omega and Goon sat in a low-key van, catty corner from the Bank of America in Evansville. Bulletproof vests covered their chests and semi-autos laid across their legs It was 12:15 in the afternoon and the traffic in the center of town was mild. Omega started to perspire under his arms from the nervousness he felt from the crime he was about to commit. He wasn't scared, he was more like excited. He picked up the TracFone he purchased from Walgreens from the next town over and dialed 911.

"This is 911, what's your emergency?" the operator stated.

"Listen, this is not a game. There is a bomb inside of the elementary school in the town of Evansville in Wisconsin. I repeat, there is a bomb at the elementary school in the town of Evansville in Wisconsin." Omega pressed end on the phone, terminating the call. He then logged on to the My Scanner app on his iPhone, which he already had turned in the frequency in the city of Evansville. Putting in his Bluetooth, he waited to hear what he was listening for.

This is Emergency Central Control. I just had a bomb threat called in at the town's elementary," the operator said over the airwave.

"That's it right there, my nigga, let's get to it. Remember give me sixty seconds exactly," Omega said, putting a red Wisconsin Badger fitted cap over his head, then a pair of sunglasses over his eyes. Goon put the van in drive and pulled off, en route to the bank. Sirens could be heard getting closer, as the town's elementary was located on the next block from the bank.

Goon pulled up in front of Bank of America and parked. Police cruisers raced past them on their way to the elementary school. Goon put his long dreads in a ponytail and then put a Green Bay Packers hat on top of his head. Taking the Glock off his lap he placed a 30-round extended magazine in the butt of the weapon.

"Remember, Goon…sixty seconds," Omega repeated again, then exited the van. Walking smoothly to the entrance of the bank his palms began to sweat inside of a brand-new pair of Ken Griffey, Jr. baseball gloves.

"Hi, how are you?" an elderly white woman greeted as she passed Omega in the corridor of the bank entrance…he paid her no mind. Once inside the small, almost empty bank, Omega pulled the .45 from the waistline of his Army fatigue cargo pants.

"This is a robbery, get on the ground." A customer stood in line looking stupid like he was hard of hearing. Omega rushed him and brought the four-nickel down on top of his bald head, causing the skin on his head to separate. He fell to the ground, his head leaking like a faucet. The teller behind the counter who was servicing the man that had just got his head bust to the white meat let out a piercing scream.

"Shut up, bitch, before I pop your dumb ass…Matter fact, come here," Omega growled pointing the pipe in her face. He reached over the counter and grabbed her by the collar and practically pulled her across the counter by her shirt just as Goon rushed in, pointing his Glock in an aggressive manner. Omega forcefully pushed the bank teller to the ground.

"Y'all two bring y'all ass from behind that counter." Omega pointed the gun in their direction. The two white ladies walked from around the counter with their hands to the sky, scared to death.

"Lay down, muthafuckas…lay down," Goon threatened with murderous intent. Omega scanned the lobby and found just who he was looking for… the bank manager. Omega knew the cover might be blown. He rushed over to him, snatched the phone out his hand and hung it up.

"Get you stupid ass up." Omega grabbed him with force by his collar and assisted him with aggression in getting out of the chair. He placed the large cannon under his chin, then whispered in his ear. Now, we going to the money room, then we going to the vault. If you give me so much as a small problem, I'm going to blow your fucking head off. Are we clear?"

"Yes-yes," the bank manager stuttered while they walked to the money room. Goon used zip ties to secure the tellers and the few customers' hands behind their backs, then posted by the entrance of the bank, just in case anybody came in. He was on point while Omega went to get the money.

Omega sneered, "Open it," pressing the gun to the side of the bank manager's rib cage. The scared manager took the key chain off his neck and inserted a key into the lock mechanism, turned it and tried to open it but it remained locked.

"You get one more chance, old man, then I shoot you and open it myself," Omega sneered, looking at his watch, they had been in the bank exactly three minutes. Omega wasn't tripping about the time. Every police officer, detective and fireman was at the elementary school, trying to evacuate it. Omega had his Bluetooth in his ear. No alarms went off pertaining to a bank robbery in progress, his morale was up. The bank manager tried another key and put it in the lock mechanism. the door opened. Omega pushed him in the back, into the pitch-black room.

"Turn the fucking light on, don't make me smash your ass," Omega threatened. The manager flicked a switch on the side of the wall, the light invaded the small room and when it did, Omega almost had a stroke at the sight of the thick-plastic-wrapped, stacked bricks of cash that sat neatly on a small table. He had never seen so much U.S. currency at one time.

"Get on the ground, pops," Omega ordered the manager to lay face down on the floor. Looking around the room, he saw a dolly laying up against the wall. He tucked the gun on his waist and walked over to the table of money and picked one of the large bags up. It was heavier than he expected. After getting the ten bags off the table and on the floor, he went to get the dolly. Omega loaded the dolly up with the dead presidents. He then went in his cargo pants pocket and retrieved the plastic zip ties, knelt down to the bank manager and secured his hands behind his back.

"Please, you don't have to do this, young man," the bank manager pleaded.

"Shut up, old man, this ain't your money. You not taking no loss, so if I was you, I would keep quiet." Omega thought about clearing out the teller station, but he knew it would be a good chance he could get some bait money, a dye pack or a tracer, and he wasn't trying to take a chance with any of that.

The money he now had in his possession was untraceable. Omega kicked the bank manager in the face, his steel-toe Timberland knocked three of his teeth out and had them spinning on the floor like dice. Afterwards, he took the dolly and rolled it to the front lobby where Goon was keeping the hostages in order with the Glock. Goon almost lost his breath at the sight of all the money loaded on the dolly.

"Come on, fam, we got to get this in the van. But we can't just roll this shit out like this, we gotta cover the bread up," Omega said, looking around the bank for something to throw over the money before they took it out the bank. He saw a table with a blue tablecloth on it that had pamphlets about the banks and its programs laid across it.

He rushed over and yanked the tablecloth off the table. "This should do," he said out loud, then came over and covered the money with the tablecloth. Omega looked through the blinds in the window. Police were everywhere making their way to the elementary school to assist with the bomb threat.

"Goon, check it out… stand in the corridor and give me some security while I get this in the van," Omega said.

"My nigga…you don't see all the laws cruising around this bitch?" Goon retorted, sweating nervously like he was about to walk to the gas chamber.

"Fuck them, they not on us. We gotta get up outta here…we can't stay up in here, we gotta make our move…Just hold me down, it's do or die, my nigga," Omega replied and started rolling the dolly out not waiting for Goon to reply. Goon followed Omega but stayed posted in the corridor, looking out at the street while clutching his gun and silently praying the police didn't intervene, because it was going to be a deadly situation. It took Omega two minutes to load the money in the van before he rolled the dolly back into the bank.

"Come on, Goon, we gone lock them in the money room, plus it's another bundle back there." Omega and Goon got all the hostages off the floor and forced them at gunpoint to the money room.

"Everybody on the ground," Omega commanded, pulling the .45 off his waist.

"Where the rest of the money at, fam?" Goon asked, looking around the empty room. Then it hit him like a ton of bricks, he knew he shouldn't have trusted Omega. He turned around only to see Omega pointing his hammer in his face. *Boc* Omega squeezed the trigger and the sound from the .45 sounded like thunder inside the small, confined room. The bullet penetrated Goon's cranium, blowing his thoughts out in a spray of brain tissue and skull fragments. His body hit the ground with a loud thud. Crimson red blood formed a thick puddle under his head.

One of the tellers began to scream in horror at the sight of murder. Omega turned off the light and closed the door behind him. Casually, he walked out the bank, got in the van and pulled into traffic, with a van full of cash that was going to ultimately turn his life around.

Later that night, Omega was in the crib sitting with Jenny on the couch watching TV. The 10:00 news had just aired. The robbery and homicide at the Bank of America was broadcast across all local stations in Wisconsin. Dane County, Rock County, as well as Winnebago County in Rockford, Illinois, were all on high alert, looking for the armed suspect responsible for the brutal homicide.

Jenny sat quietly in shock after learning about the murder. She never wanted anybody to get hurt in the process, now she was starting to feel guilty about putting Omega on the lick. The video surveillance showed a picture of Omega. It was hard to identify him, but Jenny knew it was him on video. The news said the authorities had Evansville blocked off as they tried to follow all leads of which they had none.

Omega sat calmly, smoking a blunt, watching Jenny intently, her actions making her seem suspect. No more did he see "Ms. ride or die with my nigga" Jenny. After seeing the news, that Jenny was replaced with, "Oh my God what am I going to do? I'm a tell on his ass" Jenny. Omega peeped game.

"Come on, Jenny, let's bounce up outta here," Omega said, blowing smoke through his nostrils. Jenny slowly turned her head to face him, her sad puppy dog eyes a dead giveaway to her weakness…she had just become a liability.

"Baby, why did you kill your friend? Omega, I never wanted anybody to get hurt," Jenny said in a soft guilty tone. Omega put the blunt out in the ashtray.

"Friend? That nigga just got what he had coming. He the reason my friend is in the cemetery. I'm just returning the favor. Now like I said…let's bounce the fuck up out of here," Omega said through clenched teeth. Jenny shook her head in the negative.

"Omega, I don't want anything to do with murder, I can't go with you. I'm scared, baby." A lone tear escaped her eye.

"Fine then, shorty, I guess we done then. Don't call my phone, trying to get up with a nigga…I knew you was a weak ass bitch. You don't deserve no nigga like me. I did this for you and this how you treat me?" Omega said, standing up, playing victim.

"Baby, it's not like that…I love you, Omega. Please don't leave me," Jenny cried. Omega turned his back to her, walking toward the door as he slowly took off his designer belt. Jenny put her head in her lap crying her eyes out. Her life was spinning out of control, she had lost her job and she was sure they would come questioning her about what happened at the bank. Omega figured that as well. He crept up behind Jenny with his hands behind his back.

"Jenny, I love you, baby girl." When Jenny looked up, Omega attacked like a king cobra, wrapping the leather belt around her neck and applying massive pressure. Jenny reached for her neck in an attempt to pry the belt off as she began to lose breath. Omega used all the strength he could muster while Jenny jerked and kicked, His force was so strong from the chokehold, it crushed her windpipe. After sixty seconds, Jenny lost all fight she had, and her loving soul traveled to the afterlife.

Omega laid her limp body on the couch, took his belt from around her neck and put it back through the loops of his jeans. He knew he had to get outta there and fast. He went in the kitchen and looked under the sink and grabbed a towel and a bottle of Clorox bleach. It took an hour and a half to wipe down Jenny's apartment. He made sure he wiped down anything he possibly touched.

Omega grabbed his belongings after doublechecking his work and left the apartment, as well as Jenny's body, a memory. Getting

84

inside the van, Omega put his gun on his lap and pulled out of the apartment complex's parking lot. he knew Evansville was hot as fish grease because of the murder at the bank. All he had to do was make it to the highway and he was on his way.

He came to a stop light on Enterprise Street. Omega looked catty corner and saw a squad car sitting discreetly inside the BP gas station. To make matters worse, another cruiser had just pulled up behind him. Looking though his rearview mirror, he could see the officer on his walkie talkie.

"Shit," he cursed to himself, now clutching the gun. "Whatever happens, I'm not going out like a lame to serve all day in the penitentiary, they going to have to work," Omega mused out loud. He had just committed two homicides and he wasn't going alive. The light turned green and he calmly pulled off, making sure he did the speed limit. The cruiser remained behind him for six city blocks. Omega was sweating profusely. He was coming up on an overpass, where he could get on I-94.

Omega was about to smash the gas until he saw the cruiser turn off. A smile plastered across his lips as he jumped on the highway. He started to beat on the steering wheel in joy. He had gotten away, had a van full of cash he hadn't even counted but knew by eyeballing it was more than a half million in cash. The first part of this plan had been executed, his money was up, and he had finally left Goon stanking for his disloyal act to the gang.

Now he was about to get his weight up, get his shooters on deck and take the G.B.C. to war. Omega was about to soak the Chicago streets with blood. Quavon and his men had killed the wrong nigga from the wrong squad. It was about to be drill season for them for putting their hands on Ace.

S. ALLEN

Chapter 8

Two months later

Yayo was at home comfortably at the condo he shared with Shakira. He had been released from the federal halfway house and was now free. The only thing he was to do now was abide by the rules of the federal parole officer. Yayo was to serve three years of supervised release that started the moment he signed his release papers from the halfway house. Yayo set on the black leather sectional sofa watching one of his favorite movies called *I'm gonna get you Sucka*, staring the Wayans brothers.

Watching the movie brought back childhood memories, some good, some bad. Shakira sat next to him, looking through a magazine called *Kite*. She didn't have any hair appointments today, so she took off work to relax with her man. It was a Friday afternoon, and they were sitting back chilling, enjoying each other's company. The eight long years had put a mental strain on their relationship and now they were just trying to rebuild what the federal government had tried to destroy.

It was the end of the movie and the credits now invaded the screen. At the same time, Yayo's phone vibrated in the pocket of his True Religion joggers. Looking at the caller ID, seeing who it was, he sent the caller to his voicemail and put the iPhone back in his pocket. Shakira saw the activity through her peripheral vision.

"Who was that?" she asked, without even looking up from the magazine she was browsing through. Yayo chose his words carefully before he spoke, knowing that how he articulated his words would set the tone for the conversation that he dreaded to have with Shakira. He was a grown man with nothing to hide, so he would be honest and assertive about this situation.

"That was Amanda, she called me pertaining to Jamarie and the blood test. She just wants what I want," Yayo explained.

"Well, why you didn't just answer the phone? Seem like you hiding something," Shakira said, putting the magazine on the table.

"I just didn't feel like talking…we chilling," Yayo responded.

"Yeah whatever, Yaton…but let me ask you something…and be honest with me."

"Of course, baby."

"Do you have feelings for her? And don't lie to me."

"Feelings for her? Why would you feel like that, Shakira?"

"Just answer the question, Yaton…Please," Shakira said sternly, waiting for him to answer. Yayo shook his head, smiling at her.

"Shakira, that's crazy. How you just ask me that, after all we been through? We even talked about this and you said you was supporting me through this, now this how you coming at me? No, I don't have feelings for her. I just want to see if Jamarie is mine, so I can step up like a man and take care of him, as he will be my responsibility. That's what real niggas do, it has nothing to do with her," Yayo retorted sounding agitated from Shakira's insecurity and questioning his love and loyalty to her.

When Yayo had sex with C.O. Sanchez, he was serving a life sentence, was vulnerable and was strained from the day-to-day life of prison. Shakira wasn't there to comfort him with the nourishment of a woman's love. C.O. Sanchez was, and it was a strong possibility that Jamarie was the outcome of their fifteen minutes of lust. What happened had happened and couldn't be taken back. Then, having unprotective sex in that situation was irresponsible, but now it was time for them to make the right decisions…all parties involved.

Shakira had told Yayo while he was in prison that she would support him in dealing with this situation, but now that he was home and it was in her face, she was starting to feel insecure. She had seen Amanda Sanchez on Facebook and was beginning to feel threatened by the beauty of the busty Latina. She just prayed that Yayo would remain loyal to her and their family, as she also prayed that when the blood test did come back, it would prove Yayo was not the father.

"Yaton, I can't believe you did what you did…we wouldn't even be going through this bullshit. She gone fuck up our family…baby, this is not fair." Yayo couldn't believe how Shakira was coming out of left field. He pulled her close to him.

"Shakira, you are my wifey. What happened with me and Amanda happened, and it had nothing to do with feelings. I was in prison without a release date. All I want to do is see if shorty is mines. My heart belongs to you as well as my loyalty. I want to marry you, Shakira. I want more children with you. Baby, all I want is you, your stanking attitude and all."

Yayo spilled his feelings then planted kisses on her neck, causing her to smile from his genuine assuring words. "You can even come with me when I go down there to take the blood test, so Amanda can meet my better half," Yayo concluded while he caressed her legs through her leggings, making her pussy wet.

Yayo kissed her lips softly. They were both caught up in a passionate lust until his iPhone vibrated again. He put his finger to his lips signaling for her to be quiet as he looked at the caller ID. Shakira snaked her neck with fake attitude, while Yayo got up from the couch and walked to the kitchen for some privacy before he answered the phone. Shakira got up and followed him.

"As-salaam Alaikum, Ock," Yayo answered.

"Walaikum As-salam, Yaton…How are you, brother?"

"I'm peaceful, just at the crib chilling, what's good?" Yayo greeted, watching Shakira get on her knees and pull his dick from his joggers and start to lick the tip of it.

"You have been out the halfway house for a week. I think it's time to start moving toward our plan, don't you think?" Yayo tried to pry Shakira off his tool, his attempt was futile.

"I'm with whatever, Ock. When you want me to get up with you?" Yayo asked, staring Shakira in the eyes while she gave him head. He had to bite the inside of his jaw to stop from making any type of sexual noise, while his baby mama tried to suck the sleeve off his dick.

"Why don't you meet me downtown in the Burger King parking lot right by Congress, let's say…in about an hour. I want to introduce you to some important people."

"Alright, see you in a minute, Ock," Yayo replied and hurriedly ended the call before he grunted like a wild animal as he exploded inside of Shakira's mouth. She swallowed all that was released like a champ, before she gave the tip of his dick a final suck.

"Damn girl, what's with all that?" Yayo asked her with a satisfying grin on his face, putting his deflating cock back in his jogging pants. Shakira stood up, ignoring what he just said.

"Where you going?"

"Damn, Nosy Rosy, all in the business…But na for real, I gotta go meet up with Kawann. I'll be back in a minute." Yayo said trying to kiss her on her lips, she turned her face away from him letting him kiss her cheek.

"You a be back, uh-uh. I'm not about to be stuck in this house doing nothing. Plus, I got to go get Shamira from Honey house. Either your friend gone come get you, or I'm a have to drop you off, but I need my car, Yaton," Shakira stated matter of factly.

"You know what, tomorrow or Saturday, we going to Western. It's time for me to get some wheels up under me, I'm going to get a whip ASAP. You playing Uber driver ain't hitting on nothing." Yayo playfully pushed Shakira upside her head, before he jetted upstairs to take a quick shower, so he could get in traffic to go meet up with Kewann. Shakira took off behind him to get her lick back.

An hour later, Shakira pulled her Audi into the Burger King parking lot on Congress Street. "Park by that shiny blue Lincoln, baby," Yayo stated, noticing Kewann's car.

"I'm about to go chop it up with my mans and then I'm a give you a call when we gone link up…ok?"

"Ok, baby, try not to make it too late. I told Shamira we was taking her to Home Runn Inn Pizza. You already know how your daughter loves her pizza."

"I'm already hip, give me a kiss." Yayo gave Shakira a soft kiss on her lips before he got out and jumped in the Lincoln with Kewann.

"What it do, Ock?" Yayo greeted.

"As-salaam Alaikum, Yayo." Yayo watched as Shakira pulled out of the parking lot, as Kewann backed out of the parking space and out of the lot.

"So, where we headed fam?" Yayo probed.

"As I told you on the phone, I have some very important brothers I want you to meet, brothers who are very conducive to what we are trying to achieve," Kawann explained.

Twenty minutes later, Kewann got off on Independence Street on the west side of the city. The ride was a quiet one as Yayo looked out the window, watching the grimy west side streets pass him. The entire west side seemed to be in poverty, with abandoned buildings, the potholes all through the street, and the homeless invaded every corner. They would walk up to cars at stop signs to beg for change, only to get it and go to the nearest dope boy to cope some dog food to feed the savage demons that caused their lives to come to complete ruin.

Young men stood posted on blocks with dreads and braids. Three-hundred-dollar Jordans laced their feet and thousands of dollars were confined in their Balmain's. It was a fifty-fifty chance one of the young blacks in that crowd wouldn't make it through the weekend, as there was another black man only a few blocks away plotting on a way to take his life with a semi-auto. Riding through the city streets, Yayo really saw the streets of Chicago as a battlefield. "It looks messed up out here, Ock," Yayo said, breaking the silence.

"It don't just look messed up out here, Yayo, it's definitely messed up out here. It's been like that out here for a while. Everybody sees it, but don't nobody wanna step up and try to fix it. Everybody got a job to do, but everybody waiting on somebody…anybody to do the job. In life, brother, it's all about initiative. If a man doesn't possess initiative, then he possesses nothing but failure. You know why Trump is the president of the United States of America?" Kewann asked Yayo as he stopped at a red light on 15th and Kedzie.

"Because he got money, he bought himself into presidency." Yayo retorted. Kewann shook his head in the negative.

"No, brother, don't get me wrong. We all know Trump got that bread, he's a shark with the business, a monster with the money, but he been having money like that for over twenty-five years. But he wasn't the president, was he? His money didn't get him in the White House, the initiative he took to step up to even run for president got him in the White House.

"That, and his ambition, whatever it was fueled by. Now, imagine if we could get in the minds of some of these brothers to use initiative and ambition righteously for something positive what they could accomplish," Kewann said, pointing at a small group of men standing on the corner of 15th and Kadzie, a hood run by the Black Gangster, a deadly drug gang on the west side. The light turned green and Kewann pulled off. He continued to kick knowledge.

"Yayo, we as black people all possess the choice to use initiative, these young brothers use it every day, Every day they get up to cook and bag up their drugs and post up on the corner to sell it. Every time they put a clip in a Glock, pull up on their enemy and squeeze that trigger to end a life, they are using initiative. Every display of action, settling an issue. Now what if they used that same initiative energy for something positive?

"Going to college to be a brain surgeon, a real estate giant, CEO of a major promoting company, each these occupations gross no less than a hundred and fifty geez a year. But these young brothers don't go after these occupations. You know why? I'll tell you why, because nobody is telling them these occupations make this much paper.

"All they being told is that you can get a kilo of coke for thirty stacks, sell ounces for twelve hundred and forty-four thousand two hundred, make a quick fourteen-thousand-dollar profit. Or, spend sixty-five hundred to cope a hunnid grams of dope and make twenty bands in a period of two days. Sounds good to a shorty who living off a hundred and fifty dollars of Aldi groceries every month.

"But what they not being told is that fast money don't last and that same kilo of coke or the same hundred grams of dope can have you spending thirty years in somebody's federal prison, or being laid in a casket and buried at Burr Oaks Cemetery, with only their parents and the preacher attending their service. They don't know until it's too late, feel me?"

Kewann's intellect and realistic dialog sent a chill down Yayo's spine. He knew what Kewann was speaking was fact, as he had seen firsthand how playing the streets could end up. He understood, he just wished Quavon would open his eyes and see the same thing. Quavon was smashing the gas to a grueling demise and he was too blind to see it.

Kewann pulled up to a furniture store called Mikes Furniture on Milwaukee and Ashland Street and parked. "Come on Ock, let me introduce you to the rest of the movement," Kewann said and got out the car. Yayo followed suit, following him inside the furniture. Kewann led him to the back of the store, they entered a dark hallway that led to some steps. Walking down the stairs, they headed to the basement of the furniture warehouse.

Once down there, they came up to a door. Kewann knocked on the door before a slide opening slid back. The person behind the door looked out to get a visual of the ones on the other side. Bolt locks on the other side were unlocked. The door opened and a heavyset, dark-skinned brother stood before them with a huge smile across his face.

"As-salaam Alaikum, Ock."

"Walaikum As-salaam," Kewann greeted the man then entered the room. "Yayo, come in brother," Kewann said, noticing Yayo still standing in the doorway. Yayo walked in the dimly lit room and they heavyset brother closed the door behind him and put the dead-bolts back on the door. Yayo looked around the room.

A large flat screen television was plastered on the wall turned to *CNN*. A giant poster of Larry Hoover when he was in ADX Supermax Prison, was also on the wall. Four men sat at a table in the center of the room, a map spread across the table. When Yayo entered the room, they ceased the conversation they were having and all looked up at him.

"As-salaam Alaikum, brothers," Kewann said, greeting the men.

"Walaikum As-salaam," they all responded in unison.

"My brothers, this is the brother I have been telling you about. Yayo, these good brothers are the voices of the Save Our Youth Campaign. This brother right here," Kewann pointed to the heavyset brother who opened the door. "His name is Malik. Malik is a retired Black P. Stone from 87th and Cottage Grove. He has been with us for a while."

"What's good, bro, nice to meet you," Malik said genuinely.

"Likewise." Yayo nodded his head toward Malik, showing respect. Kewann walked over to the table.

"This brother right here I'm proud to say, is aggressive in our campaign, but yet righteous in all his endeavors. This is Kali." Kewann put his right hand on Kali's shoulder. Kali nodded his head at Yayo but remained silent. Yayo returned his nod, but didn't speak either, matching Kali's demeanor. Kewann kept moving around the table, now standing behind a bald man with a gray beard. He wore a pair of Cartier frames over his eyes. "This fine brother right here, his name is Doc." Doc got up and walked around the table to shake Yayo's hand.

"It's good to finally meet you, Bernard speaks very highly of you, tells me you are an honorable man," Doc stated, shaking Yayo's hand.

"You know Bernard?" Yayo asked Doc.

"Sure do, that's my nephew…my sister's oldest boy," Doc informed him. At that moment, Yayo remembered one of the many conversations he held with Mr. B and he recalled him telling him that he had family in Chicago. Doc and Mr. B even held some of the same features.

Kewann was now standing behind another one of the men. He had long French braids in his hair, was light-skinned and had a distinctive tattoo on his neck of a crescent moon and five-pointed star. He didn't look like he was a Muslim, but a street nigga.

"This intelligent, brilliant brother right here is Musane. Musane, this is the brother, Yayo." Musane smiled, his grill lit up with flawless diamonds.

"Yayo's what good? Nice to meet you."

94

"You too, bro," Yayo greeted back, feeling a positive vibe from Musane.

"Last but not least, this brother right here is named Muhamad. Muhamad is the only one of us who is not from Chicago. Muhamad is from North Philly."

"As-salaam Alaikum."

"Walaikum As-salaam," Yayo said to Muhamad. Yayo noticed that all the men he was introduced to all wore black T-shirts, on the front in bold white letters read, *As Together* on the front, and on the back, *We Are Stronger*. Kewann noticed Yayo reading the words on Doc's shirt. He walked over to a small table in the corner of the room where a stack of T-shirts sat. Kewann grabbed one and tossed one to Yayo. Yayo caught the shirt in midair.

"Put that on, brother…it's our uniform." Yayo took off his Polo shirt and replaced it with the shirt Kewann had just given him.

"Now that we are acquainted as family, Yayo, I want to tell you who we are and how we politic. First and foremost, we are all here for the same reason, to save our race from self-genocide in the streets. Like I told you, it's only one way to curb this pandemic and that's to get in the minds of the youth. We have to get them out the streets and into colleges, into hospitals, restaurants, the corporate world.

This is Mr. B's… as you call him… vision, and his vision is our vision. How we are going to do that? We are going to march into these ghettos, into the jails…in these group homes and speak.

"We all know words hold power, all they have to do is hear them. A lot of them will ignore these powerful words, but some will adhere to them. If we can just save a few, then our efforts will not go in vain." Kewann walked around the table with his hands clasped behind his back as he continued.

"Yayo, our voice has to be heard loud and clear. Now even though we are moving with a positive message, we are also making a lot of enemies."

"How are we making enemies and we are doing good things in the community?" Yayo asked confused, not understanding how trying to get young men in the ghetto to change their lives for the better caused beef.

"Very good question, Yayo. look at it like this… if you are a drug dealer in the hood and you use these young juveniles as lookouts and pack runners, or have them stand on the corner, promoting your drugs for peanuts and gym shoe money. Then here comes some righteous brothers, waking up the youngsters showing them a better way. They wake up and get off the corners and start doing positive things in the community, prosocial things.

"Now the dealers and gangs have nobody to use, they have to put in the work themselves and risk going to jail…Something they are to coward to do. So, they will resent us, animosity will be built, and could end up deadly," Kewann said, staring Yayo in his eyes.

"So, if we gone be in the streets causing that much animosity…we gone be in the streets, in these dudes' neighborhoods naked without protection?" Kali stood from the table and removed the two nickel-plated FNH pistols from his waist and laid them gently on the table.

"Nah, Ock, I'm here for the protection. We promoting a peaceful demonstration, but make no mistake about it…we not going for the fuckery, we motivated by a higher force, if it's disrespect or violence, then blood will be shed," Kali let it be known before he sat back down. Yayo nodded at him respecting his gangster, then returned his attention back to Kewann.

"So, when do we start?" Kewann walked over to Yayo and put his hand on his shoulder.

"Yayo, we have been started, but you will start today. Today you will ride with us and watch how we do things, today you will just get your feet wet." Doc walked over to a walk-in closet in the basement and came out with four bullhorns. He passed one to Musane, Malik, Kewann and kept one for himself.

"Let's go, Yayo, it's time to see if we can save a few youngstas lives," Kawann said and led the way as they left the furniture store, to see if they could captivate the minds of Chicago's most dangerous and lost.

Chapter 9

It had been two months since Omega robbed the Bank of America in Wisconsin, leaving two bodies in the course of the violent crime…Goon his once comrade-in-arms and Jenny, his girlfriend of two years. He felt no remorse for his actions, as the money from the robbery killed any regret, he might've had for taking the two lives.

It took three hours to count, running all the bills through the money machine, but he couldn't believe he hit a sting for so big. Omega counted one-point-five million dollars in U.S. currency and so far, had gotten away with it. Now that he had his money, it was time to put the second part of his deadly plan into action. Omega needed some work, so he went to holler at Rico, his Latin King plug he had been buying his coke from for the past two years. Rico sold weight, but he didn't have enough to secure Omega's order. He was trying to spend five hundred thousand in cold cash.

Rico, originally from Medlin, Texas, called his uncle who worked for the Madin Cartel in Mexico and told him he knew somebody who was trying to spend a half-mil on the Peruvian flake. Numbers were exchanged, prices negotiated, and Omega was able to walk away with paying twenty-five stacks a brick, getting fifty kilos of uncut coke. Not to mention, since he came with straight money and King Rico vouched for him, the cartel sent an extra fifty bricks on consignment, putting the consignment dept on Rico.

Rico would take nine ounces out of each of the fifty bricks, replace nine ounces with nine ounces of isotole and then recompress the work. Rico would get twelve-point-five kilos off the muscle, so he was benefitting greatly off the deal. Omega had a hundred keys sent to him. He couldn't care less about the extra fifty bricks. or Rico for that matter. He had no attention on paying the Mexican back anyway. Omega knew if he wanted to take the G.B.C. to war, he had to get his hammer game up, so he reached out to a cat he met in the state prison who went by the name of Dino.

Dino was from Indianapolis, Indiana and was in the business of gun running. Omega found him by way of Facebook, slid in his DM and told Dino he wanted to holler at him and left his number. The next day, Dino called and they made plans to meet up in Calumet City. Omega went to get a U-Haul full of firepower. He was now equipped with FN's, Draco's, AR's and fully auto Glock 17's, along with enough drums, 30-round sticks and ammunition to arm a small army and that exactly what he planned to do.

It was Friday as the sun shined over the city of Chi. Omega was riding around hitting blocks in his fresh, off the showroom floor, matte black 2019 Mercedes-Benz AMG. He had just left Royal Redemption off Clark and Roosevelt, purchasing a Sky-Dweller Presidential. He had dropped seventy thousand on the time piece that now surrounded his wrist. Cartier diamond-studded frames covered his blood-shot eyes, he called them his hater blockers. A track from Calboy and Lil Baby pounded from the 4-15's in the back of the truck, while twin fully-auto Glocks laid across his lap as he headed to the west side, K-Town.

Omega pushed the "ALT" button on the fifteen-inch touch screen, silencing the music. Grabbing his cell phone, he scrolled through his contact list till he found the number he was searching for. Once he did, he hit "sound." The phone rang twice before it was answered.

"Who dis?"

"This Omega, nigga that be grabbing that loud from you."

"Oh, what's good, Joe? What's the bizness? You trying to get right?" Fonzo asked, anxious to make the serve, as he knew Omega would probably want the ounce for the five hundred, a quick lick as the money was moving a lil slow today for some reason.

"Yeah, my nigga…Just keep it five hundred with me because you already know keeping a hundred in the streets don't mean shit no more," Omega said, speaking in code.

"Alright, that's a bet. Pull up."

"Fifteen, Joe," Omega replied, indicating he would be there in fifteen minutes. Twenty minutes later, Omega turned the corner of Keystone Street, shaking the concrete as he shined on the twenty-six-inch Forgiatos. It was hot outside, so the block was in full rotation. A crew of females dressed in barely anything, were in awe when the exotic truck turned the corner.

Omega pulled up and parked in front of crowd of dealers getting their grind on in the middle of the block. He noticed Fonzo looking as if he was trying to see through the dark tint. He rolled the window down. "Check it out, scud," Omega yelled out the truck. Fonzo, seeing it was Omega, made his way over to the vehicle. "Hop in, fam."

Fonzo jumped in the passenger seat of the Benz truck. Looking around the automobile, he said, "Damn nigga, this you? This bitch look like a spaceship," amazed.

"Yeah, this ain't hitting on nothing," Omega retorted like it was nothing and he wasn't riding around in a hundred-and-fifty-thousand-dollar vehicle. Fonzo pulled the ounce of Moon-Rock from his pocket and handed it to Omega. Omega went in his pocket of his Givenchy jeans and pulled out a ridiculous wad of blue faces and peeled off a stack of ten, crispy hundred-dollar-bills, and gave it to Fonzo. Fonzo looked at the money confused.

"Why you didn't tell me you wanted two?" Omega let out a slight chuckle.

"Nah fam, that other five hundred…that's you, put it in your pocket," Omega said. Fonzo just hunched his shoulders and pocketed the blue notes. "Aye fam, what you on? I need to holler at you on some business, let's bend a few blocks real quick."

Fonzo looked over at Omega. He definitely didn't remember seeing him like this. Last time he was in an old Dodge Intrepid, now he was in a 2019 Benz Wagon, thousand-dollar jeans and had no less than fifty on his wrist. The only thing that made Fonzo a little nervous was the two plastic Glizzy's that laid on his lap in plain view. But nevertheless, Omega was looking like new money. *Fuck it*, he thought.

"Yeah, we can hit a few blocks," Fonzo replied.

"Roll up, my nigga." Omega tossed the ounce he'd just paid for in Fonzo's lap before he pulled away from the curb. Omega turned down Washington Street.

"So, what's good? Y'all over here getting plenty money, huh?" Omega probed, glancing over at Fonzo slyly.

"You know, we over here doing what we do… the loud move feel me?" Fonzo replied while he broke the exotic strain in the middle of a split Backwood.

"Yeah… I hear that, my nigga, but that shit don't move like the coke." *Givenchy Kickin* from Calboy and Lil Baby and pumped in the background from the 4-15 Rockford Fosgate subwoofers. Fonzo licked the blunt to seal it, before he responded. "That coke move quick…but shid…the profit ain't shit. They want forty geez for a brick. It ain't worth it," Fonzo said, using a Bic lighter to dry the blunt, before he lit the tip and took a strong pull from the gas. The THC put a vice grip on his lungs, causing him to cough uncontrollably as if he was diagnosed with the coronavirus. Omega smiled at him, accepting the blunt.

"Forty a brick? What if I told you I could get 'em for twenty-five bands and I could front you ten?" Omega stated, taking a pull from the wood while he glided the Benz through the congested streets of the West side. Fonzo looked over at him, greed apparent in his eyes.

"Twenty-five a brick? Ten bricks?"

"That's what I said, my nigga."

"What I gotta do?" Fonzo asked, his palms starting to itch. He was getting plenty of paper moving the loud, but he had to grind extra hard. Not to mention, he wasn't getting his own pounds. He was working for one of his potnas who was getting pounds shipped through the mail from Colorado, and he was only catching five to ten at a time. He would break them down and issue packs out to the homies, in all aspects Fonzo was nothing more than a pack runner…Omega knew this.

"You GD, right?" Fonzo retorted.

"Who run your area?"

"A nigga name Weed. He ain't even from out west. The nigga from the hunnids somewhere," Fonzo vented. Omega could hear the resentment he held for Weed in his tone, it was evident he didn't care for him. Omega smashed the gas. "Sound like you don't fuck with buddy." Omega hit the weed before passing it back to Fonzo.

"He cool... he just goofy as hell, and I don't feel like a nigga shouldn't have no authority in our area if he ain't never put no work in over here. But you know how that go, a board member put him in play over here, what I'm supposed to do? I'm subordinate to the laws of this organization," Fonzo replied his eyes glossy from the blunt. Omega looked over at him, looking like the devil.

"Kill his ass, shorty," Omega encouraged him, like murder was nothing. "I'm just fucking with you, scud. How many people feel the same way you feel?"

"Shid...damn near the whole count," said Fonzo. Omega knew this was going to be easy as shit.

"How many of y'all on count?"

"It's like a hundred of us easy...we got K-Town on smash, been like that for a while," Fonzo informed him.

"Alright, my nigga, I'm a be as assertive as I can be. What would you say if I told you I would give you ten kilos to flip?"

"Flip to what?"

"From GD to H.C."

"What the fuck is H.C.?" Fonzo asked.

"Homicide Crew," Omega sneered. Fonzo now knew he was in the presence of a killer. He remembered a couple of years ago, it was the Homicide Crew's name constantly ringing in the streets on the robbery and murder tip.

"I can't do that shit... the folks a kill me."

Omega laughed at him like he had just told the biggest joke in the world.

"Fam, in a minute, every nigga that's in the streets gone be Homicide Crew. Those who not, gone be dead or broke. I'm offering you a seat at the table so you can eat with me. The ten bricks is nothing. I got enough work and guns to flood the city. Your days of standing on the block will be over, it will be replaced with you riding foreign whips, taking trips to Vegas and fucking the finest bitches. And not only will you be running your neighborhood, but the entire west side. You will have enough dope, guns and soldiers to do it."

Fonzo started thinking about what Omega was speaking. He was definitely tired of block hustling, even though he made decent money. but he was thirty-five years old and still working for another nigga, it was time for him to step up and be his own boss. He looked over at Omega as he drove. He had no shirt on, his jewelry hung around his neck glowing like it had batteries. Whatever he was doing must have been working, because Omega had come all the way up, with ten kilos of cocaine he was going to use to put himself in a position of power. And for that power, he would be willing to go against anything and everything he had grown to believe in, and at that moment he made a decision.

"All right, bro…I'm a take you up on that. I'm a go holler at the guys and let 'em know what business is. You already know it's gone be a few that ain't gone be with it. But they gone be the minority," Fonzo said, flicking the blunt roach out the window. Omega stopped at a light on Pulaski Avenue, looked over at Fonzo then passed him one of the fully automatic Glock 17's with a 30-shot extension.

"Then put they ass to the concrete, let 'em know this a dictatorship, not a democracy," Omega commanded through clenched teeth. Fonzo accepted the Glock 17 and tucked it on his waistline. Omega continued riding around the west side with Fonzo, talking money, drugs and expansion and after two more blunts of the Moon-Rock, Omega pulled back on Keystone.

"I'll hit your phone tomorrow to let you know where to come pick up the ten demos. Remember, let them niggas know the plates are full and it's dinner time, time to eat." Fonzo nodded his head in understanding and gave Omega some dap before he hopped out the truck. His morale was up as he was about to rise from the trenches.

Omega pulled from the curb and turned the music up. This was just the beginning. He was about to flip a whole hood of Gangster Disciples to Homicide Crew and was going to use Fonzo to do it. Indeed, he was going to put Fonzo on. Fonzo had just traded on his own organization. An organization he had put in work for, and for ten kilos of coke, he was going to betray their loyalty. Which, in Omega's eyes, made him expendable. Fonzo wasn't to be trusted.

Omega had his eyes and vision set on a few more dangerous areas throughout the city he wanted to take over. Once all the pieces of the puzzle were put together, he was going to wage war on the Get It Boy Clique. And for Ace, who was resting in peace, he was going to mop the streets with their blood.

Yayo sat in the back of Kewann's Lincoln, Doc occupied the passenger seat. They were trailed by the rest of the Save Our Youth squad, who were in a cocaine white Dodge Durango SRT. They were headed to Wentworth Gardens, some projects on 35th and State, located on the South side of Chicago. The Wentworth Gardens Projects sat off the Dan Ryan Expressway. *The Chicago Tribune* said these projects where having a lot of drug overdoses due to the dealers using fentanyl to stretch the heroin. It was the same projects where a thirteen-year-old boy was found shot to death. Police said the murder was gang-related, and for that reason, Kewann wanted the residents in this community to hear the voices of Save Our Youth.

It was 7:30 at night when they pulled into the parking lot of the Wentworth Gardens. Kewann parked the Lincoln on the side of a beat-up Ford pick-up, the Durango pulled on the side of the Lincoln and parked. Kewann killed the engine. "All right, brothers, let's see if we can save some of these youngstas out here." They all got out their whips. Yayo looked around and could see the drug activity as he saw a long line of dope fiends standing in a single-file line, leading to the back of the brown row houses.

It was a hot summer night, so the projects where in full swing. Teenagers roamed around the project grounds smoking, drinking, and everything else involved in adolescence. Kewann popped the trunk and grabbed the bull horns just as Malik, Kali, Musane, and Muhamad walked up to the Lincoln. He passed one to Doc, Musane and Malik and kept one for himself. The Save Our Youth team made their way through the entrance of Wentworth Projects. Kewann got on the blow horn and began to speak as they made their way through the rusted front gate.

"My young brothers and sisters...we have come in peace and prosperity to let you know we care about each and every one of you.

We understand you may not have mothers and fathers… we understand you have been steered down the wrong path in life. But my young brothers and sisters, we are here to tell you that you can be anything in life you want to be. You all possess the power to choose." A small crowd began to form as the men walked through the projects.

Doc began to speak through his bull horn. "Young brothers and sisters, do you know that we African Americans maintain ambitious mind frames? Look at Simone Biles, Venus and Serena Williams. Venus and Serena both came from an urban ghetto just like this. But now they are worth millions upon millions of dollars…they made it out of poverty because they took initiative to do so. They didn't accept the limits society placed on them, they placed all of their energy into making it out.

"We can all do that because we come from a strong bloodline. Our ancestors went through four hundred years of slavery, but we made it through. Harriet Tubman was a great woman, she refused to live the rest of her life in forced confinement…She escaped slavery…You know why? Because she made the choice to take initiative to get out her predicament. That's the bloodline that you all come from, all you have to do is want better and take the initiative to do better."

The loud projects had now become remotely quiet to hear what these Black men with black T-shirts were speaking on. A man hanging out the window shouted, "Man, get the fuck outta here with that Martin Luther King shit," and threw a forty-ounce bottle out the window, which crashed on the concrete as they continued to walk.

Musane then started to speak. "Listen y'all, if anybody can feel your pain and what you going through, it's me. When I was younger, I used to post up on these same corners, sell drugs and gangbang. That's right, I used to be affiliated. I was a Black Disciple from the Calumet Building. I got indicted by the feds when I was twenty-one years old for selling heroin. They sentenced me to a hundred and twenty months in federal prison and I was sent far away across the country and had little contact with my family.

"I had no support, the same gang I sold drugs for never sent a money order, picture, Christmas card or nothing. I had nobody, Allah took everybody out of my life, but he did it for a reason. He wanted me to focus on me and to make a decision to either live…or die. My brothers and sisters, I chose life. I had to find my talent or purpose in life, as we all have one. I made the decision that I wanted to be a better man, better son, better brother, uncle, grandson and to be a positive person in my community…in the world.

"I found my God-given talent as a writer and started to write about my life…our lives. I remained relentless in my writing, shot my story out to a publisher and was granted a contract. Yes, my brothers and sisters, you are hearing the words from a published author. I'm no different from you, we are the same as far as skin, ambition and blood, I accomplished something great and you can too, all you have to do is take initiative to take control of your lives and do better," Musane testified.

A chill ran down Yayo's spine as he listened to Musane, and was shocked to find out Musane was a published author, something he was trying to achieve. Musane definitely held the attention of a lot of individuals from his testimony. They kept moving through the projects trying to get anybody and everybody to hear their message, until Yayo saw four men with white T-shirts on come walking briskly from behind the row house, where the drug activity was being trafficked. All four men had their hands under their shirts, walking directly toward them with menacing facial expressions.

"Aye, look y'all…look like we got trouble coming our way," Yayo said, putting everybody on point. Yayo peeped one of the thugs pull a gun out. Kali peeped game and now his hand rested on the handle of his own pole as the thugs walked up.

"I don't know who the fuck you goofy ass mugs is, but y'all need to slide from over here with all that Jehovah Witness shit. Y'all causing undue heat, fuck around and get yo shit pushed back over here, scud," the thug threatened. Kewann put his hands up in a surrendering manner.

"Listen, my brother, we come in peace. Just trying to spread a positive message, that's it, that's all."

"Well, spread that shit somewhere else…and this my last time saying it." The goon with the gun out pointed it in their direction, with his finger tight on the trigger, ready to let it blow.

Kali's jaws tightened, he was ready to up and bust. Malik noticed it and put his hand on his shoulder and whispered, "Be easy, Ock, everything all well."

"Alright brothers, no need for violence, y'all be safe and have a good night. God bless," Kewann said and motioned for his men to follow suit. They left the Wentworth Projects after leaving their testimonies. If only they woke up one of them, then their work didn't go in vain.

Chapter 10

Quavon's plane landed at LAX Airport at 6:00 p.m. He was there to check on his dispensary in L.A. He had three in all, one in Beverly Hills, one in Oakland and one in Los Angeles. He would check on them individually at different times of the year. Quavon had been introduced to the California weed game from an old friend of his that attended Kennedy King College when he and Davon was enrolled there. Quavon was a small-time weed hustler, selling forty-dollar grams, then once his line got to booming, T.B. started fronting Quavon five to ten pounds. The more he moved, the more T.B. fronted him. That was his past.

A lot had changed since then, he had elevated in the streets and was now responsible for sixty percent of the drugs that touched the streets of Chicago. Rio was one of the guys Quavon sold those forty-dollar grams to back in the day while attending Kennedy King. Rio was from 95th and Wentworth and was a basketball star at King. After graduating from college, he went overseas to play ball until he ruptured his spleen, bringing his promising career to an end. Not wanting to return to the violent unpromising streets of the Chi, Rio relocated to Los Angeles with his aunt.

Being involved in the night life, Rio's smooth character got him introduced to some Cali heavyweights in the marijuana field. So, he started to hustle, moving high grade weed. He would get the exotic strains for the low and get it sent to Chicago where he would make an ugly profit. Rio was getting the pounds for twelve hundred a pop and taking it to Chicago, selling them at thirty-five hundred to four thousand a pound.

Quavon heard about the exotic gas floating around the city and his intel led him to 95th and Wentworth, as he found out Rio was the one flooding the streets. After getting a line on Rio, the two of them made plans and ended up meeting up. Rio was intrigued to find out Quavon had the streets on lock and key with the dope and coke and was also involved in the film industry. He put Quavon on game and two years later, Quavon owned dispensaries in California and was checking a bag from the hustle.

Quavon walked out LAX pulling his Louis Vuitton luggage.

Where the fuck this nigga at? Quavon thought, scanning the sea of cars looking for Rio. Quavon got his I-phone to via FaceTime Rio.

"Man, where you at, thug? Got me out here looking stupid and shit," Quavon said jokingly, seeing Rio's face on his phone.

"Nigga, you ain't in L.A yet," Rio responded.

"What you mean, I ain't in L.A., goofy ass nigga. Where I'm at then?" Quavon waved his iPhone around so Rio could see the airport in the background.

"Ok then! My nigga on deck!" Rio said, geeked up his mans was in the city.

"Aye look, fam, give me about an hour. I'm on my way," Rio said, getting out of the California king size with three Latina chicks he was just sexing. Quavon saw one of the females get out the bed, thicker than a Snicker.

"Aye shorty, who is them thots? And what you mean an hour? Man, just pull up on me, I'm about to catch a cab and get a room at the Ritz Carlton. Hit my phone when you get downstairs...you on bullshit, my nigga."

Rio just laughed at him before he said, "I'm on my way playboy, I'm a make it up to you. You in L.A., this my city!" Rio said and ended the call so he could shower and get dressed so he could go swoop his potna.

Forty-five minutes later, Quavon was at the Ritz Carlton. After passing the Uber driver a crispy blue note, he grabbed his luggage and exited the vehicle and made his entrance to the motel. Walking inside the hotel lobby, Quavon was approached by a young thug who seemed to be no older than twenty-one years old, dressed head to toe in Balenciaga. Quavon could tell he was a hustler before the first words he spoke even left his mouth.

"Aye, what's good, player? My name Trap...if you looking, my nigga, I got that gas...that Gorilla Glue," Trap said, promoting his product.

"Oh yeah? What you got, shorty?" Quavon probed. He didn't have any weed and he knew it would be a minute before Rio got there. And after the long flight he was in a dying need to smoke.

"I got whatever you want...quarters, ounces, halves, pounds whatever."

"What you want for a quarter?"

"A huncho," Trap replied, meaning a hundred dollars.

"Alright, Joe, what's your number? Once I check in, I'm a hit your line and let you know what floor to meet me on...Bet?"

"That's a bet, my nigga." Quavon gave Trap a pound and after getting his number, made his way to the counter to purchase his room.

"Hi...welcome to the Ritz Carlton. How can I help you?" the receptionist asked with a Colgate smile.

"What's good, I'm trying to get a standard room," Quavon replied. The receptionist started typing on the computer.

"Ok sir, we have a standard room on the 37th floor for a thousand dollars a night. Are you fine with that?"

"Yeah, that's cool...I'm a need the room for the weekend."

"And how will you be paying for the room, sir?"

"Cash," Quavon retorted and pulled a thick wad of Benjamins from his Givenchy shorts, peeled off twenty bills and passed it to the receptionist, along with his ID. After checking Quavon in, she handed him back his ID with his receipt.

"Enjoy your stay at the Ritz Carlton," she said with a flirtatious smile.

"Appreciate it," Quavon replied not believing he had just come off of two stacks for a room for two nights. Fuck it, he thought. Quavon got on the elevator and made his way to the 37th floor of the Ritz Carlton. Getting off on his floor, a dude almost bumped into him...not looking where he was walking.

"My fault," the man excused himself. Quavon was shocked to see who the man was. The man that almost bumped into Quavon was basketball great Jalen Rose, who worked for *ESPN*, which was located across the street from the hotel. Jalen Rose apologized and got on the elevator. Quavon made his way to his room and used the key card to enter the spacious room. Looking around the room, Quavon was pleased, as he now felt the room was worth the two bands he just dropped.

Everything seemed to be trimmed in gold. The view was magnificent, overlooking the City of Angels. His view gave him a perfect view of the Staple Center. Los Angeles was beautiful. Quavon tossed his luggage on the king size bed and made his way to the bathroom, where he saw the walk-in shower, a massive hot tub and gold toilet. Quavon got his iPhone and dialed Trap's number.

"Hello?" Trap answered.

"What's good, this Quavon. I met you in the lobby. Meet me on the 37th floor, fam."

"On my way," Trap replied.

"Aye scud, if it's not too much to ask, could you grab me a pack of Backwoods? I got an extra fifty for you."

"Don't even trip, cuz, I got you." Trap hung up the phone. Fifteen minutes later, Quavon met Trap in the hallway, as he didn't want him knowing which room he was in. He was in killa Cali…and Cali niggas was known to get grimy.

"What's good, shorty, you got that issue for me?' Quavon asked, walking up, giving Trap the one-fifty.

"I told you I got ya, cuz, enjoy your lunch." Trap passed Quavon a Burger King bag, accepting the one-fifty. Quavon glanced inside the bag and saw a Whopper, fries, a pack of Backwoods and the quarter-ounce of loud. Satisfied with the contents in the bag, he gave Trap a pound and made his way down the hallway as Trap got on the elevator. Once inside the room, Quavon wasted no time breaking down a Backwood and filling it with the potent Gorilla Glue.

He was nervous about sparking the blunt because he knew the smell would be loud and he didn't want to cause undue heat to his room. *Fuck it*, he thought and went inside the bathroom. He turned the hot water on in the shower, filling the bathroom with steam to try and muffle the loud smell. Quavon fired up the blunt and took a strong pull, filling his lungs with the exotic strain. The ridiculously strong THC flowed through his bloodstream, putting him immediately in a hazy state, causing him to take a seat on the toilet.

Quavon sat on the toilet, chiefing on the blunt, getting his mind right. He was all the way up, was flooding the streets with work, but he was starting to think about what Yayo was saying. He loved his brother and had always looked up to him.

Yayo came home different than how he went in. He was positive and wanted nothing to do with the streets. Quavon was the streets, and to be at odds with his brother would have Quavon all the way off balance. He waited eight years for his brother to come home, and now that Yayo was home and they were living different lives, it seemed as the two brothers were becoming strangers...Something Quavon wasn't comfortable with.

Quavon figured in due time he would amend things with his brother, but as of right now, he had to stay focused on securing his future. And at the same time, start to plot and strategize to make his exit out the game, but still remain on top.

Quavon put the blunt out on the sink, he was too high, unable to finish smoking the wood. Shaking from his thoughts that he had drifted into, Quavon stripped naked and stepped in the hot shower. He had to hurry up and get fresh before Rio arrived. After taking a ten-minute shower, Quavon got dressed, throwing on a new pair of Amiri fitted jeans, matching Polo shirt and a pair of red and white Balenciaga gym shoes. Quavon was in the midst of putting his Patek Phillipe watch around his wrist when his iPhone came to life...seeing it was Rio, calling he answered.

"What up?"

"I'm downstairs, my nigga...let's bounce."

"Here I come," Quavon replied and ended the call. After putting his diamond chain around his neck with the fifty-thousand-dollar platinum and diamond cross, he sprayed on some Versace cologne and left the room.

Quavon walked out the entrance of the Ritz Carlton, only to see Rio posted up on the side of a powder blue Maserati Ghibli sitting on twenty-four-inch Rucci rims. He smiled at his friend. "Man...Joe, you got this fast-ass whip and it took you two hours to get here? Lame ass nigga," Quavon said jokingly, walking up and embracing his childhood friend.

"Nigga, your goofy ass making plans at the last minute like you Obama or some shit. A nigga start getting a lil money, don't know how to act," Rio replied, throwing a slug back at Quavon, both of them happy to be in each other's company. "Come on, my nigga, let's bounce." Rio jumped in the driver's seat. "So, what's the business, what the plan for the night?" he asked, stopping at a light on the Boulevard.

"I need to go holler at this white boy real quick and go check on my shit. then it's whatever," Quavon answered, strolling through his contact list on his iPhone.

"You already know it's Friday night, the Sun-Set gone be cracking. We can slide through, pop a few bottles, grab some thots and bounce back to your room," Rio said, planning the night for them.

"Hold up, fam." Quavon held his index finger up with one hand, holding his phone to his ear with the other as he listened to the phone ring. "Hello?"

"What up, white boy, where you at?'

"Quavon, what it do? I'm on location, come on and slide through," the person on the line said.

"I'm on my way…be there in like thirty," Quavon replied before ending the call.

Rio looked over at Quavon. "To the warehouse?"

"Yep."

Rio slid the Mozzy through the traffic of los Angeles in route to the warehouse Quavon owned. "So, what's up with Davon, what he been up to? I see he don't fuck with a nigga no more," Rio inquired, playing but serious at the same time. He and Davon was cool when they attended Kennedy King, as they had a few classes together. Quavon laughed lightly. "You know bro got a lot going on, He work for EA Sports, designing video games and shit…He chasing that bag. I know you played that NBA 2020…you know bro helped put that shit together."

"Straight up? Hell yeah, I played 2020. I got it! Man, tell Davon I send my love and respect and when he get a chance, check on a nigga."

"I got you, fam," Quavon said, relighting the blunt he had put out in the room. Rio pulled into the parking lot of a warehouse on the east side of L.A. and parked on the side of a Rolls Royce Wraith.

"You want me to wait in the car while you handle your business?" Rio asked Quavon.

"Nah fam, come on...I want to show you something real quick." Quavon and Rio entered the remotely empty warehouse lobby. Quavon led Rio to an elevator, once they got on the elevator it took them to the top floor. The door to the elevator opened and they stepped off into an area that looked like a small club.

In one section, a group of Asians sat at a large table breaking down what looked to be about three hundred pounds of marijuana while in another section, some white boys where at task, vacuum scaling pounds upon pounds of weed. Quavon had come to see a fat boy named Fat Louie. Fat Louie sat on a large sectional sofa, with two exotic females on each side of him. His Cuban diamond chained shined brightly in the dimly lit room. Louie worked for Quavon, overseeing his operation.

Quavon not only grew his own strain called G.B.C., but he also allowed other growers to sell their product through his dispensaries, as he had the best clientele...Rick Ross, Snoop Dogg, Lil Durk and Lil Boosie, just to name a few. Other growers were allowed to move their pounds through Quavon...for a price of course. Quavon would charge the growers five hundred dollars a pound and growers had to move no less than five hundred pounds to be able to even warrant the chance to fuck with Quavon's dispensary. Louie made sure the business got handled and the numbers was right. The other two dispensaries were also run in the same strategic corporate manner.

"What it do, gym shoe?" Quavon greeted, walking up to Fat Louie with Rio.

"Excuse me, ladies, let me holler at my people real quick," Louie told the two females. They both stood up and straightened their short skirts. One of them gave Quavon a seductive look before she walked off, but Quavon paid her no mind, his mind was on his money. He took a seat next to fat Louie. "How was your flight?" Louie asked, taking a sip from his bottle of Ace of Spades.

"Same as always, long and boring. Ay, this my man Rio. Rio this Fat Louie and you can see why they call him Fat Louie." Quavon introduced the two men, throwing jokes at Louie's weight. Louie was almost four hundred pounds. The two men shook hands upon introduction.

"So, what's up, you ready to handle this business?" Quavon asked Louie, ready to get to the reason he had flown all the way to Cali from Chicago.

"Yeah, let's get to it. Rio, make yourself at home, feel free to sample anything you see here, it's on Quavon," Fat Louie said, patting Quavon on the back.

"I appreciate it," Rio replied and sat down on the sectional and started breaking down some exotic that was on the table in front of him, while Quavon and Fat Louie made their way to the back of the warehouse where the pounds where located. Once inside the large room where the pounds were stacked wall to wall, Louie grabbed a clipboard and ink pen. Walking over to a section where a large sign read "Cookies," there were pounds of high grade stacked to the ceiling.

"Ok, Quavon, it says here we have two thousand pounds of Cookies in inventory. This quarter, we sold a thousand pounds and this quarter, we sold eight hundred pounds at fifteen hundred a pound." Fat Louie then led Quavon over to another section of loud, where the sign read "Skittles." Quavon followed him with his hands clasped behind his back.

"We have about six hundred pounds left of this and moved two thousand pounds. The Skittles did good this quarter." Fat Louie then walked over to the OG Kush. "We have eighteen hundred pounds of the OG in inventory and we sold five thousand pounds at a thousand dollars a pound." Quavon smiled like a proud father, hearing the numbers Louie was kicking.

Louie walked him out to the Purple Haze. "The purple we got about six hundred pounds left. This quarter was kind of slow, we

114

only moved three hundred pounds, but things should pick up soon. A customer in Alaska just pre-ordered a thousand pounds and said he might need more."

"Man, what about the G.B.C....what them numbers looking like?" Queen asked, cutting Louie off, inquiring about his own strain. Louie looked at him with a smirk on his face.

"My dude, we completely sold out of the G.B.C....We ran out and sold three thousand pounds at eighteen hundred dollars a pound."

"That's what the fuck I'm talking about, fat boy! Louie, you the best, nigga!" Quavon yelled, geeked up and pumping his fist in the air.

"Yeah, yeah, yeah. So Quavon, we have sixty-two hundred pounds in inventory, which we will be restocking at the end of the month from the growers...And the quarter gross was..." Louie looked down at the clipboard again. "My dude, we grossed one-point-six million." Quavon hugged Louie like he had just found a lost loved one. In three months, Quavon had managed to gross almost two million dollars without selling a bag. He was extra excited that the G.B.C. strain was doing numbers. To say he was geeked was an understatement.

"Alright Louie, this the business." Quavon said, calming himself down. "Once the inventory is restocked, I need five hundred pounds of the G.B.C. sent to Chicago, a thousand pounds of the OG sent to Memphis. Oh yeah, send five pounds of the Cookies to the Chi as well." Louie jotted down what Quavon had just said.

"Where do you want them sent?" Louie asked.

"I will send all drop-off locations via email at the end of the month."

"Everything should be ready by then... Anything else?"

"Nah everything good, Louie. I'm a snatch a pound of this to blow on while I'm down here." Quavon grabbed a pound of Cookies and made his way out the room, with Louie following behind.

"Come on, scud, we up outta here," Quavon told Rio, who was high as a kite and surrounded by some fine ass women. He took one more strong pull from the blunt, then passed it to the right to a chick who resembled Gabrielle Union before he got up.

Quavon and Rio left the warehouse. Quavon's morale was all the way up as well as his paper. He was making a killing off the loud as he supplied different states in America with the exotic strains. Quavon also controlled the drug trade in the Midwest on the dope and coke. The numbers where immaculate, but along with the riches succumbed accumulated from the dope game also came murder, and when the bodies started dropping, then the feds would step in. Quavon knew he was on the federal radar, as he had already caught a federal money laundering case, in which he was only given federal probation.

But getting caught with the three-point-two million had the feds on his line, that he was sure of. It was now time to make a decision. A decision to make his exit out the dope game. With the numbers he was seeing off the loud, he didn't need the bricks, he and the G.B.C. would continue to eat off the marijuana. At that moment, Quavon made the choice to leave the dope game before it was too late, and he was fed-bound.

First thing he was going to do when he landed back in the Chi was schedule a sit-down with his plug, Castilino, leader and boss of the Madin Cartel. But as of right now, he and Rio were about to go to the Sun-Set strip club on the Boulevard and turn up. He had close to twelve bands in his pocket and he planned on leaving with none of it.

Chapter 11

Yayo and Shakira where on I-44, headed south. They were on their way to Shreveport, Louisiana. It had been about a month since Yayo went to the doctor to conduct the blood test for paternity of Jamarie. the test came back ninety-nine-point-nine percent that Yayo was indeed the father. Yayo had mixed feelings, a part of him was proud Jamarie was his blood, but yet another part of him felt guilty because he had a kid on Shakira behind her back. but what was done was done and he couldn't take it back if he wanted to. Shakira sat in the passenger seat as Yayo drove the rental on the way to Louisiana to meet his son.

Since finding out Yayo was the father, Shakira had been on an emotional rollercoaster. She wanted to be supportive for her man, but her heart was torn to pieces knowing that she had to share Yayo with another. Not just with Jamarie, but also Jamarie's mother, Amanda. Shakira was secure with her position as wifey. Yayo had proposed to her, putting a Charles Krypell stylized eighteen-carat engagement ring on her finger, but Shakira still felt somewhat intimidated by Amanda and saw her as a threat to her family.

Yayo could tell Shakira was feeling some kind of way. Since they found out Jamarie was his, she had been distant and her conversations had started to become shorter and shorter, making it hard for him to read her. He felt the more he needed her love and support, the more she was starting to pull away from him. Yayo even suggested they bring Shamira, so she could meet her little brother, but Shakira felt it wasn't the right time. Yayo didn't understand her actions, but at the same time he didn't want to argue with her. He would deal with Shakira and her emotions at a later time. As of right now, his main objective was getting to Jamarie.

Twenty-five hours later, Yayo and Shakira pulled into the town of Shreveport. It was a hot summer day as they drove through the muggy slums of Louisiana. last time Yayo had come through these parts he was on a bus loaded with vicious criminals headed to the United States Penitentiary in Pollock, Louisiana with a life sentence on his back, a nightmare he was blessed to awake from.

Yayo picked up his iPhone and dialed Amanda's number. After she gave him the address, he logged it into the GPS and twenty minutes later he was pulling up to a small, one-flat brick house in the middle of town. Yayo turned into the red dirt driveway and parked behind a gray Honda Civic. Turning the ignition off, he turned to Shakira.

"You cool, baby?" he asked, noticing she was still in her feelings. She remained silent and just nodded her head, indicating she was alright. Yayo leaned over and kissed her softly on the cheek, trying his best to reassure her that she had nothing to worry about.

"Come on, boo…let's go meet *our* son," Yayo said, emphasizing "our," wanting her to know they were one, and were in this together. Yayo got out the car with Shakira following suit, slowly getting out the car. Yayo walked over and put his arm around her shoulder as they made their way up the driveway. Amada came out on the front porch, holding four-year-old Jamarie on her hip, walking down the steps to meet them. Yayo could tell just by looking at Jamarie that he was his blood, as he reminded him of Shamira.

"There go your dada," Amanda whispered in Jamarie's ear and put him down. Yayo bent down on one knee and held his arms out to Jamarie. Jamarie didn't know who the stranger was but ran to him like he had known him his whole life. Yayo swooped Jamarie into his arms, spinning him around like the proud father he was.

"What's up, lil man?" Yayo planted kisses all over his face.

"What up?" Jamarie responded back. Amanda looked at the exchange between her only son and his father, causing her to tear up. Shakira stood off to the side, watching all three of them with her hand on her hips. She looked at Amanda, sizing her up from head to toe. Amanda had her long silky hair in a neat ponytail. She rocked a short tank top that exposed her flat stomach, her flower print Gucci shorts made her ass look like two basketballs stuck together. Her thighs were toned as if she did squats on a daily basis, while her nails and toes were manicured to perfection, matching the flower print on her Gucci shorts.

At the moment, Shakira was definitely feeling insecure in the presence of the Latina beauty standing before her, Amanda looked like she was gracing the cover of a *Straight Stuntin Magazine*. Yayo looked over at Shakira while he held his son. He could see the steam coming from off her and used this time to introduce them.

"Oh, my fault...Amanda, this is my beautiful, soon-to-be wife I been telling you about...Shakira. Shakira, this is my son's mother, Amanda," Yayo said, introducing the two of them. Amanda wiped the tears from her face and walked over to Shakira, extending her hand.

"Hi, nice to meet you. Yaton has told me so much about you, it's nice to finally meet you," Amanda greeted, genuinely shaking Shakira's hand.

"It's nice to meet you as well," Shakira started dryly, her tone oozed attitude but in reality, she was happy to hear Yayo had been speaking on her name, letting her position be known. She looked over and smiled at Yayo who was walking toward her, holding Jamarie.

"Say hi to Shakira, Jamarie."

Jamarie wiped his eyes before he said, "Hi, Shakira," then reached for her. Shakira took little Jamarie in her arms and kissed him on his cheek.

"Hi, Jamarie! It's nice to meet you, baby boy." Shakira said, tickling him causing him to giggle uncontrollably. Yayo was happy, happy that Shakira was happy and accepting Jamarie.

"Come on y'all, come inside. I know you had a long ride, so I made some good food for you," Amanda said, leading them into her home. Yayo and Shakira followed her inside. Once inside, the smell of fried chicken smacked Yayo in the face.

"Dada...come see my room!" Jamarie excitedly yelled, pulling Yayo by his Polo shorts.

"Ok, lil man." Yayo followed him to the back room that served as Jamarie's bedroom.

"Shakira, you can make yourself at home, I'm going to go in the kitchen and prepare y'all food." Amanda gestured, making her way to the kitchen.

"I'll help," Shakira offered, following her. "You have a nice home. Have you been living here for a while?" Shakira asked, starting conversation to lighten the mood.

"Yeah, I actually grew up in this house. After my mother passed, I just kept it…I love this house," Amanda replied, grabbing some plates from the cupboard.

"So, I see. How have you been working in corrections?" Shakira inquired.

"Well, I used to work at the state level for about three years and federal for four years."

"Girl, you better than me. I couldn't be around all them crazy ass niggas at one time," Shakira stated.

"It's an easy job and they offer a lot of overtime, so the money is good," Amanda said, filling the plates with fried chicken, and mac and cheese with Grands biscuits.

"So, was Yaton the first inmate you had relationships with, or is that something you do…fuck inmates?" Shakira asked, being assertive with her communication. Amanda stopped what she was doing, put her hands on her hips and snaked her neck around, now looking at Shakira as she felt disrespected.

"Listen, Shakira, so I won't have to repeat this again. When Yaton was at U.S.P. Pollock, he was assigned to my unit. Yes, I found him attractive, I was single. I was infatuated by not just his looks, but the way he carried himself…like a man…a boss. Long story short, I gave him some pussy, something I have never done my entire career working in corrections. So yes, Yaton was the first inmate I ever had sex with. You can believe me or not, your opinion of me don't mean shit. And when I found out I was pregnant, I felt stupid as hell.

"How was I supposed to bring a child into the world by a nigga serving a life sentence? But you know what, I decided to keep my baby. And that was before Yaton gave back the life, may I add. I contacted him and told him it was a possibility he could be the father, but like the boss nigga he is, he kept it a thousand and told me he had a wife and daughter back in Chicago, and he would let nothing come between that. He wanted a blood test once the baby was born and said if the test came back that he was the father, then he would step up to the plate.

"As I can see, he is a man of his word. Yaton is a good nigga...I wish I had met him before you, but I didn't, and I respect the face he has a wife and daughter. I ain't on no bullshit trying to home wreck, long as my son knows who his daddy is, then I'm content. But if you can't respect that or respect me in my house, then it's whatever! I'm definitely trained to go," Amanda said, taking her earrings out her ears, ready to get active. Shakira put her hands up as a sign of peace.

"Amanda, I didn't come here to fight with you. or disrespect you and if I offended you, I apologize. But make no mistake, sweetie pie, I'm from the Chi. I'm with all the dumb shit if you want to go that route. The only reason I came down here is because Yaton asked me to. Do I feel some type of way? Yes, I do. What woman wouldn't, finding out her man got a chick pregnant while he was in prison, and they're on the streets holding shit down, taking care of their child singlehandedly. Not to mention, he is serving a life sentence. You would feel the same way. How I feel can't be changed overnight, it's going to take time, that's just the fact of the matter. But I do respect you and your situation. I just ask that you respect mine," Shakira stated.

"Shakira, trust and believe, I respect you as well as your situation. I'm not with the drama...to me, it's all about Jamarie. That's it, that's all," Amada replied and got back to making the plates. Shakira got up and walked over to help out.

"It's all good, girl, through Jamarie we now a part of each other's lives, so we basically family," Shakira said, making peace.

Amanda stopped what she was doing and looked over at Shakira before she stated, "That's what it is then...we family," and they gave each other a hug. "Now, let's go feed our men." Amanda and Shakira grabbed the plates of food and took them out to the dining room table, just as Yayo and Jamarie were coming from the back room after playing a video game.

"Hope y'all hungry," Amanda said, placing plates on the table. The four of them demolished a fantastic dinner that caused Jamarie to get sleepy.

"Yaton, look like Jamarie ready for bed...you want to tuck him in?" Amanda asked, picking up the plates and taking them to the kitchen. Shakira helped her clear the table.

"Come on, lil man...time to get ready for bed." Yayo picked Jamaie up and took him to his bedroom and laid him in his bed, tucking him in.

"Dada, can you read me a book? Mama always reads me a book," Jamarie asked. Yayo looked around the room and saw a shelf with a small library of children's books on it and grabbed one and began to read to Jamarie. After the third page, Jamarie's eyes were completely closed as he drifted into a peaceful sleep. Yayo rubbed his son's head, full of black curly hair from his mixed heritage, and kissed him on the forehead before he stood up. Jamarie's voice caused him to freeze in place.

"Dada?"

"What's up, lil man?" Yayo said, turning around to face his son, who still had his eyes closed.

"Dada, are you going to be here when I wake up in the morning?" Jamarie asked. Yayo kissed his son on the head.

"Son, I have to go back to Chicago...But I promise, I will be back real soon, and next time I'm going to bring your sister. Ok?"

"Ok, Dada. I love you."

"I love you too, son," Yayo replied. He wanted to take Jamarie with him so he could be with him every day. He and Amanda were going to have to work something out so he could be a part of Jamarie's life, which he knew she would have no problem with.

Walking in the living room, Yayo was greeted with the smell of high-grade marijuana. Shakira and Amanda sat on the couch smoking a blunt of loud, laughing and giggling like two childhood friends. Yayo covered his nose with his shirt, making sure that he didn't catch any contact. If he caught a dirty UA, his parole officer would surely violate him and send him back to prison.

"What's up, Shakira, you ready to hit the road?" He asked.

"Yaton, ain't no way y'all about to drive back to Chicago tonight, it's too late. And plus, I told Shakira we was going to the mall tomorrow," Amanda stated. answering for Shakira.

"Yeah, let's kick it down here for a couple days...Ain't no rush to get back to the city, is it?" Shakira asked him.

Whatever, baby...whatever you want to do," Yayo replied, he was actually happy Shakira wasn't in a rush to get back to Chicago, now he could have more time with Jamarie. Yayo left Shakira and Amanda to their high school sleepover, while he went back to Jamarie's room and climbed in bed with him. Jamarie must've felt his father's presence as he laid his head on his chest. Yayo stared into the darkness consumed in his thoughts, while his son slept. It felt good to have Jamarie in his life, it was like Jamarie completed him.

Things were starting to look up as God's blessings continued to rain down upon him. He couldn't wait to get back to Chicago to push the line with the Save Our Youth campaign. He had his first taste of the movement when they went to the Wentworth Gardens Projects, as he could see things could get violent as everybody wasn't with curbing the pandemic of murder and drugs in the city. But Yayo had promised Mr. B, who was only about an hour away in U.S.P. Pollock, that he would do all he could do to Save the Youth. He owed Mr. B...Mr. B had saved his life and gotten his freedom. Now Yayo just prayed silently as he held his son, that the same life Mr. B saved wouldn't be took in the process of trying to save the lives of others.

S. ALLEN

Chapter 12

Omega stepped out of the Benz Wagon, dressed in all black...a mini, Draco AK-47 hung from a Louis Vuitton strap over his right shoulder. He was at Sherman Park on 55th and Garfield on the city's south side. He was there to attend a function he labeled the Meet and Greet, where he would introduce the new regime of the Homicide Crew. For the last month, Omega had demonstrated ruthlessly and singlehandedly, a recruitment movement with different gangs throughout the city of Chicago, offering them money, guns and drugs to leave their own organizations, only to align with the Homicide Crew.

Most of these men traded sides for money and power, where the rebellious individuals within their own crews. They broke the ties that bonded them by laws and policies of their organizations, only to find home with the H.C. in which they lived by only one creed...murder and mayhem. Omega recruited these rebellious gang members from different areas of the city, 59th Bishop, 69th and Justine, 39th and Prairie, 53rd Troop as well as the K-Town section of the west side. He flooded these areas of the city with bricks of cocaine and enough guns to start a war with Russia. With the money, guns and drugs, Omega was able to gain blind loyalty from gangsters throughout these areas, all of them willing to rob, steal and kill for him.

Times had changed dramatically, what used to be loyalty that bonded men, was evilly replaced as the loyalty went to the man holding the bag...and Omega held it.

It was a hot summer night and Sherman Park was almost packed to capacity with gangbangas...Weed smoke hung in the air like fog. Omega was met by Fonzo.

"What up, fam?" he said, shaking Omega's hand.

"Same ole' shit...different toilet. You got that for me?"

"Yeah, I got it." Fonzo replied and walked over to a clean 1990 box Chevy, sitting on twenty-six-inch Rucci rims...compliments of Omega. Fonzo popped the trunk, reached in and grabbed a blow horn and passed it to Omega, then shut the trunk.

"Now, let's go handle this Nation Bizness." Omega walked over to the large crowd that occupied the park.

"Homicide Crew, what's the business?" Omega said, his voice loud and clear through the bullhorn. The goons all responded with chants and throwing up gang signs, repping their blocks and areas. Omega continued. "I want all y'all mutherfuckas to look around you. Look to the left, look to the right. The niggas you surrounded by, remember they face and where they from. Because as of right now that nigga is your family," Omega said, watching the men shake hands, give daps and embrace each other.

"Now, listen up…We all here for a reason, and that reason is to dominate these muthefucking streets and everything in them. From this point on, anybody who is not at this park right now, is not part of this family…they are the opps." Whispers could be heard throughout the crowd. "In order to have complete dominance, we must be in total control. With no resistance from none of these hoe ass niggas out here, including the Get It Boy Clique and that bitch ass nigga, Quavon."

"Fuck the G.B.C.!" a youngsta in a white T-shirt and long dreads yelled. His animosity toward the Get It Boy Clique made Omega smile, as he moved forward with his speech.

"Yeah, that's right, family…fuck the G.B.C., 69th and Wolcott is a red-zone. I want that shit blew off the map. For every nigga y'all shoot from that area, whoever put the work in will be rewarded with two stacks…the nigga die, then it's twenty. As for their leader, Quavon, a hunnid geez to whoever bust his head. I want that shit on Wolcott to look like a ghost town. In the end we gone be at the top of the food chain. We all gone have the bag. As you see, the work is no issue. I'm plugged with the Sinaloa Cartel, we ain't gone never run out," Omega lied, He couldn't care less about money, all he wanted was revenge for Ace and K.I.

He wanted the G.B.C. dead like yesterday and he was going to stop at nothing until they were all disposed of. Omega continued to preach venom to his subordinates for another thirty minutes or so, until he adjourned the meet and greet. He had manipulated the minds of all that attended, to do one thing…And that was to kill G.B.C. gangsters.

Lonell was on the block of 69th and Wolcott, sitting on his mountain bike smoking a blunt of loud doing security. It was midnight and the flow of fiends was thick. Choppa had sent message that all blocks where the coke was being sold were to remain open twenty-four hours. All heroin blocks opened at 5:00 am and closed at 10:00 am, then opened back up at 3:00 until 8:00 pm.

Lonell was working the graveyard shift on the coke block and was being paid five hundred dollars a shift. Security had been beefed up since Mud and lil Von got killed in front of Fat Albert's restaurant early that summer…they didn't want the opps to catch them lacking, so security toted MAC-11's. Everybody had to be on point and on the same page in order to secure this drug turf. Lonell's iPhone sprang to life and seeing it was Mika, he answered.

"What's good with it, ma?" he answered with smoke escaping from his nostrils.

"Where you at? My girl said she got fifty dollars and she trying to get something to smoke on, plus I'm trying to see your sexy ass. I got an itch that need to be scratched," Mika said. She had a thing for Lonell and how he fucked her in the ass. Her asshole was the itch that needed to be scratched.

"I'm on security right now, I'm a see if I can get one of the guys to relieve my post then I can slide your way. Matter fact let me see that pussy, give me something to look forward to, FaceTime a nigga and let me see something," Lonell said, watching a car turn into an alley off Wolcott, he adjusted the baby MAC on his waist and was about to go investigate until his iPhone beeped from Mika's FaceTime request. Lonell pressed "send," accepting the request. the screen on his phone now showed Mika's fat twat as she fingered her wet sloppy pussy. Her friend giggled in the background… *These freak ass hoes*, Lonell thought as he posted up, watching the show on his phone, totally off point.

"Hurry up, my nigga, so we can get up outta here," Slug said, turning the headlights of the Chevy Malibu off. He was talking to his potna Pharoe who occupied the passenger seat, pulling the draw strings to his Marc Jella hoodie that covered his head. Slug and Pharoe was from 39th and Prairie from a hood called New Town and was now aligned with Omega and the Homicide Crew.

The two gangsters were in the process of running a drill on the opps and trying to cash in on the twenty-thousand-dollar bounty Omega had put on the heads of the Get It Boy Clique gang. Armed with a fully automatic Glock with a 50-round drum and red beam, Pharoe was ready to blow something down.

"On Chuck Grave, I'm about to nail this pussy to the cross," Pharoe vowed with a sinister smirk on his face before he cocked the Glock and got out the car. Slug had his head on swivel as he scanned his surroundings, He was paranoid as he knew he was on 69th and Wolcott...the heart of G.B.C. territory. Pharoe crept through the gangway between two houses, moving stealthily in a crouching position, holding the Glock at his side. He now had Lonell in his vision. Raising the pole, he aimed it toward the corner where Lonell sat on his bike, glued to his phone and lined him up, put the beam on him and tightened his finger on the trigger.

"Alright boy, that's enough...now can you please hurry up and bring us some weed?" Mika said, pulling up her Dereon jeans, done with her little freak show.

"I got you, shorty, just give me about thirty minutes. I got to wait for one of these niggas to come through. I'm definitely on my way," Lonell told her, his hard dick trying to bust through his skinny jeans from the light porn Mika had just given him.

Boc Lonell jumped from the loud gunshot, dropping his phone on the ground. He felt a burning sensation on the side on his stomach. *Boc, Boc, Boc, Boc, Boc, Boc* the 9mm slugs ripped through his body in rapid retorts, knocking him off the bike. Pharoe emerged from the gangway, running toward him pointing his weapon and squeezing the trigger. Lonell's nerves were shocked, causing him to be paralyzed as his killer stood over him.

"Please, fam...don't kill me...Please," Lonell pleaded, gurgling from the thick blood caught in his throat. Pharoe watched his enemy beg for his life through his bloodshot eyes. He grinned, then pulled the trigger, putting Lonell's brains on the pavement and sending him to his maker. Pharoe looked around before he ran back through the gangway he had come from, leaving Lonell DOA.

Jumping back in the Malibu geeked from the act of murder he had just committed, he told Slug to pull off. Slug pulled out of the alley calmly, en route back to their hood, just as some G.B.C. gangsters ran down the block with guns drawn, only to find one of their own laying in a puddle of blood next to his MAC-11 on the corner of 69th and Wolcott. Their opps had slid through and scored…little did they know this was just the beginning, and a lot of lives was about to be added to the city's murder rate.

"What the fuck you mean they just slid through? How they just slide through? That's what security is set up for, so shit like this don't happen, simple minded muthafuckers," Choppa vented. He was at a project called the Calumet Building, discussing the incident that happened on 69th and Wolcott. Another one of their men had died by the hands of their opposition, and it was making it seem like he wasn't conducting his position as chief of security for the Get It Boy Clique properly. Reggie G and Crusha was also in attendance.

"I just don't understand how nobody seen nothing. Niggas was on the block and nobody witness the shooting? Make that make sense," Reggie G intervened, directing his question to Span and Low-Low, who were on the block serving fiends at the time of the murder.

"We ain't see nothing, fam, all we heard was the shots. We ran down there, and we found fam laying on his back. Shid, he was supposed to be on security securing us, not the other way around," Span retorted. Choppa slowly turned around facing him, with a look of evil plastered across his face before he walked over to him, all while pulling a .357 off his waist. Grabbing him by his collar, he put the cold barrel under his chin and cocked the hammer.

"Nigga, did we ask you what the fuck he was supposed to be doing, huh? Say that shit again," Choppa hissed, ready to pull the trigger. Span remained silent, knowing that Choppa was crazy enough to take his life. "Yeah, that's what the fuck I thought." Choppa pushed Span with brute force, causing him to fall back in his chair. Crusha put his hand on Choppa's shoulder.

"Come on, fam, it's not their fault, that could happen to any-body. Let's just move objectively, get the facts and find out who responsible for this and take care of the business." Choppa knocked Crusha's hand off his shoulder.

"Nah, this shit couldn't happen to just anybody, it definitely wouldn't have happened to me, you know why? I'm a tell you why…because I know we at war, so I be on point. I'm a muther-fucking demon, I ain't letting these bitch made niggas murder me, I do the murdering. Niggas better know what they a part of. This the G.B.C. and if niggas heart and soul ain't in this shit, move the fuck around…We need killas on the squad. Fuck all the excuses, how I'm supposed to explain this shit to Quavon?" Choppa spat venom-ously, pacing back and forth clutching the .357 tightly.

"You two brothers can be excused, shut the block down until further notice. Nobody but security is to be on the blocks. We on Code Blue, High Alert," Crusha commanded, taking control. Span and Low-Low got up and left the small apartment to go follow their orders.

"I shoulda popped that stupid mutherfucka just to send a mes-sage. Now I gotta call Q and let him know we just took another L on the land…He gone be pissed," Choppa said as he dialed Quavon's number.

"Speak on it, family," Quavon answered.

"Aye, what up, G? This the business, niggas just slid through and scored."

"Who got hit?" Quavon probed.

"Lonell." The phone got quiet for a few seconds.

"Outcome?"

"DOA," Choppa answered. Quavon shook his head, Lonell was his lil mans, his heart began to hurt. Lonell was only twenty-one years old and the wicked city of Chicago had claimed his young life. This was what Quavon was trying to escape from, all the murder and violence that plagued the city. He wasn't in the game to kill…he was in it for the bag, and now that he had the bag, it was time for him to make his exit.

Listen, where Crusha and Reggie G?" Quavon asked.

"They right here…you on speaker phone, bruh."

"I need y'all to meet up with me, we need to have a staff meeting. I got to put y'all up on something pertaining to our future…where y'all at?"

"We at the Calumet Building, where you want us to come?" Crusha asked.

"Look, meet me up north on Clark and Towley, it's a park behind that Walgreens called Pottawatomie Park. Meet me there in about two hours," Quavon said.

"Alright, that's a bet…we en route," Choppa retorted and ended the call. Quavon sat his head back on the sectional sofa. The news he just received about Lonell getting whacked had him vexed. It was now time to make the call he was dreading to make. He didn't know how he was going to take the news that he was going to lay in his lap. Quavon knew when you messed around with these kinds of people, the contract was signed in blood, and it was no getting out once you entered their world, as the only way out was death. This was something he was willing to die for. Quavon scrolled through his contacts and pressed "send." The most powerful drug lord in the world answered… Castilino Madina, leader and boss of the Madin Drug Cartel.

Chapter 13

Yayo and Davon sat in the basement playing *Call of Duty* on a large projection television. The projection screen was so large, the men on the screen looked to be the same size as actual humans. Yayo tapped on the controller frantically, knocking his enemies down on the battlefield, his character was shooting his pistol like Cane was in *Menace to Society*. Davon sat next to his brother, enjoying his time with him. He had missed the times he and Yayo shared playing video games before Yayo was sent to prison.

Davon was doing well at EA Sports, being promoted to executive director, he was now living on a hundred and fifty thousand dollars a year salary.

"Damn!" Yayo cursed as he had just lost his life on the game, getting killed by an enemy fighter with a FNH assault rifle. He put the controller down, frustrated. Davon continued shooting shit up, the gunshots from the game sounding real from the surround sound speakers posted in different positions in the furnished basement.

"Come on, Yayo, pick the controller back up so we can finish punishing these clowns," Davon encouraged. They were playing online and the others they were playing were trash talking.

"I'm cool, lil bro...we been playing this game for the last four hours. Matter fact, what you said you wanna holler at me about?" Yayo asked. Davon had called him early that morning, saying he needed to talk to him about something important and for that reason, he was at Yayo and Shakira's condo, but they just ended up playing the PlayStation. Davon paused the game and turned to face his brother.

"Oh, yeah...Yayo, remember when you came home and we threw that party for you?"

"Yeah, what about it?"

"You and Quavon was on the patio talking to Reggie and Crusha."

"And?" Yayo said.

"Well, I was listening to what you was talking about and for real, bro, you was speaking some real shit. The streets is messed up out there, and like you said, it's mostly the youth. A lot of my friends I went to school with that chose the streets are either dead or in jail, Yayo. I got a friend named Rodney and we went to school together. He went to school for business management, his grade point average stayed high. He graduated from college.

"He didn't get into the gangs or the drug dealing stuff, he got involved in fraud, selling bogus C.P.N. numbers, swiping credit cards and identity theft, came up quick. He was on Instagram at a strip club, throwing a hundred geez. When he got back to Chicago, he got kidnapped and held for ransom. They took three hundred bands from him, then shot him in the head, and you know the worst part, bro?"

"What's that, Davon?"

"It was his own blood cousin that robbed and killed him. Bro, we need more people like you out here to get in the heads of the youth, they will Listen to you. You are a success story. You was involved in the negative stuff and now you live a positive life. You have a lot to offer the community, and I think I can help you and the Save Our Youth Movement."

"How is that, Davon? Holler at me, lil bro, I'm definitely hearing what you speaking."

"It's like this. I have this friend named Katrina. I used to go to school with her back in the day. She grew up to be a counselor at the Audi Home. I was telling her about you and the Save Our Youth Movement. She was intrigued with your story and she sees you as a pillar in our community.

"She thought it would be a good idea if you could come to the Audi Home and speak to the youth about your trials and tribulations, in hopes to persuade them away from a life of crime, and I feel it would be a great idea as well. Katrina said she was going to contact the Cook County Sheriff and the Mayor of Chicago to see if she could make it happen. Matter fact she supposed to have a sit down with Cook County next week…what do you think, bro?"

Yayo smiled at Davon's intellect as well as his networking connections. Yayo could remember serving time at the Audi Home for Boys where he was sentenced to juvenile life for murder. At that adolescent age, he was nothing but a troubled youth with no direction. Some of the juveniles at the Audi Home were as young as eight years old.

Tossed into the system, only to be warehoused and taught criminal ways that would pave their way for the problematic, impulsive, violent criminal lifestyle. Resorting them to death or years upon years in and out of state and federal correctional facilities. What Katrina had proposed was genius. Yayo knew Kewann and the rest of the Save Our Youth would be with it.

"Damn, baby boy! I think that's a good idea and I'm definitely with it. We might not be able to save all of them, but I think we can save a few and that few is worth the work. All you gotta do is let me know when your friend is ready. Save Our Youth is on standby. We work twenty-four hours, three hundred sixty-five days of the year, bro," Yayo said, giving Davon some dap, excited about what they had just come up with.

"Don't even trip, bro, I'm a keep you posted. But right now, let's finish putting this work in on these chumps," said Davon, picking back up the controller. Yayo just shook his head, smiling at his brother he picked his controller up. The two brothers continued to blast away at their enemies, playing *Call of Duty*, until Davon had to go to the crib to get ready for work the next day. Yayo was glad his brother had come over to spend some quality time. Davon had just given him some more ammunition to arm himself with, to fight for the lives of the youth in the city of Chicago.

Quavon pulled up to Pottawatomie Park on the north side in a lowkey Audi RS3 and parked behind Choppa's Range Rover. He had a lot on his mind. He had just scheduled a face-to-face meeting with his plug, Mr. Castilino, and had even purchased a plane ticket to Midland, Texas. He would be picked up by some of Castilino's men, and driven across the border to Juarez, Mexico to meet with the boss. Castilino had asked Quavon what the cause of the urgent meeting was, Quavon responded by telling him it was something that he had to discuss with him face-to-face.

"Very well, my son, I will see you soon," was all Castilino said. Quavon just hoped and prayed after he gave Castilino the business, that Castilino would release him from the grasp of the Madin Cartel and allow him to make it back to the United States without incident.

Quavon got out his whip and started walking through the dark, empty park. He could see three shadowy figures sitting on a bench on the side of a sliding board. A bright orange cherry from a blunt or cigarette glowed like a lightning bug in the darkness. The closer he got, he could tell it was Choppa taking the strong pulls from the blunt, as the closer he got, the stronger the pungent scent of the high-grade marijuana invaded the atmosphere. Quavon walked up and shook hands with his loyal G.B.C. faculty.

"What's up with y'all?"

"Ain't shit, just waiting on you," Crusha replied, shaking his boss's hand.

"What up with you?" Quavon asked, looking at Choppa who held a look of murder, his eyes the color of a "stop snitching" sign. Choppa passed his iPhone 11 to Quavon.

"Press play, scud," Choppa said, taking a pull from the blunt. Quavon reviewed the *Instagram* video. The video showed Pharoe and Slug boasting about the drill they did on 69th and Wolcott.

Yeah, you pussy ass niggas, y'all see that work call…Bitch niggas, it's drill season, get down or lay down, Homicide Crew Crazy, RIP Ace!" Pharoe said behind an all-black ski mask, flashing the twenty stacks he had been rewarded for busting Lonell's head to the white meat. Slug stood beside him bare-faced, pointing two Glocks with extended 30-shot clips at the camera.

"Faggot ass Homicide Crew," Choppa sneered. Quavon looked at his men in confusion.

"Homicide Crew? I thought all them niggas was dead," Quavon said, giving Choppa back his phone.

"They say it's a nigga named Omega running around, offering bricks of coke to niggas in the city to align with him and his politics," Crusha intervened.

"Politics…what he supposed to be politicking?"

"Our demise," Choppa answered, flicking the blunt roach. "Word on the street is he want us dead because I nailed that hoe ass nigga a couple years back. Now they wanna get back on that…we can definitely get back on that," Choppa fumed, ready to drill some-thing.

"Wait a minute…you said he recruiting shooters from all over the city? Who is these niggas and where they from? Because if what y'all saying is true, we can be at war with the whole city. Where them niggas from on that video?" Quavon asked.

"Word is they from New Town on 39th and Prairie," Reggie G said, shedding some light on the situation.

"New Town? That's Vamp hood. We ain't beefing with them niggas, I fuck with him and his brother Carlos. That don't make sense."

Choppa stood up from the bench. "Big homie, you ain't listen-ing to me. This nigga Omega going to different areas, recruiting random niggas to flip for guns and coke…Niggas is switching sides on *they* gang for money…Shid, we don't know who gone come gun-ning, we warring with a ghost," Choppa explained, breaking it down so Quavon could understand what kind of fight they were up against. Quavon tried to remain calm, even though his anger was starting to emerge, he had to stay level-headed and in the mind frame of a leader in front of his team. He shook his head in under-standing.

"Alright brothers…listen, these suckers just cast the first stone. We all know that don't nobody lay hands on any member of the organization…period. Them two lames boasting all on the *'Gram*, I want them niggas dead. I'm gone slide through New Town and see if I can get up with Vamp and Carlos and see how they feel about they men flipping and offer them something they can't refuse. Ei-ther they give us the green light on Tom and Jerry, or they suffer the same fate. And that nigga Omega, let the streets know I got two hundred racks on that nigga head!" Quavon said, leveling with his squad.

Yayo had always taught him the game was chess, not checkers. He had to give Omega his props on the recruitment tactic, but he didn't see Omega as a threat. He knew whoever Omega was, his pockets weren't as deep as his. As Quavon knew, money won wars, and in due time, Omega was going to be just another article in *The Chicago Tribune.*

"Now moving forward, I just got off the phone with Castilino."

"And?" Choppa asked, ready to leave the park so he could get in the battlefield.

"After this, we gone be done with the coke and dope." Crusha, Reggie G and Choppa all looked at each other with perplexed looks on their faces, before looking back at Quavon.

"Done with the work? You made a decision like that without consulting with the whole table?" Crusha asked, feeling his title within the G.B.C. entitled him to more respect than that.

"Let me finish, Crusha," Quavon said, putting his hands up in a surrendering motion. "Check it out, family…We don't need the hard drugs, that shit ain't doing nothing but keeping us in the streets to deal with the shit we dealing with now. The main objective of the game is to get in and get out. We been in this shit too long, my niggas. Look at us, we drive whatever the fuck we want, dress in all the latest designer and can lay our head in the plushest shit in the city. Well hell, the world.

"My nigga we run shit, but how long will it last? I say we bow out gracefully and on top while we still can. These hating, bitch ass niggas, they broke. They gunning at us out of envy, because of what we have become. We feasted and feasted good, let these serpent niggas crawl on they bellies and survive off the scraps we leave them." Quavon was trying to get his men to see the bigger picture.

"Quavon, we all straight and got our bag up. But if we hand the streets over to these niggas, how we gone eat?" Choppa probed, cutting Quavon off.

"Choppa, that's what I'm trying to tell y'all. Just like we flooding the city with the coke and the defense, we gone continue to flood the gates, only we gone flood the city with the loud. We can eat like giants from the weed. In three months, we made one-point-eight million, my nigga. And I say we, because what's mine is yours. It's three dispensaries in all in Cali. It's time to make our move out the city, move to Cali and get fat! Fuck all this busting and thugging. The whole city knows our murder game official, we don't got nothing to prove to these off-brand niggas, it's time to take it to another level."

Cusha sat quietly rubbing his thin goatee, digesting what Quavon was speaking. And it all made sense. If they stayed in the city, continuing to slug it out with all the up-and-coming rivals, the same tactics they applied to get Chicago in the vice grips of the Get It Boy Clique would be the same murderous tactics to be the cause of their ruin. And all the blood, sweat and tears would die in vain with them. Crusha stood from the bench and put his hand on Quavon's broad shoulder.

"Quavon, what you decided is the smartest decision you have made since you have been sitting on the throne. I totally agree with you, youngsta. I'm forty years old and too old to be out here playing with the pistols. You have grown, Quavon. Yayo is going to be proud of you. I'm with you, youngsta, you have my love and support," Crusha said, pulling Quavon in to embrace him. He had more respect for Quavon more now than ever. He had watched Yayo's lil brother climb the ranks of the G.B.C. righteously, gaining a position of authority by adhering to the laws and policies of the Get It Boy Clique.

Quavon used his head to plot and scheme to exploit the imposters within the G.B.C. and then ruthlessly cover their demise, gaining total control and leadership over the Organization. He wasn't the type to use his authority and position to exploit the guys. He looked at everybody as equals and in accordance with G.B.C. laws as he preached love, life and loyalty, the three principles the G.B.C. was built upon...causing the gang to love Quavon wholeheartedly. Crusha would do a hundred years...or die at the hands of the opps for Quavon.

"Thank you, Crusha, it's all well," Quavon told Crusha then turned his attention to Reggie. Reggie G, how you feel about all this?"

Reggie G looked Quavon in his eyes, grinning like a proud father. He loved Quavon as if they had come from the same womb and shared the same bloodline. To Reggie G, Quavon was one of the sharpest young niggas to play the game, from the way he dressed, spoke, and used finesse to climb to the top of the under-world in the most violent city in the country.

And he did it all by using his head. The way he played Top Cat and his crew of killas was classic. Taking the three thousand bricks of heroin, then going back to the plug with all the money that Top Cat owed took balls of steel.

Those same balls secured him a plug with the most powerful drug lord in the world. He took initiative to kill T.B. while he was in the height of power because T.B. was using the G.B.C. for his own personal gain. It showed the rest of the gang that Quavon was righteous and would always stay loyal to the Get It Boy Clique's code of conduct, whether leader or foot soldier. Reggie G knew Quavon was from a rare breed and would follow him through hell and back. He stood and bowed his head as if Quavon was a god, showing his undying loyalty. Quavon laughed at him.

"Man, if you don't get up outta here! Bowing your head like you a sensei or some shit...Come here, fam," Quavon said and grabbed Reggie G in a thug embrace.

"I'm with you, Quavon," was Reggie G's only reply, mere words need not be explained.

"I'm already hip, fam, we gone eat forever. And that's on gang!" Quavon then turned to Choppa, who was mean mugging.

"Don't even ask me, Quavon, I ain't moving to California, I don't give a fuck what y'all talking about! I ain't put in all this work and get to where I'm at, just to throw it all away. And niggas still trying to slide like it's sweet? Like my drill game ain't shit? I'm ready for war!" Choppa said through clenched teeth, meaning every word.

Quavon felt Choppa's pain. If it wasn't for Choppa, his militant mind-frame and deadly trigger finger, the G.B.C. would not be where they are today. Choppa had a body count that exceeded TJ's, Yayo's second-in-command that died at the hands of his enemies. Choppa's soul was embalmed by evil, making him murderous and sickly dangerous, and an A-list killer in the city of Chicago. Quavon loved Choppa and wanted to show him a better life, a different side of the game and minus all the killing.

"Choppa, brother, I feel you. Trust and believe all that work will not go in vain. But listen, it's about the bag, that's why we are all here. When Yayo started this thing, it was about the money. Remember the time I told you, Yayo told me when I was a shorty, the money bring the murder, as money and homicide coincide...huh?" Quavon asked. Choppa nodded his head yes.

"Then you also remember I told you he said murder is used as a tool for peace. I'm trying to make it where you ain't got to be out here like that, My nigga, one-point-eight mil in ninety days! You ain't got to be out here running drills, make that make sense. You want Al Capone status or Donald Trump status?"

Choppa's chest was heaving as he said, "I want Pops Johnson's status. You know why? Because he stayed loyal and true to the code he lived by, willing to die when the feds wanted him to flip on the GD's. He told them crackers to go to hell and give him the needle. I want Yayo status...niggas like that, that's true to the game. We been out here fighting unapologetically to own these streets. Now that you find out it's a nigga out here with a lil bread coming at our necks, now y'all wanna run to California...when we should be laying our lick down, punishing these hoe ass niggas. Now make *that* make sense," Choppa fumed. Quavon walked up to Choppa so they were face-to-face, nose-to-nose.

"Choppa, first and foremost, watch your tone when you speak to me, family. Running? We not running, we outsmarting these goofies. You making reference to 'Pops.' Indeed, he was loyal to the guys, but you know where 'Pops' at now? I'm a tell you. He somewhere on the West Coast in a federal penitentiary, where he will die an old man. As for Yayo, you already know his story, had it not been a blessing from God he would a died behind the wall. That's the outcome you want, fam? Then so be it, But the rest of us getting out...and we getting out winning. You either with us or you not, Choppa," Quavon said, stepping back from Choppa, awaiting his response.

Choppa's reply would determine if he lived or died. Quavon was smart with the game, there was no way he and the rest of the staff would make an exit out the game and leave Choppa in the Chi.

He loved the young goon, but if Choppa decided to go his own way, then he would have to be put to rest, he knew too much and when Quavon left, he was leaving no strings untied.

Choppa analyzed Quavon's words, he didn't want to die in the streets with his blood leaking in a sewer, nor did he want to die slow in a United States penitentiary. But at the same time, he didn't want his name tarnished in the streets for ducking rec in the midst of a gang war. He didn't want his guys to leave him in Chicago. He was with them wholeheartedly, but he had to convince Quavon to let him stand on the G.B.C. brand and let them go out with a bang, knocking Omega off and the rest of his Homicide Crew flunkies for testing their gangsta!

"Quavon, when Yayo got me off the streets, I had no family. He looked after me and taught me the meaning of love and loyalty, integrity as well as dignity. When he went to the feds, my loyalty to him was never lost. You stepped in and being his brother, my loyalty to you was equal and solidified. Fam, the Get It Boy Clique is my only family. I know what it is to be loved now and that feeling is a feeling I never want to depart from. So yes, I'm with y'all, but only on one condition," Choppa said.

"What's that, bro?" Quavon asked, smiling like a Cheshire cat.

"You give me the green light to put these fake ass niggas in Burr Oaks Cemetery before we bounce." Quavon cocked his head to the side and laughed.

"Nigga, is you crazy? I know you wasn't thinking we was gone leave without handling that Nation Business…where they do that at? I told you I'm about to get up with Vamp and see what's to them two niggas on the video. Make no mistake about it, the city gone feel our wrath, for years to come. This shit chess, not checkers. You just get the Blackout Squad on standby. And when I push this button, I want y'all to soak this bitch," Quavon said, embracing Lil Choppa. Quavon now had the G.B.C. on the same page. They were going to swiftly make their opps pay dearly for the disrespect and then make a move for the betterment of their future and longevity. He had given Choppa the green light to lace up his boots. If niggas in the Chi thought the G.B.C. was sweet, then they had another think coming. *They mommas better have life insurance on them, or they were going to be paying out their pockets for their sons' funerals.*

S. ALLEN

Chapter 14

Yayo sat in the passenger seat of Kewann's Lincoln. They had just pulled into the parking ramp. They were on 11th and Hamilton on the west side of the Cook County Courthouse, also known as the Audi Home for Boys. Davon sat quietly in the back seat. He had contacted Yayo and told him that Katrina had gotten the ok from the mayor as well as the Cook County sheriff and granted Yayo to do a public speaking at the juvenile facility. And today was the day the speech was to happen. Kewann parked on the second floor of the parking camp. They all got out and made their way to the entrance of the building. Yayo's stomach was in a balled-up knot…He was a nervous wreck as he had never spoken in a large crowd before.

The large lobby of the courthouse was crowded. It was 12:15 pm and a lot of the people who worked at the courthouse was in a slight panic, rushing to get to or back from their lunch breaks. After the men cleared the metal detector, Yayo was met by Katrina, who was waiting patiently on a bench. She noticed Davon coming through the metal detector, stood and straightened the wrinkles in her brown, tight-fitting, two-piece business suit. She was caramel-skinned, five-four, a nice size and had a professional look to her. Katrina walked up and gave Davon a hug and Yayo could tell by their interaction that they were indeed good friends.

"Hi, Davon, I'm glad you all could make it. Is this your brother?" Katrina asked, now walking up to Yayo, extending her hand for a handshake.

"Yep. That's him," Davon replied.

"Nice to meet you, Katrina…Davon has told me a lot about you. I appreciate this opportunity," Yayo said, shaking Katrina's hand.

"No, I appreciate you. I think these young men in here need to hear from somebody like you. Somebody who has been through the trenches, overcame trials and tribulations and bounced back on a positive note," Katrina concurred.

"I definitely have a story to tell. I just hope it wakes some of these brothers up and see there are no happy endings to the life of crime. By the way, this good brother right here is Kewann, CEO and co-founder of the Save Our Youth Campaign," Yayo said, introducing them.

"It's an honor to meet you, Kewann. I'm sorry I couldn't get all of the Save Our Youth to attend, it was like trying to pull the mayor's tooth just to get him to sign off on this. As you know, everybody doesn't see the bigger picture, or the vision we do. But I'm sure in time things will turn around," Katrina stated, shaking Kewann's hand.

"It's all good, Katrina. I completely understand. Long as we make progress in this movement, and we can change some lives, that's all that matters," Kewann replied.

"I totally agree, it's all about taking the initiative, igniting everybody's will to do better. Now, if you don't mind, we are running late. They are only giving us an hour for the speaking. They should have all the boys in the gym room, follow me," Katrina said, leading the way. Yayo, Davon and Kewann followed Katrina to an elevator.

Looking around, Yayo remembered the Audi Home just as if it was yesterday, instead of twenty years ago. The same pictures hung on the wall, the same smell he remembered vividly. He could almost feel the coldness that invaded the brick cells, had a flashback to the nights he tossed and turned at night, from the stress of not knowing if he was going to ever make it back home a free man. The guilt he felt for firing the weapon that claimed the life of a five-year-old girl. All these feelings and thoughts started to surface as they rode the elevator to the basement floor of the Audi Home.

Yayo knew it was many young men going through the same thing he had gone through when he was last at the Audi Home. Knowing this gave Yayo the morale he needed to get through to these young adolescent individuals. The elevator stopped on the basement floor and they all exited the elevator. They followed Katrina down a dimly lit hallway and stopped in front of two large double doors that said, "South Gymnasium" in big black broad letters. Katrina turned to look at the three men before she said, "Y'all ready?"

"More ready than ever," Yayo responded. Katrina smiled then, opened the door to the loud gym room. Two correctional officers called tenants, stood on both sides of the entrance into the gym. Yayo was greeted by a sea of young violent criminals, their hardened eyes fixed on them as Katrina led them to the front of the gym, where there was a wooden podium with a microphone. At the front of the gym room were seven more tenants, they were there to keep order and control inside the gym in case anything popped off.

The entire gym was packed to capacity, with young GDs, BDs, Vice Lords, Latin Kings, Unknowns, Latin Folks, just to name a few and they were all from different areas of the city. South side, west side, up north and the low end to the wild-wild hunnids…All these convicted felons committed to their gangs and neighborhoods, and anything was bound to pop off. The administration of the Audi Home was taking no chances, so the tenants were armed with handcuffs and pepper spray.

Yayo followed Katrina to the small stage where the podium sat. As he walked past the teenagers, he heard one of them say, "Light baldhead, chicken leg looking boy!" Then the boys erupted in laughter.

"Man, dude better get his Sherman Hemsley looking ass up outta here. Oh, I wish I was y'all age but I'm not looking ass nigga!" Another said, then more laughter.

Yayo just shook his head smiling, remembering the days he and Pudge used to jones and crack jokes like when they were younger. He paid them no mind as he made his way to the stage and stood behind Katrina as she took to the microphone. She tapped on it three times, making sure it was on.

"Testing, testing…Ok, y'all need to quiet down."

The boys continued to chat and make jokes, ignoring what Counselor Katrina was saying. Seeing they were not adhering to what she was saying, she snaked her neck, put her hands on her hips, then yelled into the microphone. "I said, quiet down!" Her voice boomed throughout the gym, causing all the boys to cease their conversations. All the boys respected Katrina, she been working at the Audi Home for three years and had been battle tested. The boys all had a crush on Katrina but knew not to play with her, as she was quick to send them to the hole for not following the rules.

"Thank you...now that I have y'all undivided attention, I want to introduce to you all three special important people. These men have come to speak to y'all about the importance of change and bettering your lives. They speak from personal experience and would like all of you to take a look at them and their lives, and how they were in the same predicament as a lot of you. Please pay attention to these men's words of wisdom...Give a round of applause for the Save Our Youth Movement," Katrina said, then moved out the way to give Yayo the floor.

Kewann had already told Yayo today was all about him and his testimony. Today it would be Yayo's chance to take a shot at captivating the minds of Chicago's most notorious juveniles. Only a few clapped as Yayo took to the microphone.

"What's up with y'all...how you fellas doing? My name is Yaton. But when I was in the streets, my name was Yayo—"

"Where you from?" a youngsta with short dreadlocks shouted out, cutting Yayo off, Before Yayo was able to respond, Katrina stepped up.

"Y'all can ask questions at the end, right now just listen," Katrina said sternly. "Go ahead Yayo," Katrina said, sitting back down.

"To answer your question, lil homie, I grew up on 69th and Wolcott." Yayo noticed a lot of the youngsters whispering to each other after finding out Yayo was from the infamous Englewood area on the south side. He continued.

"That's right ...I'm from the hood just like most of you. I want to share something real quick with you brothers. When I was young, I was physically abused by my stepfather. I felt my parents didn't love me. My world was black. Nothing but pain and misery. Then, I moved with my grandmother on 69th and Wolcott. Back then, that hood was ran by a gang called the 69th Street Gangsters. I would watch as they pulled up in the flyest cars, hopped out dressed in the best threads, and wore the best jewelry money could buy.

148

"I wanted to be a part of that life. So, I joined the gang...I started selling drugs. I felt the gang loved me and I definitely loved them back. But, you know what...the same ones that claimed they loved me...when I put in some work and the heat came down, they snitched me out. I was convicted of murder and sentenced to juvenile life in this very gym room we are at now. I played basketball on these same rims, before I was sent to St. Charles to serve a juvenile life sentence. While I was doing my time, my best friend was shot to death over a pound of weed.

"My heart was broken, I wanted revenge, so sitting in my cell I let my demons overcloud my judgement and I started to plot about starting my own gang. I stayed in jail until I was twenty-one years old. When I got out, I set out to do exactly what I planned and started my organization, we robbed and sold drugs all for money...we made it to the top of the game. We had all the money, cars and clothes, and drugs...and we rode around as if we owned it. We were living a gangster's dream...But guess what?

"My man's moms was murdered, then later he was killed. Our whole operation fell to the ground. To make it worse, an individual we treated as family was working for the FBI. End result, I was indicted on kingpin charges, sentenced to life in prison and sent to serve my sentence, in some of the most venomous prisons in the country. While I was living in the murderous psychotic environment, my baby mama was out there struggling to raise our daughter singlehandedly. She suffered in silence from my actions.

"I have a little brother who followed in my footsteps, stepping into the bowels of hell. This young man right here is his twin brother, also my little brother. He was shot and paralyzed just for being with his twin, even though he had no dealings with the street life. It's only the grace of Allah and his strong will that he overcame adversity and learned to walk again. What I'm trying to tell y'all is there is no fairy tale ending in a life of crime. Only death, destruction, loneliness and misery. We were all infatuated by the money.

"Do you know how much a doctor makes? A doctor makes no less than a hundred fifty grand a year. Y'all like rap, don't you? Lil Durk come from the same ghettos as y'all, but he found his talent and put his energy into exploiting it. He took the initiative to make it. Initiative is making a decision to do something and then taking action. Once you put something in your mind, you can achieve it. Put it in your mind, believe and it will be. Always remember before great success comes, you will surely meet with temporary defeat.

"Never quit at anything, the most common cause of failure is quitting. Never quit. When you dream, always dream big, never stop short of reaching the top. Set high standards for yourself, don't limit yourself to being average. Stay on your toes and be focused. We not gone always have it sweet…success takes commitment and hard work. Find your strengths and exploit them. fire your weakness and I promise you will never feel or remember the blows, you will only feel the victory.

"As a black race, we come from a strong bloodline. Our ancestors passed this bloodline to you all. But, my young brothers, just know gangs, guns and drugs will only be the cause of your ruin. I love you all and I will be here for you if you ever need me. I believe in all y'all…you just have to believe in y'all selves," Yayo spoke, being genuine with his words.

"I thought you said you had a life sentence. How the fuck you get out of jail?" a youngster blurted out. Yayo knew this question was going to be asked and couldn't wait to answer it.

"My young brothers, when I came into the federal prison system, I was sent to one of the worst prisons to date. I was young, wild, rebellious, full of hate and resentment. I resented the judge for giving me a life sentence, I resented the person that took the stand, and raised his right hand and swore to tell the truth. I felt as if I didn't have anything to live for until I ran into a gentleman from Memphis, Tennessee, serving two life sentences for drugs. He had exhausted all of his appeals, which meant he is going to die in federal prison. This great man was a genius with the legal work.

"Even though he couldn't save himself from the clutches of the federal government, he used his precious unique skills to help other brothers like me with their cases. This man took a liking to me and wanted to help me, as he knew I had some loopholes in my case. He made me a promise if he helped me on my case and got me free,

150

that I would pay it forward and help save the lives of our youth. He was able to get the life sentence off me, for continuing a criminal enterprise…which is basically a kingpin charge.

"The feds found some guns in my house, so the gun charges stuck. I was sentenced to a hundred and twenty months, ten years for the pistols. I had already been down four years and I had to pull eight years and six months on the ten. I did that and got released," Yayo explained. The youngsta that asked the question nodded his head in understanding.

"Aye, Yayo. What you gone do now that you not in the streets getting money and running your gang?" another one of the teenagers asked. He was dark-skinned with dreads and reminded Yayo of TJ.

"Well… you know, brother, besides reach out and try to help y'all anyway that I can, I'm going to start publishing books. When I was in prison, I wrote a few urban books. So, I'm going to be doing that and raising my two kids and live a prosocial lifestyle."

"What's your books about, Yayo?" another asked.

"It's about the streets…the struggle. It's about brothers like us and what we going through out here in the city," Yayo said.

"I want to read that shit. I got a double life sentence, I ain't got nothing but time to read," the youngster said like his death sentence was nothing. Yayo's heart was broken, he was speechless as his words got caught in his throat. His eyes began to water. Yayo looked into his young soulless eyes and knew the Save Our Youth Campaign had a major fight ahead of them that would probably end up being never-ending, and he was more than willing to take on the fight. Katrina looked at her Movado time piece and saw it was time to end the speaking. She motioned to Yayo to wrap things up by tapping her watch.

"Alright, my dudes, I think my time's up. I wish I could holler at y'all all day. I'm a try to see if I can come back to check on y'all soon."

"Yayo…you a boss!" one of the boys shouted out.

"I wanna be like you, my nigga!" another one shouted.

The gym room erupted in claps as well as whistles. Katrina smiled.

"I love y'all…Remember, dream big, never stop short of reaching the top…one love!" Yayo said and stepped from the podium. Katrina got on the microphone.

"Alright gentlemen, remain seated until your unit is called for you to go back." The units were called, and the juveniles were led out of the gym. Yayo, Davon and Kewann were able to stand at the door and shake hands with the young men. Some of them even gave Yayo hugs, showing him a lot of love. He could tell his words had touched a lot of their hearts. It made him feel good, as if the trials and tribulations he endured was well worth it.

Chapter 15

Quavon's plane landed in Midland, Texas at 5:30 pm on a hot summer day. Getting off the plane, he walked through the small airport and out the front gate, where he was met by an older Mexican man. He introduced himself only as Oscar and worked for Castilino Madin and was sent to escort him to Castilino Mansion in Ciudad Juarez. Often known as just Juarez, it has been called the most violent zone in the world, outside declared war zones! It was 2020 and the murder rate was one-thirty-two per hundred thousand citizens, the worst in the world.

Oscar led Quavon to a clean Ford Bronco…Two men stood outside the vehicle with AR-15 machine guns slung over their shoulders. They were there for his protection…Castilino and the Madin Cartel controlled two hundred forty-eight miles, or four hundred kilometers of the border. It was estimated he shipped over sixty tons of heroin and cocaine into the United States from the border a year. Castilino was from the old school, but the new breed of enemies and narcos gunning for his throne were flamboyant, openly defiant of authority, impulsive and unpredictably violent.

Quavon got in the backseat of the bulletproof Bronco. Once he got in, Oscar passed Quavon a loaded XDM .45 ACP. This was routine when he would come to visit Juarez. Castilino would use different men to escort Quavon to his estate, but the protocol always remained the same. Castilino knew that at any time his men could be attacked by rival narcos, so he felt it was best to have Quavon armed and protected, as he was protecting a healthy financial investment. The hour-long ride to Castilino Mansion was a long, bumpy one. Castilino's estate sat close to the rigid mountains of Ojinaga, Mexico, a small town outside of Ciudad Juarez. The driver of the Bronco pulled into the circular driveway and parked behind Castilino's Rolls-Royce Phantom and killed the engine. Three armed guards in black suits stood posted, sunglasses covering their eyes from the blistering, baking sun. Quavon handed Oscar the pistol back, and then got out of the SUV and walked towards the three security guards in front of Castilino's entrance to his home. Oscar followed close behind. One of the guards, who went by the name Diego, greeted Quavon.

"Que honda way, Quavon?" Diego said, patting Quavon on his shoulders.

"Diego, what's good, my nigga? Where's old head at?" Quavon asked Diego. He and Diego were cool. When Quavon would come to Mexico, it would be Diego who was assigned to by his personal security. He was used to Quavon coming around and felt comfortable with the American drug boss.

"Right this way, mi nigga," Diego said, trying to imitate Quavon, then led him inside Castilino's home. Castilino's beautiful wife Marca met Quavon in the massive dining room.

"Quavon…como estas, my son? Castilino awaits you out back. Are you hungry? I have made enough food to serve an army," Marca said, walking up and hugging Quavon, she looked at Quavon as he was family.

"Yes ma'am, I'm so hungry I could eat a horse," Quavon replied.

"Well, a horse you shall have," Marca joked, then made her way to the kitchen to make Quavon something to eat, while Quavon made his way to the back patio. Castilino sat comfortably in a large plush chair, reading a Mexican newspaper called *Sol de Culiacan,* a large Garcia Vega filled with a potent strain of weed hung from his lips. A glass table piled high with marijuana was in front of him.

"Mijo…How was your trip?" Castilino asked, calling Quavon his son as Quavon walked up behind him.

"Same as always, big homie, but bumpy and long," Quavon retorted, taking a seat in a lawn chair across from Castilino. Castilino took a long pull from the Vega, laid the newspaper on his bare hairy chest, then removed the Cartier sunglasses from his bloodshot eyes and passed Quavon the Vega, which Quavon accepted and took a pull. Castilino blew out a thick cloud of smoke.

"It's good to see you again, Quavon, but something is telling me this visit is not for pleasure, si?" Quavon hit the weed then passed it back. He held the smoke in his lungs for a few seconds, then let the smoke escape from his nostrils. The strong and powerful THC immediately flowing through his bloodstream.

He stared Castilino in his eyes before he said, "Casilino...I'm out, it's over with. I got a lot going on in my life right now and I just want to focus on that." Quavon was as assertive as he could be, but felt his heart was beating a thousand times a minute as he waited for Castilino response. He stared at Quavon for what seemed like an eternity. A smirk now was plastered across his lips. He shook his head in the negative.

"You know, Quavon, things are not just that simple. This thing is not something you can quit whenever you get ready. There are rules to this level of the game, and the number-one rule is blood in, blood out," Castilino said sternly. Quavon rubbed his hand over his three-sixty waves.

"Castilino...in these past few years, I have made you and the Madin Cartel millions of U.S. dollars and—"

"You think you are the only one who has made this family money? You killed a man I personally had grown a good business relationship with, to gain your position in the game. I could've easily had your life took," Castilino said, cutting Quavon off.

"And I could've easily not come to you and returned the money for the three hundred thousand bricks of raw...I had three hundred thousand bricks in my position, and it was all free. You were the one that told me to take initiative to be my own boss, and that's what I did. I bust Top Cat's head and secured the plug...Straight gangsta shit! No harm, no foul...like EA Sports, it's in the game.

"But Castilino, while you out here living in the big ass house, thousands of miles away from the battlefield, I'm in Chicago, the most notorious city in the United States of America, holding it down. Every day, it's some niggas popping up, willing to come at me and my team to get what we have worked so hard to obtain. And these niggas is willing to die for it. Castilino, I have some good men with me. I love them, they are my muthafucking brothers. It's because of them you are getting these millions up outta Chicago. I know you ain't think I was doing this shit by myself. I am accountable for my brothers. We have made enough money for us to leave the game and invest our paper in different endeavors.

I don't want my brothers' blood to be the next to soak the city's streets, or worse, end up with a life sentence in a federal penitentiary. If you want to kill me for walking away, then so be it, but my death will save the lives of my brothers and that's all I want," Quavon said, waiting for Castilino to nod to one of his henchmen to come put an AK-47 to the back of his head and pull the trigger. Castilino studied Quavon as he took another pull from the blunt. If Quavon walked away from him and the Madin Cartel, his pockets would feel the impact. He was sending Quavon thousands upon thousands of kilos to Chicago and in return, Quavon was sending him millions of U.S. currency.

Castilino had a lot of respect for Quavon, he had come to Mexico alone to tell him face-to-face that he wanted out, he could easily have told him over the phone, ran off or anything. But yet he respected him enough to cross the border to tell him personally, knowing it was a chance he could be killed and never seen again. Castilino saw Quavon as a man, a friend and definitely a gangster…he was smart, loyal and ready to die for his team, it was a drought in the game on guys like Quavon.

Quavon was the last of a dying breed. Castilino's face softened as he passed Quavon the blunt. He knew that letting Quavon go, he was letting go a thoroughbred. He would never meet another like him. But in reality, he wanted nothing to happen to young Quavon. Death or jail…it would be a waste of brilliance and good talent. With the way Quavon moved, thought, and held a heart of a lion, whatever endeavor he chose, he would approach and conquer it. He knew Quavon would flourish into something great.

"Mijo…my heart is broken knowing you will be leaving me, but I see you have made your decision. I love you like a son, Quavon, and I would never step in the way of your growth and happiness. My inventory says you still owe me eight-point-three million. Send me my money ASAP. I wish you the best of luck, Quavon," Castilino said and stood up. Quavon also stood.

"Your money will be sent no later than Friday. I love you as well, Castilino, and I appreciate the opportunity as well as your wisdom and guidance. Your teachings will be forever be embedded in me." Quavon extended his hand.

Castilino took it and pulled him in close and embraced him and whispered in his ear, "Just know, Quavon, that once you walk out this door…it is over completely, there will be no coming back."

"Castilino…thank you for everything…it's all love," Quavon responded and let go of Castilino, whose eyes began to water as he watched Quavon leave. He was letting go of one of the realist niggas he ever met. He knew if Quavon kept a clear head and continued to move like a boss he was, in the near future he could possibly become more powerful than El Chapo.

Quavon sat on the plane on his way back home to Chicago. He was glad the meeting with Castilino went well. Things went better than expected…he was going to miss Castilino and the business they conducted. Just being able to be affiliated with the drug lord was an honor in itself. But now he was putting that chapter of his life in the rearview, and it was now time to focus on the future of the Get It Boy Clique. It was time to start lining things up in California, where he and his men would ball legitimately out of control.

Yayo was going to be proud of the decision he just made, he couldn't wait to tell him. But first, the G.B.C. had some unfinished business to attend to regarding Omega and the Homicide Crew. He was going to holler at Vamp and his brother Carlos and try to get some kind of understanding and see if they could get a location of their enemies. The G.B.C. were the alpha males of the streets of Chicago and when the smoke cleared…the alpha males they would remain…that he knew.

Chapter 16

"Fucking puta," King Rico cursed in Spanish. He was frustrated as he continually tried to call Omega. It had been two weeks since he was supposed to have his uncle's money off the fifty kilos of cocaine they had sent on consignment. The total tab was a quarter-million dollars. Rico's uncle Hector put the bill on him, because Rico had vouched for Omega. Hector worked for Castilino Madina, and once he found out Omega was spending a quarter-mil of his own paper, he figured he would talk Castilino into fronting another fifty kilos...tying Omega into the vicious web of the Cartel, in which he would be able to benefit off the deal. It had been three months and Rico had not sent a red penny of his uncle's money, which had him perplexed, making him put the press game on his nephew.

What's wrong, papi?" Rico's girlfriend Sabrina asked, while Rico paced back and forth, chain smoking a Newport Long, worry stretched across his face.

"Shit...the pussy mothafucka playing games, that's all. He think shit sweet...I'm a fucking Latin King! On King Gino, I can't wait to catch that nigga, I'm a put him and his family through a woodchipper," King Rico vowed, dialing Omega's cellphone number again in an attempt to gain contact. The phone rang four times, each time irritating Rico even more, knowing Omega wasn't going to answer. He was about to throw his burnout phone against the wall until somebody answered.

"Hello?" Omega answered in a groggy voice.

"Omega? Ay, my nigga, what kind of time you on? I been trying to call you for the past two weeks...fuck you ain't been answering the phone for?" Rico yelled through the receiver.

"Chill, Pinocchio...I been a lil busy...but what's up?" Omega replied smoothly as a thick, red-boned chick snorted cocaine off his six-pack abs, while another chick ran her tongue down the sides of his hard shaft.

"What's up? Muthafucka, you talking like you don't owe me no paper. Matter fact, what's your location, I'm on my way to see you."

"Aye, señor? Think you need to take it easy, you talking to me all crazy, like you don't want to get paid or some shit. I think you need to check your vocals and calm the fuck down," Omega said, his hand tangled in the blonde's hair as she went down on him, giving him head.

"Fuck nigga, you got me fucked up…listen muthafucka, that two-fifty is owed to some very important people. You got twenty-four hours to come up with that bread or I'm green lighting you, stupid ten percent nigger," King Rico threatened…ready to send his shooters.

Omega laughed before he responded, "Aye, fam…on the two-fifty I owe you? You just forfeited that shit. You hit, it's a wrap, Jack. See me in the streets, but on my dead homie, don't come faking pussy," Omega sneered and pressed end on his Galaxy Android and tossed the phone to the side…leaving Rico with silence in his ear.

Rico was beyond pissed. He had fucked up in a major way, vouching for Omega. He thought Omega was righteous, he had been serving him crack cocaine for the past two years…without a situation or incident. He thought Omega was valid. Now Omega had just put him in a deadly predicament. He owed his uncle and the Madin Cartel for fifty kilos of raw. Even though he was blood, Hector's sister's son, blood meant nothing when it came to money and drugs as he knew. Rico had to think his way out of his violent situation and quick. Rico dialed a number. He had to hold a meeting with the Latin Kings in Humboldt Park.

There was no way Omega was going to ride around the city getting money that was owed to him. He had to find Omega, ASAP. The Latin Kings had been peaceful all summer getting to the money, but Omega had crossed the line, now it was time to put the drugs up and bring out the artillery…it was time for the Kings to make their presence felt in the streets. He called his potna Pito and told him to round up the Kings and meet at the park in two hours.

After giving his orders, King Rico went to the closet and pulled the bulletproof vest off the hanger and strapped it on his chest. After putting a white tee on, he grabbed his .40 tucked it on his waistline and left out the crib to go rotate in the battlefield of Chi-Raq. The Kings had to find Omega and the dope, before his uncle sent a hit squad to put him in the ground for eternity.

Omega tossed his phone to the side, grinning like a Grinch that stole Christmas. Rico had played right into his diabolical plan. He had no plan of paying Latin King Rico for the fifty kilos anyway. By Rico fronting his move on the phone, getting off with the bricks wouldn't even sit on his conscience. He had been cool with Rico over the years, even in prison. But times had changed, the game had changed, as well as the playas. Omega wasn't worried about Rico or the Latin Kings, Omega was becoming powerful in the streets he had money, guns, and shooters on deck. Not to mention, he kept his pole on him.

He had already declared war on the Get It Boy Clique, they were his competition. Rico and his boys were nothing. At the nod of a head and a brick of coke, he could get Rico knocked off by a thirteen-year-old, itching to make a name in the city. Omega had more important things to worry about, like murking any and every-body involved with the G.B.C. He wanted Quavon's head on a stick. In the end, the Homicide Crew would be the crew to be reckoned with.

Omega reached over to the plate on the dresser that had six ounces of cocaine on it. Grabbing a hundred-dollar-bill, he rolled it up, put it to his nostril and sniffed from the pile. The inside of his nose was raw from the habitual drug use. His heart began to beat rapidly as if he was about to have a stroke. The euphoric feeling from the powder made him feel invincible to his opposition. The money made him feel as if he was God, as the acts of homicide invaded his inner being with evil.

Omega put the plate back on the dresser and laid back on the king size bed and let his *Backpage* whores continue to please him. He knew Ace and K.I. were smiling down from the heavens, watching him put on for the Homicide Crew.

The Ida B. Wells Projects were remotely quiet. It was 11:30 at night and only the dope fiends and crack addicts walked around, trying to cop drugs to get the itching, heavy gorilla off of their backs. Quavon pulled into the dangerous Ida B. Wells Projects in all-black Dodge Hellcat. Choppa sat in the passenger seat, two FNH hand pistols lay across his lap. They were coming to meet up with Vamp and his younger brother Carlos to see what they could find out what was to the two individuals who was boasting on *Instagram* about killing one of the Get It Boy Clique soldiers.

The Ida B. Wells Projects was called New Town and run by the Black Disciples and Vamp was the minister for the gang. Quavon made a left on 39th and Prairie and turned into the project's parking lot. The Hellcat crept through the parking lot slowly. A group of men stood on the sidewalk, their attention now focused on the Hellcat, as they tried to see through the tint of the whip. which was impossible. Choppa peeped a few of them pulling out hammers.

"My nigga…they pulling out pipes," Choppa said, tightening his hands on the handles of the FN's, looking around checking his surroundings, his adrenaline beginning to rush.

"Be cool, shorty…I fuck with these niggas," Quavon replied, and pulled up to the clique of BDs and rolled the driver's side window down.

"Aye, scud, where Vamp and Carlos?"

"Who want to know?" a dark-skinned dude with shoulder-length dreads said, bending down, trying to look inside the vehicle from the curb. He was clutching a MAC-11 in his hand, ready to spray something.

"Tell 'em Quavon looking for him," Quavon said out the window. The guy with the dreads said something to one of his homies…who said something to some more of the guys. They then formed a small circle around the Hellcat, guns drawn. The one with the dreads got on his cellphone.

"I don't like the way this shit look, Quavon," Choppa said.

"I said chill, fam…this shit just protocol," Quavon said calmly.

"Alright…BD," Quavon heard the dude on the phone say, then put the phone back in his pocket.

"Aye, Vamp about to pull up in five minutes, he coming down King Drive right now. You can park right here, fam," the guy with dreads said and then pointed to the open parking space. "Vamp say he gang. Watch out, let him park," the dude said, signaling to his crew that Quavon was cool and they could put they poles up. Quavon parked the whip. The BD's continued doing what they were doing but watched the Hellcat. Eight minutes later, Vamp pulled up through the rearview mirror.

"Choppa, let me get your phone real quick." Choppa passed him his iPhone with the *Instagram* video already on it. All Quavon had to do was press play.

"Now look, fam. Stay in the whip and watch these niggas. I'm a get out and holler at this nigga real quick. If I shake his hand at the end, it's all peace...If I dap him, jump out and start blowing these niggas down."

"Say less," was all Choppa said as Quavon got out the car. Vamp parked the 'Lac truck and walked over to where Quavon was standing at the curbside.

"Quavon, what it do, killa?" Vamp greeted, walking up shaking Quavon's hand. In his other hand, he held a bottle of Ace of Spades. He offered it to Quavon.

"Nah, I'm good, family...what's good with you though? I see you getting to a bag," Quavon said, referring to the designer Vamp was rocking and the 2020 Cadillac truck he pulled up in. Vamp took a swig from the bottle. He wiped his mouth with the back of his hand.

"You already know. the block doing about a buck a night, a hundred grand...so I can't complain. But I know your rich ass ain't come to the slums to talk about my pockets...what up, Joe?"

"Yeah, you right, bruh. Walk over here with me right quick. I want to show you something," Quavon said and he and Vamp walked a few feet away. Quavon pulled the phone out and pressed play. Vamp watched as Pharoe and Slug exposed themselves on *Instagram*, taking credit for shooting and killing a G.B.C. member. Vamp watched the video all the way through. He passed the phone back to Quavon.

"Them your niggas?" Quavon asked.

"Yeah, that's Slug and Pharoe, they gang. I don't know why they did a drill on your team…I didn't authorize it, if that's what you think," Vamp replied honestly.

"Vamp, me and you go way back, we ain't never had no beef. But let me put you up on something…you say them niggas gang? Family, them niggas ain't BD's. they flipped Homicide Crew. A nigga named Omega going around flipping the guys, giving 'em, coke and pipes to flip. This same nigga that started Homicide Crew gunning for the G.B.C. One of my lil homies blew one of they ass down a couple years back, now these niggas starting to resurface…that money that nigga flaunting on the *'Gram*, he was paid that to kill my people."

Vamp just shook his head, digesting what Quavon was telling him. His anger was starting to rise now, knowing Slug and Pharoe switched sides on them. "So Quavon, if you know I ain't greenlight that move…what you want from me? Because as of right now, I got some Nation Bizness to handle. Niggas ain't just gone flip from BD like that. I ain't going, for it," Vamp said, ready to go get up with Slug and Pharoe, which Quavon knew was going to be the outcome.

"Vamp…listen to me, brother. This shit way bigger than what Slug and this character did to my lil homie. Then switching sides is a total violation to the code, but as you know, they young…they money-hungry shooters…they loyalty lies with no one but their greed. They were just following orders and cashing in on it at the same time. Omega is the cause of it all, and that's who I hold accountable. While he sending shooters to run drills for money and drugs, his coward ass hiding in a hole like a groundhog. I got to find that hoe ass nigga like yesterday, scud. So, I'm asking you to hand them boys over, so we can get to the bottom of this shit and slide on this cat, Omega…feel me?"

Vamp stared Quavon in his eyes, he wanted BD's to handle BD business, but Slug and Pharoe had pancaked and flipped, they were no longer Black Disciples. Vamp was about hustling, getting to the money and he needed all his soldiers on deck to protect his drug turf. He didn't need them getting popped off on a bullshit murder beef, for some bullshit niggas. He could let Quavon and the G.B.C.

handle the business, it would all come to the same result, with Slug
and Pharoe dying in the streets, which they deserved. At that moment, Vamp made the decision to throw Slug and Pharoe to the
wolves.

Vamp smirked at Quavon before he said, "Alright Quavon, you
got that, scud. Them niggas is now y'all issue. The dude Pharoe got
a bad lil baby mama, her name Fatmama. They stay on 87th and
Gilbert Court, it's a dead-end block, first house on the right. Slug
sister name Rashida. She stay north, on Clark and Davon in that red
brick building across from Chicago-Style Hot Dogs. He be posted
up over there a lot. Now what y'all do with this information is on
y'all. I don't want this conversation brung up again...I'm out of it."

"Say less, family...that's all I wanted to hear you say. But
dig...I'm about to bounce and you BD be safe out here. Keep your
boys on point, it's about to be a lot of heat on the south side, the
murder rate about to skyrocket. It was good seeing you again. Oh
yeah, I got them pounds for the low," Quavon said, shaking Vamp's
hand.

"That's a bet, Quavon. I might get up with you on that...Be
safe," Vamp retorted.

Quavon jumped back in the Hellcat and pulled out of the parking lot of the infamous Ida B. Wells Projects. He had all the information he needed to retaliate for Lonell's murder. But killing the
culprits was just the beginning. Before he left the dope game, he
was going to make sure Omega was dead.

"So, what's the business, big homie?" Choppa asked him from
the passenger seat as he rolled a Backwood. Quavon made a left at
the light on King Drive.

"The nigga on the phone talking all that Homicide Crew shit
name Pharoe. He got a baby mama that stay on 87th and Gilbert
Court. Pay them a visit...since he want to talk all that killer shit
make sure everybody in that bitch stop breathing ...fuck 'em. The
other nigga name Slug be north on Clark and Davon. He stay with
his sister across from Chicago-Style Hot Dogs. Bring that nigga to
me, anybody else, you know what to do.

"We about to show these lil boys they dealing with some grown ass men and shit ain't sweet…And that block on 59th and Bishop, bust them niggas' head too, make sure they stay in line. We the G.B.C., it's got to be an aura of fear around this bitch," Quavon said, speaking like the commander-in-chief he was. Choppa just nodded his head in understanding, putting the lighter to the tip of the blunt. After lighting the Backwood filled with Gorilla Glue, he sent a text to the Blackout Squad. It was time to get active.

Chapter 17

It was 9:30 at night. Pharoe was at his baby mama's crib on 87th and Gilbert Court. He had just come back from Las Vegas gambling. He had lost thirteen stacks, tricked off two bands on prostitutes and was down to his last. He had five thousand in cash and a half-brick of cocaine, it was now time to bet back on the block and grind. Pharoe had sent his baby mama and daughter to Walmart to do a little shopping, while he cooked up some work.

Pharoe grabbed the Visionware Pyrex from the kitchen cupboard and filled it halfway with warm water. After weighing up four ounces of cocaine, he dumped it into the Pyrex and stuck it in the microwave and put it on ten minutes. While the cocaine was cooking, Pharoe measured four ounces of baking soda. Looking in the microwave, he saw the drugs begin to bubble inside the Pyrex and took it out.

He dumped the baking soda inside, stirred it with a silver spoon, then stuck it back inside the microwave. Pharoe watched as the drugs cooked, the oil from the cocaine separating from the coke and rising to the top of the Pyrex. Pharoe then went to the sink and turned on the cold water. Taking the Pyrex out the microwave, he went back to the sink to let some of the cold water seep into the Pyrex and began to stir the drugs. The cold water caused the cocaine and the baking soda to lock up. Pharoe continued to whip the drugs until it became a mushy substance...like mashed potatoes.

Pharoe let the drugs sit while he laid a newspaper across the kitchen table, then ran upstairs to grab his digital scale. When he came back downstairs, he turned the Pyrex upside down and hit the bottom of it, causing the cocaine, now crack, to drop out of the Pyrex. After weighing up the crack, the weight on the scale display nine-point-eight ounces of coke. For the next hour, Pharoe bagged up eight balls of crack cocaine...he had to hurry up before Fatmama and his daughter got back home. Pharoe cleaned up the kitchen and washed the dishes he used to cook and mix the drugs then went in the living room to play NBA 2K20 on a large television. He couldn't wait for his BM to get back so he could get in traffic to get his hustle on.

Choppa and Killa were patiently waiting on the side of Pharoe's home in all black, armed with pistols. They had sat in a rented Ford Fusion across the street from Pharoe's crib, about to run a demonstration, until they saw a woman and a child leave the house. Choppa had Vietnam followed her to see where she was going, knowing that she and the kid would return and when they did, Choppa and Killa would use her to gain entrance to the house.

Vietnam had called Choppa, who was tailing Fatmama and her six-year-old daughter, letting him know they were on their way back to Gilbert Court. Choppa watched the headlights of the car turn into the driveway and park. Choppa and Killa moved stealthily on the side of the building toward the beginning of the driveway, Glocks with extensions in their gloved hands. Choppa watched through his ski mask as Fatmama got out the driver's seat then went to the trunk to retrieve the Walmart bags, her daughter Nella got out the backseat.

"Nella, help Mami with the bags." Nella went to the back, where her mother gave her a light bag. They both made their way to the front door. Fatmama was about to put the key in, until she felt something cold press against the back of her neck. Her daughter was about to scream at the sight of the big figures in black masks, until a gloved hand cupped her mouth...muffling her scream.

"Shhh...you follow instructions, you and the kid gone live. We here for your man. You disobey my command... I'm killing all y'all...do you understand?" Choppa threatened through clenched teeth. Fatmama nodded nervously, mentally cursing herself for dealing with her crud ball baby daddy.

"Now, open the door, bitch." Choppa sneered. Fatmama did as she was told. Choppa held the collar of her Polo shirt in a vice grip with the Glock in her back as they made their way inside the house.

Pharoe was tapping on the PlayStation controller, when his baby mama and daughter entered the living room. A man in a black mask held his daughter in his arms, with a pole under her small chin. Fatmama had tears in her eyes as the other gunman was behind her with a gun to the side of her head. He dropped the controller on the floor. He had just got caught lacking. Choppa pushed Fatmama forcefully in the back, causing her to stumble forward and fall on her face. Killa put young Nella down and mushed her in the back of the head. She ran over to her mother.

"Please, man. I got some bread. And I got like a half of brick of work. C-come on, man, don't hurt my family," Pharoe stuttered, pleading for his family's safety. Killa closed the front door and locked it. Choppa pulled his ski mask from his dreaded head.

"You bitch ass nigga, you laid hands on G.B.C.?" He sneered before he rushed over and slapped Pharoe with the Glock, causing his head to split to the white meat.

"I'm sorry…Come on, man…please," Pharoe cried, holding the wound that had just been inflicted, as blood leaked profusely through his fingers. Fatmama screamed.

"Shut up, bitch, before we pop your ass," Killa said with menace in his tone.

"Watch them, fam," Choppa said, then went to the kitchen. Looking under the sink, he found a box of Hefty garbage bags, grabbed them and went back to the living room.

"Nigga, since you wanna run your mouth about the gang…We gone teach you a lesson. Should've stayed BD, pussy!" Choppa grabbed little Nella and pulled some plastic zip ties from his back pocket and used them to secure her small hands behind her back. Killa did the same with Fatmama. After they had both of them secured, they placed garbage bags over their heads and used shoestrings to tie the bags tightly around their necks.

Pharoe watched helplessly and in horror as his baby mama and only child struggled and kicked from not being able to breathe. Minutes later, all the resistance stopped as their souls traveled to the afterlife from suffocation. Warm tears rolled down his cheeks, his head remorseful for his own actions that caused the lives of his loved ones.

"Now…when you see Omega in hell, you can tell him play by play how we nailed you and your people. Nigga, when you playing the murder game, always know it's levels to this shit. Pussy!"

Choppa sneered before he raised his Glock at Pharoe's head and squeezed the trigger...*Boc*

The loud gunshot echoed through the small one-flat house, blowing Pharoe's brains on the couch. The smell of death invaded the living room. Choppa used his index finger and dipped it in Pharoe's blood oozing from the large hole in his forehead and used it to write a message on the white wall. That message in blood read, "Homicide Crew Killa."

Later that night, Slug was across town on the north side of the city. He had just left a chick named Tabitha, freaking off. It had been a few days since him and Pharoe had run a drill on 69th and Wolcott, leaving one of their opps dead. Him and Pharoe had been at odds, because Pharoe didn't give him any of the twenty thousand Omega had paid them. Pharoe felt since he was the one who put the work in, he was entitled to the blood money. Instead, Pharoe gave him a half a brick of soft that Omega also gave them.

Slug vowed to never go on another murder mission with Lil Pharoe. And if he ever caught Pharoe slipping, he was going to rob him. Slug got out his Chevy Impala and made his way to his sister's building on Clark and Davon. He had a half ounce of OG Kush and a fifth of Hennessy he had copped from Kenwood's Liquor. He was turning it in for the night, he still had a few ounces of coke left and tomorrow he was going to dump it off on his mans, Pistol Pete.

Slug rang the buzzer to his sister's apartment. Without answering, she buzzed him in, which was odd to him as she would always ask who was at the door. Slug made his way up to the fourth-floor apartment. Once he got to the door, he noticed that the door was cracked open. Walking inside the dark, two-bedroom apartment, he was met by a blunt object smashing down on the top of his head, the force from the blow caused him to see a bright light as his vision was now blurry.

He fell to the floor holding his head that was now wet and starting to swell up at a rapid pace. The door was shut and the light invaded the living room. When Slug regained his vision, he was shocked to see his sister and niece on the couch, hands tied behind their backs and bandanas tied across their mouths, preventing them from screaming. Vietnam and one of the twins stood over him, pointing pipes in his face.

"What's up, Joe? My boss wanna see you. Now you can go by choice or by force, the choice is completely up to you," Vietnam sneered from behind his Ralph Lauren Polo mask that covered the lower part of his face. A red and black Chicago Bulls snapback covered his bald head, his identity concealed.

"Aye, man. What's all this about? Please, don't hurt my family. What did I do?" Slug asked in fear, blood starting to run down the side of his face, smelling like a penny. Vietnam put the barrel of the .40 to his eye socket with pressure.

"Nigga, get the fuck up and let's go before I start clapping shit!"

"Alright...alright man, just don't hurt my people," Slug said, getting up from the floor now stained with his blood. He looked at his sister, who had tears flowing from her eyes, knowing her and her child were about to die. Vietnam pushed Slug toward the door, his gun trained on him just in case he tried some funny shit.

"What about them, scud?" Twin asked with his .45 pointed at Slug's sister and niece.

Vietnam looked over at them through the eyes of a murderer before he responded, "Leave em be...let's get outta here," then walked out the apartment with the individual they came to get. Once outside the building, Vietnam and Twin tossed Slug, whose hands were tied behind his back, in the trunk of the Buick LeSabre. They pulled into traffic, en route to the Englewood area of the south side, 69th and Wolcott, land and turf for the Get It Boy Clique.

Span rode around the area of 69th and Wolcott, securing the blocks. His staff titles and duties were to make routine rounds in the hood, to make sure that everything was functioning properly. Quavon had lifted the lockdown status on the drug blocks. Even though they were still on Code Blue, High Alert, the money had to continue to flow, so extra security was set up and more guns was put out in the hood. Span was still in his feelings about how Choppa had treated him at the Calumet Building, putting a gun in his face.

Span had made plenty of sacrifices since being a part of the G.B.C. He had done hours upon hours of security on the block, sold massive packs of heroin and cocaine for the gang, and felt he was entitled to much more respect than he was given. His life and loyalty to the Get It Boy Clique had died the night Choppa pulled a gun on him. He now held hate in his heart for Choppa, which now polluted his mind with the thoughts of revenge.

Two nights prior, he was at a bar called the Laristos in Calumet City, when Omega and six of his goons came into the establishment. Their diamonds on their necks and ears and wrist glowed in the small dimly lit bar. Omega came to the bar and ordered bottles for his whole crew. At first, Span didn't know who the heavyweights were, until one of his goons spoke his name. Now, Span knew for a fact the Homicide Crew, as well as their chief, was in his presence. Span cursed himself for leaving his gun in the whip. If they found out he was a part of the G.B.C., they would shoot him dead, he was sure.

Span used this situation to benefit him and save his life as well. Grabbing his fifth of Rémy XO, he made his way over to the Homicide Crew. Omega had his back turned, laughing at something his man said when Span walked up. One of the goons stepped in front of him.

"What's good, my nigga? You know somebody over here?" the goon asked, his diamonds in his grill shining, Span was nervous, but had to keep his composure if he wanted everything to go smoothly and non-violent.

"Nah…I ain't lost, fam. I just want to holler at the big homie, Omega." Omega turned around after hearing his name.

"Who the fuck is this nigga?" Omega asked, looking Span up and down from head to toe.

"My name Span. I be with the G.B.C." One of Omega's goons pulled a .50 caliber from his waist and pointed it in Span's face…ready to blow him down. Omega grabbed his arm, telling him to lower his weapon.

"You gotta be crazy or stupid to be breathing the same air as me," Omega sneered, as a few of the customers made an exit out the bar after seeing the large hand cannon Omega's goon held at this side.

"Omega…I came with nothing but respect, let me rephrase my words. I used to be G.B.C., then them niggas got hoe in they blood. They looking bad and when they look bad, I look bad. I'm in it for the money and plus I play with them pistols. I feel my services could be used and appreciated elsewhere."

"So, what the fuck is you saying, shorty? You talking good, but my niggas don't talk, we all about that action. What, you trying to get down?" Omega asked him. Span crossed his arms across his chest.

"That's exactly what I'm saying. I can be more of an asset than a liability."

"How so?" Omega asked and took a sip from his bottle of 1800 Tequila.

"I can be an inside source. Tell you when them niggas out there lacking, when they about to put some work in. And I can set them niggas up for y'all. I can give y'all Choppa," Span said, willing to throw his gang under the bus. Omega rubbed his hand over his freshly trimmed goatee…Just the mention of Choppa's name caused his chest to heave. He had found out through the streets that it was Choppa who pulled the trigger, ending Ace's life. He definitely wanted Choppa's tough ass put to sleep.

"You funny as hell, shorty…but check this out. I'm a fuck with you, but you got to earn the right to be in this family. I want you to stay playing your role with them niggas. I already know they gone have something going on in the hood on the Fourth of July. I want to know what and when. Put this number in your phone," Omega said, taking another sip from his bottle. Span took his iPhone off the clip of his Louis Vuitton belt. Omega gave him his cell number, which Span stored in his phone.

"Now keep me posted on what's going on in that area. I want a daily report. Matter-of-fact call my number right now so I have your get up." Span did what he was told.

"Get up with me, fam." Omega said sarcastically.

"That's a bet, my nigga…Fuck G.B.C.," Span said and walked out the bar. That was two nights ago. Span had found out the Get It Boy Clique was planning to have a big Bar-B-Q at Rasta

Elementary School, a block off of Wolcott. The event was to be held on the Fourth of July. It was June third and Span knew it was time to put things in motion. He grabbed his cellphone and called Omega to give him the place the Fourth of July event was going to take place.

After hanging up with Omega, he continued to ride around the hood, doing surveillance without a tinge of guilt of what he had just done, or what was about to happen.

Chapter 18

Yayo glided the QX50 down the interstate, coming past Tennessee. Shakira was glued to her iPad as Shamira and Jamarie were passed out, asleep in the backseat. They had gotten some cheap tickets offline for Disney World and Universal Studios and were on their way to Orlando, Florida. Yayo also wanted to visit his mother, so he felt this was the best time to take a family vacation. He had Jamarie this whole summer, from the time he went to Louisiana to meet him.

Amanda and Yayo had made the parental decision for Jamarie to go to Chicago for the rest of the summer, so he could bond with his father and big sister. Yayo couldn't have agreed more. While Yayo was in the streets promoting peace with the Save Our Youth Campaign, Honey would watch her great grandson and granddaughter which she had no problem with. The Save Our Youth campaign was gaining a lot of attention in the streets. After Yayo's speech at the Audi Home, the genuine feedback from the juveniles, as well as staff, prompted the mayor of Chicago to have the Save Our Youth Campaign to come speak at the Cook County Jail inmates. WGN broadcasted it on the news.

Yayo and the Save Our Youth Campaign were getting letters and emails on their page to come speak at different prisons and county jails, as well as colleges and was getting paid fifteen to twenty thousand dollars per speaking engagement. Yayo was checking a bag and changing lives at the same time. He had spoken with Mr. B a few times and sent him six thousand to his account. Mr. B was proud of Yayo and what he was accomplishing out there, which only gave Yayo more morale to continue what he was doing.

Everything was going good for Yayo. He was on his way to sunny Florida with his family. Not even eight months ago, he was sitting in a United States penitentiary, with a homemade shank in the slit of his boxers for his own protection. That was now over, and it was as if he woke from a nightmare, only to awaken to a fairytale ending.

Twenty-one hours later, the family pulled into the beautiful Orlando, Florida. Riding the sleek streets of the city was totally different from the potholed streets of Chi-Raq. Palm trees along with the breezy eighty-degree weather was refreshing, compared to the polluted city of Chicago.

"Daddy, look, Mickey Mouse!" Shamira shouted, pointing to a large billboard promoting Disney World.

"I see it, baby!" Yayo said equally excited. Orlando Fl was beautiful.

"Shakira, put mama address in the GPS."

"Ok, baby," Shakira replied, then put Karen's address in the SUV's GPS system.

Twenty minutes later, Yayo pulled up to his mother's home in Davenport, Florida, fifteen minutes outside of Downtown Orlando. Shakira was in awe of the beachfront property. The panoramic ocean view was luxurious, the four-bath condo offered the finest finishes, a large, heated swimming pool decorated the back of the home. Yayo pulled in the large circular driveway and parked behind a Lexus E5300.

"We here, Shamira and Jamarie," Yayo said, then turned the ignition off. Karen came out the front door to greet her family.

"Grandma!" Shamira yelled then ran to her grandmother.

"Hey, baby girl...I miss you!" Karen said, bending down hugging her granddaughter.

"Grandma. Come here and see my new brother." Shamira grabbed ahold of her grandmother's hand, pulling her towards the car where Jamarie was still in the backseat of the X50 as Yayo and Shakira was getting the luggage from the back of the truck.

"Look at him. Yaton, he look just like you!" Karen said, as Yayo came from around the truck. Karen reached in the backseat and took Jamarie's seatbelt off him and scooped him up in her arms...she instantly fell in love with her new grandson.

"Hey, Ma!" Shakira said walking up to Karen with some Louis Vuitton luggage.

"Hey, baby. Y'all come on in and make y'all self at home. I'm so glad to see y'all. Lord knows I am. They all followed Karen into the house. Yayo was impressed with his mother's home that looked like it should be featured on *MTV Cribs*.

"Yaton, what's going on, son? I'm glad you all could make it."
Darrell said, descending from the spiral stairwell with a bottle of
Patrón in his hands.

"What's good, Pops? How are you?"

"I'm good, son. Just living the life till it's over. Care for a
drink?" Darrell asked.

"Don't mind if I do," Yayo replied. Darrell went to the kitchen
to get some shot glasses.

"Yaton, let me show you where you and Shakira will be staying,
because my grandbabies sleeping in the room with me," Karen said,
leading them upstairs to a large bedroom with a canopy queen size
bed. Shakira put her hand over her mouth at the sight of the beautiful
set-up. A washing machine and dryer stood stacked on top of each
other in the corner of the room. The bedroom balcony over-looked
the beach and the ocean, the big walk-in closet was spacious. And
the carpet on the floor was thick and plush, making you feel as if
you were walking on a pillow-top mattress. A fifty-five-inch smart
TV was mounted on the wall. The bedroom was perfect.

"Grandma, my daddy said we going to see Mickey Mouse, are
you going with us?" Shamira asked, jumping on the bed.

"Yes, I am going. You better believe it. That's why you have to
get some rest tonight, so we can get up and get an early start, so you
won't get tired and fall asleep and miss Mickey Mouse," Karen responded with Jamarie in her arms.

"Ok, Grandma."

The family dinner Karen prepared consisted of lasagna, garlic
bread, fresh vegetables and Karen's specialty...pineapple and co-
conut pound cake. After dinner, Shakira gave Shamira and Jamarie
a bath and took them to Karen's room, where they watched cartoons
until they both fell into a dreamful sleep. Yayo peeped in on them,
saw they were asleep and went in and kissed them both on the fore-
heads, before he quietly walked out the room and closed the door.

Yayo went downstairs the food had him full and the bottle of
Patrón he and Darrell consumed had him feeling good and slightly
tipsy. Shakira was sitting at the kitchen table with Karen, drinking
a bottle of Moscato.

Yayo walked up behind her and whispered in her ear, "Baby, the kids are asleep…let's go take a walk on the beach." His hot breath in her ear caused her to feel a tingle. She downed the rest of the champagne in her glass before she stood.

"Uh-uh…where you going? Yaton, you not about to steal her from me. We was having a good conversation," Karen said, feeling good off the liquor.

"We a be back, Ma, its nice outside. We just gone take a quick walk and get some air," Yayo retorted. Karen waved them off.

"Y'all go ahead and do y'all. You on vacation and I want you to enjoy yourself. Plus, I have to get some rest, so these kids won't run me to the ground tomorrow. Y'all can let yourself out the kitchen, just remember to lock the door back when you come in for the night. I'm going to bed. Oh, Shakira, you can kill the rest of that bottle. I'm done," Karen said, getting up from the table.

"Ok, Ma…goodnight and we'll see you in the morning." Shakira grabbed the bottle of Moscato and followed Yayo out the kitchen to the white sand beach that served as Karen and Darrell's back yard. The weather was seventy-five degrees with a slight gust of wind, the only sounds that could be heard was the waves from the ocean. The sky was beautiful, the moon was full, illuminating the dark clouds. Yayo and Shakira walked down the beach side, he held her close by her waist while she held the bottle of champagne, taking sips from the bottle.

"Yaton, this is so beautiful…oh my God," Shakira said, amazed at the view.

"Yeah, I know. I think we should consider moving down here. Me, Shamira and Jamarie," Yayo joked. Shakira punched him play-fully in his right shoulder. "Nah, I'm just playing. You know I ain't going nowhere without the queen," Yayo said, stopping now and staring Shakira in her brown eyes.

Shakira bit her bottom lip before she said, "Yaton, I want you to know that I am so proud of the man you have come to be. You are everything a woman needs. You are a king, and I am so grateful to be yours." Yayo was about to respond, until Shakira put her index finer over his lips, caging the words he was about to speak.

Dropping the empty bottle in the white sand, she started to unbutton the last three buttons of his Balenciaga button-up and placed kisses on his muscular chest. Yayo closed his eyes and raised his head to the sky. Shakira sucked on his neck, earlobes, then his lips. Her warm tongue entering his mouth, she could taste the Patrón on his tongue.

Yayo pulled the ponytail holder from her silky, real hair that ran down her back. He then grabbed her by her ass with both hands and squeezed, pulling her close, grinding his crotch into her midsection as he kissed her with passion. His dick started to swell. Yayo pulled away from their lustful kiss and removed the shoulder straps to her Dior sundress, letting the dress fall to the ground. Shakira stepped out of the dress, now only in her Victoria's Secret thong and matching bra. Yayo let his eyes roam over her flawless body while he took off his shirt, the love and lust plus the Patrón that flowed through his bloodstream, had him ready to attack her. Yayo pulled her slightly down toward the gritty white sand then laid her on her back.

"Damn. I love you, baby," he whispered, planting kisses on her face, neck and shoulders. Yayo unlatched her bra, freeing her breasts that set up like mounds. Her brown nipples were swollen, looking like erasers. They looked delicious as he sucked on them savagely, but yet tender and caring at the same time. Shakira moaned in ecstasy, with her manicured hands rubbing his bald head. Yayo ran his tongue down her stomach to her belly button.

"Ahhh, baby...I need you in me," she purred. Shakira arched her stomach upward, giving Yayo easy access to remove her thong, which he did, pulling it down and throwing it to the side. Shakira spread her thick caramel thighs giving her man a perfect view of her hot kitty cat, leaking pussy juice.

Yayo wasted no time, he pulled the hood of her pussy lips upward with his two thumbs, exposing her throbbing love button. He first used his tongue to run over her clit slowly, making Shakira go crazy. Then he sped it up, lapping at her clit like a hungry lion on a lamb chop Shakira came all over his chin, but he wasn't done. He now sucked on her clit as if he was trying to suck her soul from her, all the while using three fingers to deeply finger her. Shakira's eyes rolled to the back of her head in pure pleasure.

"Fuck me, Yaton...Please, I want to feel you inside me." Shakira panted.

Shakira reached for his Gucci belt, unbuckling it, pulling his linen shorts down. His hardness showed through his Prada boxer shorts. She got on her knees, planting kisses over his wood through his boxers, teasing him before she pulled his dick out and kissed the head of it, staring Yayo in his eyes. Shakira got in a doggy style position and arched her back as Yayo stepped to his business like the gangster he was. Entering her warm tight walls, grabbing her large ass cheeks, he slowly deep stroked her...filling her to capacity with him.

Shakira had to bite down on her bottom lip to stop from scream-ing, even though the loud waves from the ocean muffled her cries of pleasure and pain. Yayo sped up his stroke, his balls slapping against the back of Shakira's thighs as he dug in her. Her pussy was so wet and warm, he couldn't take it any longer and exploded in three strong thick spurts, releasing his seeds in her before he col-lapsed on her back, kissing on her neck until his meat softened in-side of her womb. "I love you, baby girl."

"I love you too, boo," Sharika said, snaking her neck to kiss him.

Yayo and Shakira laid nude on the beach, cradled in each other's arms, enjoying the moment. The cool breeze coming off the ocean was relaxing, and the mood was just right. They had made it through the torment of Yayo serving a life sentence in the feds. Jamarie was a new addition to the family and Shamira was happy to have him be a part of her life. The Save Our Youth Campaign was changing lives and made Yayo feel good about himself, know-ing that with all the destruction and violence he caused in his past, he was paving the way and doing all that he could to make it right.

Helping others not to follow in the same destructive lifestyle he had, Yayo felt now that he had a purpose in life. He and Shakira's wedding date was set for October second as he couldn't wait to marry her to make his life complete. Everything was all well, except for an eerie feeling he was having…like something was going to happen. He kissed Shakira on her lips and tried his best to ignore it.

S. ALLEN

Chapter 19

It was the Fourth of July in the city of Chicago, a hot summer night and the Rasta Elementary School playground was packed to capacity with kids and adults from the Englewood area. Lil Baby boomed from eight large speakers as the DJ did his thing, pumping the latest rap and R&B, keeping the party lit. Three large Bar-B-Q pits kept everybody with a healthy plate of beef, ribs, hot dogs, hamburgers and chicken wings. A full court three on three basketball game was in play, with the neighborhood players shooting three pointers and dunking, trying to win the twenty-five-hundred-dollar prize. The fourth of July event was sponsored by the Get It Boy Clique, which was done annually.

Most of the people attending the get-together was from 69th and Wolcott and surrounding areas. The Get it Boy Clique was still at war, so extra security around the park was beefed up, making sure everybody partied and had a good time. Choppa and the twins were in the corner of the park involved in a large dice game. It was 9:30 at night and in ten more minutes, they were going to let the fireworks go off. The G.B.C. had spent five bands on fireworks sure to captivate the crowd. Quavon stood by the DJ table, talking to some neighborhood thots who looked to him as if he was God in the hood. Reggie G and Crusha stood with him.

"So, what's good, you hollered at Yayo yet?" Crusha asked over the loud music, taking a bite from his hot dog.

"Na...bruh in Florida with my mama. I'm a holler at him when he get back in the city," Quavon responded. He couldn't wait to holler at Yayo about him making the decision to get out the game. He was ready to make his exit out, but Omega was making it harder and harder. When he left, he had to have his respect embedded in the streets, that's why he had ordered the execution of Pharoe and Span, to show Omega he was playing with a different breed of beast. Quavon watched as a few of his men set up the stage for fireworks.

"Aye DJ, let 'em know we about to start the fireworks," Quavon said to DJ Get Right.

"Alright y'all this the moment y'all been waiting for! We about to light up the sky," the DJ said over the mic…letting everybody know it was about to go down.

Fonzo and one of his boys sat in the backseat of a stolen Lexus. A crack head named Phil was behind the steering wheel. Omega had chosen Fonzo and one of his West side GD affiliates to run the drill at Rasta Elementary. On their laps were semi-automatic AR-15's. Span had told Omega about the Fourth of July's event, time and place. Now, Omega was about to bring his opps a nasty move.

The stolen Lexus was parked discreetly in an alley off of Wolcott, all they were waiting on was a text that would give them the green light to do what they came to do…murder.

"Alright, it's a wrap, my nigga. I'm about to watch these fireworks, I'll catch y'all in a minute," Choppa said, picking up his cash and pistol off the pavement. He put the small bankroll that consisted of thirty-five hundred in the pockets of his Balmain shorts, then tucked his pole on his waist and made his way over to where Quavon, Reggie G and Crusha was posted by the DJ table.

The phone in Fonzo's pocket vibrated from the text message from Span, who was making his way out the park and walking towards his whip. The text read, "Go." Fonzo pulled his black mask over his face. His mans followed suit. "Pull up," he told the crack head. Phil put the car in drive and slowly pulled out of the alley and pulled up on the side of Rasta Elementary. Just as the first rockets shot into the sky, Fonzo and his accomplice bailed out and raced through the entrance of the schoolyard.

"Yeah, what's up niggas. fuck y'all!" Fonzo roared, then squeezed the trigger. *Cha, Cha, Cha, Cha, Cha* The rockets burst in the sky at the same time the rifle spoke. *Cha, Cha, Cha* The assault rifle jerked in Fonzo's hand as he ran toward the crowd. A 5.62 round went through the back of an innocent bystander, shooting her heart out her chest. She died instantly.

"Don't run now, pussy. Come here," Fonzo guy sneered shooting into a crowd with his choppa. The park was now in pandemonium as the gunmen relentlessly fired their weapons at anybody in their sights. Choppa got low, at the same time pulling his FNH.

"Twin, get foenem to the whip," Choppa commanded, scanning the park to see where the shooters were positioned. Twin pulled his .40 and grabbed Quavon by the arm. "Come on, big homie, got to get you out of here." Quavon yanked his arm from Twins's grasp and pulled out his hammer.

"Fuck nigga!" *Cha, Cha, Cha, Cha, Cha, Cha.* Fonzo yelled, banging out in military fashion with his potna on the side of him trying to kill something. Choppa spotted the opps in white T's and ski masks, letting go with the sticks. He raised up and rushed them, FN extended in front of him.

Boc, Boc, Boc, Boc, Boc, Boc "Yeah niggas!" *Boc, Boc, Boc, Boc* Fonzo peeped game and turned the smoking barrel of the rifle in Choppa's direction and squeezed. A few other G.B.C. gang members, now aware of the situation, got active and let their hammers blow in their direction.

Cha, Cha, Cha, Cha Fonzo fired back, peddling toward the car before him and his co-defendant got low and raced to the whip and jumped in the backseat. Crackhead Phil frantically sped away from the scene. Choppa looked around the blood-soaked school yard at the bodies that lay sprawled out on the concrete.

"Ahh God, no...somebody help me, please...Help me," A girl yelled in agony, cradling her infant child, whose face was covered in red. Sirens could be heard getting close and closer. Four G.B.C. members ran up to Choppa with their guns out.

"Come on, fam, we got to bounce," the one named Dollar said. Choppa continued to scan the area looking for Quavon, Crusha and Reggie G. Seeing they weren't part of the carnage, he tucked his hammer and briskly walked out the park with his people and hopped in the backseat of Dollar's Range Rover. Once in the back seat Choppa grabbed his phone and dialed Quavon's number. He answered on the second ring.

"Where you at, my nigga?" Quavon asked, seeing Choppa's number on the caller ID.

"I'm in the car with Dollar. Where Reggie G and Crusha?" Choppa asked as he felt a burning sensation in his left arm. He felt where the pain was and his fingers became wet, stained with his blood.

"They in the car with me, but…"

"Aye fam, I think that was them pussy ass niggas from 59th. Look, y'all lay low, I'm about to go see something. I'm a hit y'all in a minute…love," Choppa said, then hung the phone and dialed another number.

"What's up?" the caller answered.

"Aye, unlock the trunk. I'm about to pull up."

"Say less," the person on the other line replied before he hung up. Choppa took off his Ferragamo shirt and examined his arm.

"Pussy ass niggas shot me," he sneered, seeing the hole in his arm that was now bleeding profusely.

Piggy, who was occupying the passenger seat while Dollar drove, turned on the dome light in the Range. Seeing all the blood, he said, "My nigga, we gotta get you to a hospital, you fucked up."

"Fuck that. Dollar, pull up on ADA in front of Poobee crib."

"You sure, thug?"

"Man, what I say…my nigga," Choppa gritted. Ten minutes later, Dollar pulled on 53rd and ADA in front of one of the guy's crib named Poobee. Choppa got out the back seat and went to a rusted Chevy Caprice and opened the trunk. He unwrapped some rolled-up carpet to reveal a Chinese SKS with two 30-round magazines taped together with electric tape. He grabbed the rifle and shut the trunk and got back in the Range Rover. Dollar pulled off as Choppa tied his shirt around his wounded arm to try and stop his blood from flowing like a river.

"Aye, Dollar, roll through 59th and Bishop. Piggy, here, roll something up," Choppa said and reached inside his shorts with a bloody hand and tossed Piggy an eighth of OG Kush he had been smoking. Piggy broke down a Backwood and filled it with the loud Choppa had given him. Pearled the blunt then sparked it and passed it to Choppa. Choppa took a strong pull to fill his lungs up and relax his nerves, his gunshot wound was burning like somebody was holding a Bic lighter to his arm. The potent THC plus his anger turned his eyes bloodshot red as sweat poured like water from his face from his adrenalin.

Dollar turned the SUV down Bishop Street. Choppa looked out the window with murderous intent. Seeing a group of individuals standing on the corner of 59th and Bishop, Choppa told dollar to pull up. Following Choppa's order, he pulled up and stopped in front of the crowd standing on the corner. It was at least fifteen people posted. Choppa hit the blunt and hopped out, holding the SKS with his right hand.

"Bitch ass niggas," he sneered, with the Backwood hanging from his lips. *Cha, Cha, Cha* The sparks from the gun were lighting up the corner like a Friday night disco. After emptying thirty rounds on the corner, Choppa hopped back in the Range. Dollar calmly pulled away from the curb as they left the corner of 59th and Bishop filled with death and stained in blood.

WGN News

I'm Vanessa Johnson…And I'm Tom Wolbert, and you are turned in to *WGN News*. On today's top story, a bloody Fourth of July weekend has left four people killed and at least eighteen others wounded in two different shootings on the city's south side. Police say two men opened fire on a crowd on the playground of Rasta Elementary School with semi-automatic rifles. At least fourteen people were hit in the incident, claiming the life of three. A nine-month-old child was hit in the face from the gunfire and is now at Mt. Sinai Hospital in critical condition.

"Later on that night, witnesses say a SUV pulled up to the corner of 59th and Bishop and a man exited the vehicle and opened fire with an assault rifle, leaving two dead and six wounded, before getting back in the vehicle and fleeing from the scene. Authorities believe these two senseless acts of violence to be gang related and would like anybody with information on these crimes to please notify the Chicago Police Department…

"On other news, ex-gang leader Yaton Anderson and the Save our Youth Campaign are making major attention after a positive public speaking that was held at the Cook County Juvenile Home for Boys early this month. Yaton Anderson was the leader of a violent drug gang that terrorized the city and residents of Cook County, until he was indicted by the federal government and sentenced to life.

"He overturned the sentence and returned back to society a positive person and joined the Save Our Youth Campaign. Yaton Anderson is scheduled to speak at the Cook County Jail later this week, in hopes to encourage gang members and drug dealers to break the cycle of criminal behavior and promote positive change within the community of Cook County."

Yayo turned off the TV, smiling about the news coverage he had just received about the public speaking. He had returned from his vacation in Florida, only to hear about the Rasta Elementary shooting. It hurt his heart to know he started the gang that now operated in that area. That same hood was now being held down by his younger brother, Quavon.

Quavon hadn't told Yayo personally, but by his street intuition, he knew his brother and his men were at war...with who he didn't know, but he knew he had to have a sit-down with Quavon, ASAP. The news coverage had boosted his morale, but there were people dying at a rapid pace in the streets as if Chicago was plagued with coronavirus...And he had to find a way to curb the violence...and swiftly.

Chapter 20

"Turn down this block right here, Pito," King Rico said from the passenger seat of the Cadillac Escalade. For the past two weeks he had been searching for Omega, but was coming up blank. Rico brought the CD case that had lines of cocaine on it to his nose and snorted two thick lines of the raw. The inside of his nose was sore from his drug use. His .40 caliber lay across his lap, he had been a nervous wreck ever since his uncle had given him a thirty-day deadline to come up with the quarter-mil he owed, and the cocaine only intensified his paranoia.

"What the fuck, esse…it's hot as shit around here," Rico replied seeing the unmarked cruiser posted on the corner of 59th and Bishop. "Make a right up here, brother." Pito made a right on Bishop and saw another Crown Victoria parked in the alley, incognito.

"What happened around here? Go back to the hood," King Rico said, taking another hit of the coke. Strolling through Omega's stomping ground was like driving through a ghost town. No dealers were out hustling, nor was there any fiends typing to cop work as the police activity was heavy. That meant only one thing…somebody had got their wig pushed back. Pito and King Rico made their way back to Humboldt Park to regroup and get their thoughts together. He only had a few days until his deadline was up, he was getting no closer to finding Omega or the work, and time was definitely ticking.

Choppa sat at the head of the table at a G.B.C. stash house on 151st and Low in the wild hunnids of Chicago, his arm in a sling from the shootout he had with some of Omega's men. A fully auto MAK-90 lay on the table in front of him. Ten shooters sat at the table with him. The Blackout Squad along with a few up-and-coming killers, itching to make their bones within the Get It Boy Clique, and Choppa was about to give them an opportunity to do just that. Quavon had personally given Choppa the green light to lay down anything that had to do with the Homicide Crew. Shooting into a crowd full of kids and teenagers let Quavon know the men they were dealing were indeed heartless and like disease-infected dogs, needed to be put down.

By the grace of God, the nine-month-old little girl that had been shot had made it out of critical condition and was now in stable condition. But the lack of human remorse the Homicide Crew was showing put a bad taste in Quavon's mouth, so now it was time to apply deadly pressure to the opps.

Choppa stood up to address his team of shooters. His dreads hung wildly down his back. A bulletproof vest around his chest, in camouflage jeans, and black unlaced Timberlands, Choppa was ready to get active. He took a pull from the Backwood and held the smoke in his lungs as his subordinates awaited his commands.

"What's good with the family?" he asked, blowing out smoke at the same time.

"Gang. What's good? We ready to slide, Chop," his men replied, eager to lay their murder game down.

"That's what I want to hear, because that's exactly what we gone do tonight. Now listen, since these niggas wanna come through our hood and shoot kids and shit, the gloves are completely off. But they reckless, they moving without a motive or objective, we the guys. We move strategically. These niggas like goofies, we like Navy Seals when it come to this murder shit, that's why we at the top of the food chain," Choppa said, walking around his men, making sure his words were being soaked in and understood, he continued.

"Now, this the business, we about to let these niggas know this is not a game. My investigation has come back that these cowards are operating in five different cliques on the south side. They so-called leader has recruited five different areas. Them frontin ass niggas on 71st and Marshfield are in compliance with the Homicide Crew shit. Y'all already know that's ATG hood...that shit green-lighted, 69th and Justine also jumped on the band wagon and it's crazy, because Big Chip run that. He used to be gang, but fuck 'em, we drilling that area too.

"This dude Omega got some of the stones on his squad, word is 51st and Troop cliquing with these niggas. So, we sliding through

Moe Town as well. And it's some GDs in K-Town over there on Keystone Street. All the way to Pulaski is greenlighted." The goons began to whisper amongst themselves.

"Now, this how it's going to go down. Vietnam, you and Lil Melvin gone hit 71st and Marshfield…Lil Melvin you on the trigger." Lil Melvin was fifteen years old, wild and a known shooter in the hood. Now it was time to prove himself to the Get It Boy Clique. He nodded his head, accepting the mission. "Moon, you and Hero run a drill on 57th and Troop. Hero, you putting in the work, make us proud," Choppa commanded.

Hero was a G.B.C. gangster, eighteen years old, itching to climb the ranks of the gang and was ready to put on for the Clique. "Killah, you and Poohman gone slide out west. Poohman, hop out and represent, I wanna hear how you shined with that stick." Poohman was the youngest out of the shooters. At only thirteen years old, he was the most dangerous, ready to make a name in the Get It Boy Clique organization.

"Kill-Will, you and the Twins gone fuck them niggas up on 69th and Justine. Kill-Will, you drive and let Foe'nem do what they do. Vietnam, I'm riding with you and Lil Melvin. This how it's gone play out, we all gone drill at the same time. At 11:30 tonight, y'all should be bailing out chopping. Each car has an AK-47 and a fully auto Glizzy, when then thumpers returned, I want them clips and drums empty…y'all understand?

"If y'all think y'all ain't ready, leave up out this muthafucka right now, cuz ain't no freezing up," Choppa threatened. Nobody made a move. Choppa nodded at Vietnam, who went to the sectional sofa and started taking cushions off Vietnam reached inside the sofa, pulling out AK's, six in all. He began passing them out with 50-round clips and 100-round drums, with a green Army bag full of 7.62 ammunition.

For the next forty minutes, the hit squad smoked blunts of loud and silently wiped off shell casings and loaded magazines. Everybody was in their own thoughts, as they each had one thing in their minds… murder. After loading their weapons, the crew walked out the stash house through the back, where stolen vehicles otherwise known as strikers, were parked. Giving each other gangster pounds and handshakes, showing their love and alliance to the G.B.C. they got in different cars and pulled out of the alley...headed to their designated areas to run a drill on their opps.

Quavon pulled in the driveway of Yayo and Shakira's condo on the north side, it was 11:00 at night. He had texted Yayo and told him he needed to speak with him ASAP. Yayo told him to come through. Quavon parked the Dodge Durango, put out the blunt he was smoking in the ash tray and got out. Yayo was looking out the window when Quavon pulled up and went downstairs to let him in. He had been awaiting his arrival.

"What's good with you, lil bruh?" Yayo greeted as Quavon entered his home.

"Same ol shit, fam...where my niece at?" Quavon asked, looking around the empty condo, and taking a seat on the sofa.

"She in the bed, Ock...her and Jamarie, they went to sleep about two hours ago. Everybody sleep. What's up with you, though? You looking rough," Yayo said, looking at his brother. His normally waved hair was nappy, and he needed a haircut and shave, his eyes were glassy red with dark rings under them.

His Tom Ford T-shirt was dingy and wrinkled and his Givenchy jeans looked as if he had slept in them two nights in a row. Quavon laid his head back on the couch.

"Man, bro, it's a whole lot going on," he replied.

"Yeah, I heard. Y'all over there beefing heavy, huh?" Yayo asked, already knowing the answer to his question. He could see the stress and worry from being in the murderous battlefield sketched across his brother's face. "Quavon, why don't you just let this shit go? Haven't you been through enough? I know you got your bag up, why must you still feel like you have to prove yourself? It's only two endings to this game, like when I told you when you come to visit me in the feds...It's either life in the penitentiary or the graveyard."

Yayo looked over at his brother who had his eyes closed, but he also noticed the lonely tear that rolled down his cheek. Quavon kept his eyes closed as he spoke.

"That's what I came over here to tell you, Yaton...I went to holler at my plug to tell him I was done. Don't send me no more bricks, it's over. I got some shit set up in Cali... legal shit. I'm about to bounce to the West Coast. Me, Choppa, Crusha and Reggie G. But these hoe ass niggas won't give me my peace. These bitch ass niggas just shot fourteen people...they shot a baby in the face, fam. How can I let that shit go? I got to find this nigga Omega and kill 'em. Period."

Yayo put his head down, feeling his brother's pain. He felt the same way when Pudge got killed. He felt the same way when TJ was killed, and the feeling his brother was feeling couldn't be ignored. Quavon's love for what he believed in was embedded in his heart, his tears began to flow. Yayo's heart was broken, seeing his brother go through this. Had he not given his brother the game to get to the level he was playing at, he would not be in this predicament and now, Yayo was feeling somewhat guilty for molding Quavon into the savage he had become. Yayo put his arm over his brother's shoulder.

"Quavon, you a grown man and you gone make your own decisions in life. I can't tell you what to do, all I can do is try to continue to steer you away from the lifestyle. You have a family that loves and needs you, man. Why won't you learn from my mistakes? Your own twin brother don't want to come near you. Last time y'all kicked it, he caught a bullet meant for you. I'm not trying to make you feel guilty...But damn, bro, you got a chance to get away with your money and your life, don't let your pride be the cause of your demise. Let it go while you still can," Yayo said, hugging his brother.

Quavon wept in Yayo's chest, releasing all the pain and grief in his heart that he gained in the years of being in the streets. Quavon got out of his brother's embrace.

"I owe the plug a couple dollars. I got it tied in the streets. Once I send him his money, it's over. Yaton, I'm walking away completely. That's on my family!" he vowed.

"That's what I want to hear, G. You gone be alright. I love you, lil bro, just know I'm here for you," Yayo said. The two brothers continued to kick it and reminisce about old times, until Quavon got a text on his iPhone. It read, "It's done."

"Alright, big bro, I gotta bounce. It's getting kind of late. I got to go out west and pick this lil broad up. Tell Shamira and Jamarie we gone kick it next weekend, probably shoot to Wisconsin Dells and go to the water park."

I'm quite sure she gone be happy to know that. You know how she love her uncle Quavon," Yayo retorted, walking Quavon to the front door.

"Alright, love." Quavon hugged his brother and left. Once he got in his truck, he placed a call to Choppa who had just texted him. It was a bloody Saturday night, as forty-two people had died in the streets of Chicago, all by Quavon's call. Tonight, the G.B.C. had made history in the city. It was August and the treacherous acts of violence they had just unleashed would make August of 2020 the deadliest month since the Al Capone days.

Chapter 21

The traffic was bumper to bumper, trying to get into the Factory strip club on 115th on the South side of the city. It was Magic City Monday and every dope boy, card cracker, pimp and hustler were coming to throw money at Chicago's baddest strippers. Choppa sat on the passenger side of his Lincoln Navigator as he let his new shooter Lil Melvin drive the whip. It had been two weeks since the drill session of the opps and the murders of their enemies were performed righteously, claiming the lives of 42. Everything was executed properly. The killings had made *CNN*.

Making the world news made Choppa feel like a giant and Choppa wanted to go out and celebrate the deaths of the ops. Choppa was geeked off the ecstasy he had taken and the blunts of Cookies he was smoking, while "Drip Like This" by Bankroll Freddie and Young Dolph pounded through the subwoofers. Lil Poohman and Span sat in the backseat, bouncing to the track. Killa, the Twins and Lil Tony followed behind them in the Dodge Hellcat. Everybody's adrenaline still pumping from the killing, making them feel like bosses. Choppa was going to show his lil homies a good time and show them the life they would live, being a certified G.B.C. gangster.

The gang turned into the parking lot of the Factory, shaking the concrete from the 4-twelves coming off the twenty-five-hundred-watt Orion amp. Females dressed in almost nothing focused on the men jumping out the Lincoln Navigator and the all-black Hellcat. There jewelry shining and swag on point like the true hood stars they were. The valet approached Choppa.

"I want both these whips parked in front," he stated and pulled out a ridiculous wad of blue notes from his Givenchy jeans, peeling off two hundred-dollar bills and passing them to the valet, then arrogantly walked toward the beginning of the line.

The Factory didn't sell alcohol, so you had to bring your own bottles. So, Choppa had Span grab the cases of Ace of Spades and case of 1738 from the trunk of the Hellcat to take into the club. Inside, the Factory was lit. Ballers popped bottles, vibing to the sounds of Lil Durk, turning up. Choppa and his men made their way toward the VIP section of the club. It was as if every bitch and nigga knew his status in the streets as his diamonds on his neck, wrist and ears shined in the dimly lit atmosphere. His G.B.C. chain was flooded in ice, giving niggas in the club chills in their spines.

The word on the streets was the Get It Boy Clique was responsible for the murder rate going up in the city. So, they showed homage to the killers with head nods. Will, the owner of the strip club, stood by the stairwell personally leading them to their section.

"How you brothers doing?" he asked Choppa, shaking his hand. Will knew Choppa and the Get It Boy Clique were heavyweights in the city and always big spenders at the club. So, he showed extreme generosity when dealing with them.

"What's up, old head? What y'all got going on tonight?" Choppa asked, putting ten crispy hunnid-dollar bills in Will's hand. He put the money in his pocket.

"Well, you know how it go. I own the Factory. But I think Taliban supposed to be performing tonight. Other than that, hotties and thotties," Will replied, standing in the area that sat over the bar, overlooking the large stage. Will made eye contact with Tottie, his personal assistant, and motioned toward the G.B.C. Now seeing who was in the club, Tottie got in motion to locate ten of the baddest strippers in the building, to go to the VIP to entertain Choppa and his people.

Choppa was in his zone, a bottle of 1738 in one hand, a quarter-ounce of Cookies rolled into a Backwood burning in his other hand. A thick redbone named Bria was between his thighs, trying to chew his dick through his thousand-dollar jeans, soaking the front of his pants from her wet tongue. Lil Melvin stood on the couch, throwing money from his eight-thousand-dollar bankroll. Choppa had blessed his game after deeming him official, seeing him hit an opp in the head with the "K" without flinching, and rewarded him with thirty racks and a 2015 Challenger.

The rest of the crew balled out, surrounded by big booty strippers. Span stood off to the side with a bottle of Ace of Spades, texting on his phone. The club was lit. Taliban performed on the stage, rapping his new track, "Bag Talk." as the dancers twerked to the beat. He was dressed in gold Marc Jella from head to toe.

"Damn, baby boy. I'm saying, a bitch trying to get to that wood for real, so I can show you how I really get down," Bria whispered in Choppa's ear, at the same time nibbling on the 1-carat diamond on his earlobe.

"Shorty, you chasing that bag, huh?" Choppa said, Bria's warm tongue sending sexual electricity through his body. The weed, ecstasy and drink had his dick wanting to bust through his jeans. Bria looked him in his bloodshot eyes and shook her head slowly.

"Uh-uh, daddy, this pussy is on the house," she retorted, then grabbed his hand and led him to the back, a darker corner of the VIP.

While the Get It Boy Clique was balling out at the Factory, Omega was behind the wheel of a tinted Dodge Neon. Span had sent him a text, saying he was with Choppa at the Factory strip club. This was the moment Omega had been waiting for. He was contemplating sending one of his goons, or better yet, letting Span crush Choppa. But this was personal, as it was Choppa's trigger finger that killed his dead homie Ace, so he felt it was only right that he stepped up and punish Choppa personally.

Omega pushed the whip down the Dan Ryan Expressway, headed to the Factory. Span had told him he would text him once they were on their way out the club. He could see the Factory from off the Dan Ryan and right then, he came up with a deadly idea and pulled over on the shoulder of the highway. Parking his car, he put on the hazard lights and reached under the seat to retrieve the Smith and Wesson 1911 semi-auto.

Looking in his rearview and seeing the light traffic on the expressway, he got out and tucked the gun in his shorts and jogged up the grass hill, leading to the front of the club. He hopped the small gate and entered the Factory parking lot. which was packed. Omega looked the part as he was dressed head to toe in a black and white Balenciaga short set, so he figured he would go over and holler at some of the thots to blend in with the crowd until his target emerged from the club.

An hour later, the joyous night at the Factory strip club had come to an end as the party goers made their way out the club. Choppa was pissy drunk from the three bottles of 1738 he had consumed. He had gotten some head from Bria, but the freak in him wasn't satisfied and now he wanted to fuck. Bria had no problem and obliged to go get a room with Choppa. She had even gotten one of her stripper buddies named Cream to accompany them for a threesome. Choppa had his arms around both dancers as they walked out. The Twins, Killa, Mondo and Lil Tony dragged behind them—all with something thick and ready to freak out, for a price of course.

Span slid out the club thirty minutes prior, waiting for an Uber to pull up. When he saw Choppa walk out the club, he texted Omega and gave him Choppa's description and what kind of whip he was driving. Guilt began to surface but his guilt was easily derailed when he had a flashback when Choppa pulled that gun on him that night. *Fuck 'em*, he thought as he watched Choppa walk out the front entrance.

Omega was taking a pull on a Newport, talking to a dark-skinned female named Brenda when his iPhone beeped. He looked at the text and smiled before he put the phone back in his pocket.

"Shorty, put my number in your phone and I'm a call you in about an hour," he said in a smooth tone. She stored his number in the phone and watched as Omega walked toward the front of the club, with his hand in his shorts pocket.

Choppa walked out with his people, making his way to the Dodge Durango when he heard, "Aye, scud." Turning around, he saw a light-skinned cat with a black and white Balenciaga snapback, pointing a chunky firearm at him. Bria and Cream let out a piercing scream at the sight of the large hand cannon. Choppa froze as he stared down the dark barrel of the .45… *Boc*

Choppa saw the bright flash from the barrel, and he felt nothing as the Hydro-Shock penetrated then exploded in his skull, blowing his brains out the back of his cranium. Noodles and skull fragments everywhere, Choppa fell on his back, brains oozing on the concrete. The thunderous gunshot caused everybody in the parking lot to get low and get somewhere. The strip club's parking lot was now in pandemonium. Choppa's men, unarmed, stood and watched as Omega menacingly stood over Choppa's dead corpse and fired the gun two more times, *Boc, Boc,* to the head and chest. Then, he bent down and snatched his chain off his neck and jogged off into the crowded chaotic parking lot, making a getaway to his vehicle. Lil Melvin and the rest of the crew rushed over to their boss, only to see his face melted to the concrete. Choppa's soul was the fifth that night to get taken off the deadly streets of Chi-Raq.

S. ALLEN

Chapter 22

Choppa's funeral was held at the Gatlings Funeral Home on 111th and Halsted on the south side of the city. Almost the entire funeral home was packed to capacity with people from the Englewood area. The whole Get It Boy Clique gang was in attendance to see their general off to the pearly gates. Quavon, Crusha and Reggie G sat in the front row, as well as Choppa's baby momma Tia, who was crying her heart out grieving for her son's father. Yayo sat in the second row with the Save Our Youth members.

Yayo felt a tinge of guilt staring at Choppa's pearl and gold casket. He was the one who brought Choppa into the G.B.C. years ago, had he not, Choppa probably would still be alive. Shakira wanted to accompany Yayo to the funeral to give her man support, but Yayo declined, not wanting to bring her anywhere near the street life. He sat stone-faced, while a tear fell down his cheek as he listened to the preacher preach.

"My brothers and sisters, the Lord, our Father has given us the Ten Commandments, which we are supposed to live by. One of these commandments was, 'Thou shall not kill,' Reverend Bishop C. Richards said. Yayo looked around the sea of young faces, red eyes, mean mugs and revenge sketched across the faces. Yayo knew how they were feeling. He had been where they were and he knew they weren't trying to hear anything the preacher was saying. All they wanted was blood.

Yayo stood up, straightened his Tom Ford suit jacket and made his way out the aisle. Kewann looked at Yayo with a questioning look. Yayo walked toward the podium where Bishop Richards stopped speaking, his eyes now on Yayo, who walked past Choppa's casket. It shattered his heart to pieces that he couldn't even see his lil mans. The .45 Hydro-Shock bullets had damaged his head and face to the point the morticians couldn't reconstruct his face properly to be viewed. Choppa had a closed casket.

Yayo walked up to the podium and hugged the preacher and whispered in his ear, "Reverend, please let me have a word with these young brothers." The reverend looked Yayo in his eyes.

Seeing the sincerity in him, he stepped away from the podium. Yayo took to the microphone. Before he spoke a word, he looked into the mourning eyes of Chicago's underworld…Pain, remorse, regret and heartache stared back at him.

"First and foremost, I know how y'all feel…I know what it feels like to lose a homie, a family member. For y'all that don't know, my name is Yayo. The same thug you out there riding for, dying for, getting years in prison for—The Get It Boy Clique, I started that. That's right, I started what y'all believe in. That great man lying in that casket, I brung him into this world," Yayo said, shaking his head.

"Everything that's going on in them streets, what y'all going through, I went through. The murder, the envy, the double crossing and backstabbing…I been through it. Do you even know why y'all at war? No, you don't, you can't know because when I was in the streets, I didn't know what it is for! Why are we burying each other…Why!" Yayo yelled, slamming his fist on the wooden podium, while staring Quavon in his bloodshot eyes.

"We giving these people exactly what they want, to shoot and kill each other, then fill they prisons up so they can get paid off our bodies yearly. Give us years upon years in prison, so we can't be out here with our beautiful black women to reproduce and breed kings and queens. I was just like you. Let me rephrase that, I am you. Same color, same blood, we are the same. Us killing each other is nothing but self-genocide, we killing off our own race. It took for me to go to federal prison to see the big picture.

"The money you out here getting, the cars and clothes, when you sentenced to three hundred and sixty months, you can't take it with you. No matter how much money you got on your books, you can't buy nothing nobody else in prison can't buy…You are nobody but an inmate with a number. What about your kids? I know most of you are fathers and mothers. It takes two parents to raise a child. I have a daughter and she is my world.

"When I was in the penitentiary, the stress and heartache I endured in that cold cell from being away from her was unbearable. I contemplated suicide, feeling I had nothing to live for…But that

202

was the price I paid for living the street life. People listen to me, this life is not worth it. It will only cause you death and misery."

"You say all that, but we in the ghetto. Ain't no jobs so we gotta do what we gotta do to survive, and what I'm standing for I'm dying for. And that's fact," a young man blurted out, cutting Yayo off.

"Fam, I understand. But understand this, the same time you using working your way up to an ounce from a ball, from an ounce to four and a half, and so on until you get that brick, you can spend the same time going to school for a trade, it's all about taking initiative, young brother. All you have to do is give yourself a chance, because it's only two endings in this game...death or prison."

"Man, the opposition always on *Instagram* dissing and disrespecting. Ain't no way I'm letting that ride," another young man said out loud.

"Bro...You will continue to suffer if you have an emotional reaction to everything that is said to you...True power is sitting back, observing everything with logic. True power is restraint. It's going to kill you softly if you get life in prison because of something somebody said," Yayo said, dropping jewels to his people...hoping he could encourage them to stop beefing out there in the streets.

After speaking, Yayo stepped from the podium. Quavon was the first to stand up and hug his brother. Yayo could feel the bulletproof vest that was strapped over his chest. He knew that whoever his lil brother and the Get It Boy Clique was beefing with were worthy opponents, and Choppa laying in that closed casket was evidence. Crusha hugged Yayo next. "I hope you got through to some of them. Yayo, it's getting real nasty out here and I know for a fact it's going to be more bodies dropping," Crusha said.

"We just got to save the ones we can, family...But I can't do it by myself, I need y'all help."

"I'm with you, brother," Crusha replied, staining Yayo's shoulder with his tears. Reggie G stood off to the side with his hands in the pockets of his Ferragamo slacks.

"How you holding up, Reggie?" Yayo asked, walking up to him. Reggie G's eyes were red and swollen from crying over his dead homie.

"You know this shit ain't over, G. They not gone stop till we all dead. What we supposed to do, just sit and let them pick us off like birds? We gotta get at them before they get at us, period," Reggie G stated. Yayo put his hand on Reggie G's shoulder.

"Reggie G, you from the old school. You already know this new generation come from a different bloodline. Let them have this. Quavon got the right idea. Y'all just got to make him stand on it. Pack up and get to the West Coast, y'all don't have nothing to prove to the streets. What needed to be proved has already been proven. Now it's time to retire as bosses…and bosses use this," Yayo said, using his index finger to tap his head. "Use y'all head. Get out the battlefield and get to the island. That's the whole objective. Put y'all pride to the side."

Reggie G stood silently digesting what Yayo was speaking and knew he was right, now all he had to do was convince Quavon to smash the gas and make their exit out the game, before it was too late.

The organs began to play and the people in the funeral walked past Choppa's casket, next to a big photo in a frame of him smiling as if his life was innocent instead of filled with pain, violence and tribulations. When the viewing was over, Reggie G, Yayo, Crusha, Killa, Vietnam and Lil Melvin carried Choppa's casket outside to the pearl white Cadillac hearse.

The front of Gatlings Funeral Home was packed. People were making their way to their vehicles so they could follow the hearse to Burr Oaks Cemetery, where Choppa's body would be laid to rest, when gunshots rang out. *Boc, Boc, Boc, Boc, Boc.* A red Monte Carlo SS sped past the funeral home, a gunman hanging out the window dumping, before racing down Halstead Street.

Gang members raced to their cars to get to their pipes, but it was already over. The shooters were long gone, leaving an innocent by-stander shot in the back. Even if some of the young men attending the funeral had felt Yayo's words, all that positive, prosocial speaking had just gone out the window, and now replaced with anger and retaliation.

Chapter 23

Slap

The palm connecting to King Rico's face sounded off like a gunshot in the secluded basement. Rico's deadline was up. He hadn't found Omega, the drugs or the quarter of a million that was owed to the Madin Cartel. With no other option, Hector sent his men to Chicago to kidnap his nephew. Now Rico was in Midland, Texas, close to the Mexican border. Tied to a chair in a remotely dark basement, being beaten and pistol whipped. Hector watched as his nephew's head began to swell like a pumpkin.

"Where is the money, Rico?" Hector asked him through clenched teeth.

"I told you, Uncle, I cannot find Omega," Rico replied through his bloodied split lips.

"And I told you, whoever this Omega is…does not owe me. You owe me, you stupid irresponsible son of a bitch!" Hector sneered before punching his blood relative in the jaw, breaking it on contact.

"Please, Uncle…give me more time," Rico pleaded, spitting out two of his front teeth.

"Time? I have given you enough time. You have played me, you and this fictitious character that you speak of…I will make sure you don't feel a thing." Hector nodded to one of his men and walked off. A tear rolled down his cheek as he heard the muffled sound from the silenced Glock and then the brass shell casing hit the basement floor. It pained his heart to have his nephew killed, but Hector was tied to some murderous individuals, and the rules were to be abided by.

There was no room for favoritism…or losses in the Madin organization. If Hector hadn't just made the call he just made to have Rico killed, then a call would be made on him. Hector still had to find the person who ran off with the work. He believed his nephew, but his belief wouldn't replace the two hundred and fifty thousand or the fifty kilos of cocaine. Walking up the stairs leading out of the basement, he left his sister's oldest son a dead corpse as the stench from death invaded the basement.

Omega stared in the mirror at his reflection. His shirt was off, revealing his prison tattoos that told an evil tale of his violent, ambitious, criminal lifestyle, his eyes were red from his marijuana and cocaine use. Choppa's G.B.C. diamond chain hung from his neck like the death trophy it was. He had just taken the life of the man responsible for killing his best friend, Ace. Omega felt like the weight of the world had just been taken off his shoulders, but he knew by facts that there was no fairy tale endings in the murder game. Killers kill other killers.

Omega knew it would just be a matter of time before the G.B.C. found out it was him who put Choppa down, and when they did, they would stop at nothing to make sure he was no longer breathing. The forty-two bodies that was dropped, all alliances with the Homicide crew, let him and the subordinates know the Get It Boy Clique was insane with these murder tactics, and had set the bar with the work they had just put in.

Omega knew he had to outthink his opposition if he wanted to have a chance at killing Quavon and getting away with it. The monster staring back at him was real, he was playing a deadly game and was planning on winning at all cost. Killing Choppa only gave him more motivation to continue to kill his opps. His feelings were numb to the core as dying meant nothing to him.

Omega took the Backwood filled with Purple Haze and laced with cocaine off the sink, lit the tip and took a strong pull from the blunt and exhaled. The funky smell from the loud and burning cocaine surrounded the bathroom. The drugs slowly flowed through his bloodstream as a feeling of evilness invaded his being. Omega grabbed his iPhone and went live on *Facebook*. Gripping the G.B.C. chain in his hand and his phone in the other hand, he stared bare faced into the phone with the blunt dangling from the corner of his lips and said…

"As you can see…Niggas can get touched…Ain't nobody exempt when the Homicide Crew on you. Fuck the Get It Boy Clique…Y'all see me smoking? You know what I'm smoking on?

I'm smoking on your dead homies…Bitch ass niggas…it's homicide," Omega sneered then logged off the live.

He was feeling crazy and cocky. Pulling on the blunt, he walked out the bathroom and into the bedroom, where he went in the closet and grabbed a Louis Vuitton backpack, unzipped it and retrieved the 100-round drum that was loaded with 7.62 ammunition, then went to his king size bed, lifted the mattress and grabbed his all-black, mini, Draco AK-47. Omega locked the drum into the assault weapon and got dressed.

After tying the shoestrings to his Nike ACG boots, he left out the crib. It was 11:00 at night and the drugs in his system had him feeling violent and wanting to bust a nigga's head. So, he got in his whip and got in the battlefield. En route to the area of 69th and Wolcott to try to catch some of the enemies lacking.

Smooth, Veno, Thump and a few more Get It Boy Clique gang members were on 69th and Wolcott. They had attended Choppa's funeral a few days ago and were in their feelings ever since. They had just come from sliding through 57th and Justine, shooting at some of their rivals, hitting one in the head, claiming his young life. Now they were posted on 69th awaiting retaliation, An AR-15 with no stock laid hidden in the bushes, along with a Russian SKS, as 30-round Glocks rested on their waistlines locked and loaded. The young gangsters were in a dangerous element.

"On Choppa grave, I wish these pussy ass niggas try to slide. I'm a knock one of they goofy ass down. On Foe nem," Thump said with his hand on his heat. Thump was the one who'd just shot the boy in the head on Justine and his adrenaline was still pumping. The gang mean mugged every car that came through the block, throwing up their gang sign, trying to ignite any animosity…with anybody so they could put on for the hood. A dope fiend named ED walked up the block toward the click of youngsters, two damp bills crumbled up in his hand, a twenty and a five-dollar bill.

"Who the fuck is that?" Veno sneered, turning his attention to ED, at the same time pulling the .40 off his waist.

"What's up youngstas? I don't want no trouble…J-just trying to get three bags for this t-twenty-five. That's all," ED stuttered, his eyes glued to the chunky Glock Veno had in his hand.

"Three for twenty-five? Get your crackhead ass from over here with that short money. Come back when you got five more dollars," Veno said.

"Come on, shorty…show old head some love," ED pleaded. Silently praying that the youngsters would give him a play so he could get the gorilla off his back.

"Love? Muthafucka, my big homie just got killed. Ain't no love. Now move around," Veno said, dismissing ED, then turned back and started talking to the guys.

"Fuck you, nigga. I'm a take my money over there on 59th. Y'all petty as hell on 69th," ED said and started walking off.

"Fuck you say, bitch ass nigga?" Veno turned to ED, gun in hand. Crackhead ED took off running. He didn't make it far as Veno snatched him by his collar and started raining down blow upon blow on ED's head, knocking patches of meat off his cranium with the Glock. Thump ran up and grabbed Veno's arm.

"Come on, G, that's enough…fuck that fiend." Thump pulled Veno off ED, who was leaking profusely. He slowly got up from the pavement and staggered down the block to get away from the dangerous crew of gangsters before he got himself killed. Veno walked back to the corner with Thump, his chest heaving from the pistol whipping he had just given ED.

Omega was parked on 68th and Wolcott watching the men on 69th intently. He knew they had hammers out on the block, so he needed to disarm them. He grabbed his burnout cellphone and dialed 911.

"This is 911, what's your emergency?" the operator asked.

"Yes, I live on 69th and Wolcott and I would like to report there is a group of men standing on the corner with firearms. Can you please send CPD through here to get these guns off the street?" Omega informed, then hung up and patiently waited behind the tint of the low-key Camry.

It was ten minutes later when Smooth yelled, "Ninety-nine on the lane," meaning the police was coming. All the G.B.C. ditched their firearms in the bushes and in trash cans just as the unmarked Crown Victoria came to a screeching halt in front of them and hopped out, pointing guns.

"Freeze." All of them was laid on the ground and pat searched for guns. Finding none and seeing they had come in on a bogus anonymous tip, they told the men they could leave and stay off the corner or next time they would be arrested for mob action and taken to the precinct on 51st. The detectives got back in the cruiser and pulled off. Omega watched as the police left the block, at the same time slipping his hands in a pair of latex gloves. Seeing the Get It Boy Clique make their way back to the corner, Omega pulled out of the parking space he was in and gunned the engine to the Camry. The G.B.C. had no time to react as the Camry came to a screeching halt and Omega jumped out the driver's seat, pointing the baby choppa. *Cha, Cha, Cha, Cha, Cha, Cha...*

The corner lit up with gunfire. Veno caught a slug in the throat from the 7.62 slug, almost decapitating him. *Cha, Cha, Cha...* Omega applied relentless pressure on the hair trigger, knocking life out of his unarmed enemies. *Cha, Cha, Cha, Cha, Cha...* After letting fifty of the hundred rounds go, he hopped back in the whip and sped off down the street...leaving 69th and Wolcott soaked in flesh and blood.

Chapter 24

Yayo sat in the backseat of the Town and Country min-van. Kewann was behind the wheel, as Doc occupied the passenger seat. They were being escorted by the Cook County Sheriffs into the belly of Cook County Jail to do a public speaking. The gate opened and Kewann pulled into the underground parking lot of the jail. He parked on the side of the escorting vehicle and they all got out. The nervousness that Yayo experienced the first time he did a public speaking no longer existed as this was his fifth one.

Since doing the first public speaking, Yayo's name was starting to ring in the streets, but on a positive note. The Save Our Youth Campaign was gaining national publicity and had even got the attention of the President Barack Obama, who got on TV and gave Yayo and the Save Our Youth Campaign their props for trying to reach out and change the life of those who were addicted and trapped in the street life.

The two Cook County sheriffs escorting Yayo and his people led them through the underground parking lot into the intake part of the jail where he, Kewann and Doc had to pass through a metal detector. The musty smell and funk that came from the inmates in the bullpen waiting to get processed into the jail, gave Yayo a flashback as he vividly remembered the same funk when he came through Cook County years ago. Back then, the county was more wide-open and violent. An inmate was certain to get assaulted on a day-to-day basis, either by another inmate or the jail, correctional officers, and some even involved in gang activity.

Most inmates were on their way to lengthy prison sentences for violent crimes, making Cook County Jail a violent and dangerous element for any man to be in. Yayo followed the sheriffs into a bullpen where ten other Cook County Sheriffs awaited them to give a short briefing about the jail and precautions in case anything got out of control.

"Good evening, gentlemen. My name is Lieutenant Spires and welcome to Cook County Jail. I know you men were supposed to speak to the entire jail, but as of late, three of the Division's units are on lockdown status, due to a gang war within the jail. So, you will only be able to speak with the inmates from Division 11, which is basically all maximum-security inmates."

Yayo remembered being in the maximum security when he was waiting to get indicted by the feds. He knew the caliber of men that were housed on that unit. And if he could get through to just a few of them, he knew they had influence over others and the message that he was about to send would trickle down the pipeline. After getting the rules and security regulations if anything was to pop off, Lieutenant Spires led them to the gymnasium, where all the inmates from Division 11 awaited them, to hear what they had to say.

Walking in the gym room was like walking into the gym at the Audi Home, except as the boys in the juvenile jail laughed and cracked jokes, the grown inmates in Cook County Jail sat stone-faced and serious. Some of them were gang chiefs, others were high-level narcotic dealers awaiting federal prosecution. None of them with the jokes and horse play. The warden of the Cook County Jail took to the podium and introduced Yayo and the Save Our Youth Campaign as the guest speakers, turning the microphone over to Yayo.

To his surprise, the men respectfully applauded them, which seemed to ease the minor tension Yayo felt. He waited for the convicts to stop clapping before he began his speech.

"How you men doing?" My name is Yaton Anderson. But when I was involved with the street life, my name was Yayo. I came here to speak to you brothers about something important. Something called unity. You know brothers, unity is strong when used correctly. I read *The Chicago Tribune* this morning and it hurt my heart to know that it's been eight hundred ninety-two homicides in the city of Chicago this year…sixty-two just in the month of August, with forty-two of these murders in one single weekend.

"Brothers, that's genocide…self-inflicted genocide. Most of these bodies are young men ranging from the ages of thirteen to twenty-five years old, that means we have a problem…the problem is us, the older generation. These are our sons, nephews and brothers that are out here doing all this killing in the city. And we are the problem because we not out there to show them a different way of life, or to tell them it's not right to kill. I was a product of this as well, out here on the streets doing the same things.

"But, when I went to federal penitentiary and walked the yard, looking around I was shocked to see the prison was populated with almost seventy-five percent of the prison yard being black. That's messed up, brothers. I know what it's like to be in poverty. To feel like you don't have a chance and you feel you're forced into the criminal life as means of survival.

"It's hard to be content with a nine to five job. If you're a black man with a family of three and you only making seven to ten an hour at your job a month, your take home income is probably only a thousand a month, after deductions of federal tax, state tax, Medicaid, Medicare, Social Security, and your child support is already taken out. Your rent is five to six hundred a month, electricity is one-ninety-nine, cellphone is about fifty, your gasoline is about a hundred a month, clothes is fifty a month, and let's remember, we dealing with minimum numbers.

"This already maxes out the thousand dollars and we haven't even factored in food, car notes, car insurance. Just in order to try and make ends meet, you would have to work two nine to five jobs, so I understand the frustration, making y'all pick up the sack and the Glock. But brothers, we have to educated ourselves so we can reach heights above the nine to five. We have to reach the heights of entrepreneurship. We are strong people with ambition and creativity, all we have to do is come together. That's how all the other races stay wealthy because they stay together.

"All of you have an ambitious and corporate mind frame. Some of you have blocks out there, doing no less than a hundred geez a night. And that's an off night, when everything ain't clicking right. But peep this, brothers, do you know there are forty-five million blacks in America? if every black person in America donated fifty to a hundred just one time to an African American fund or central bank, it would total two hundred and four billion.

213

"If this was done monthly, for one year, it would generate twenty to twenty-eight billion dollars in capital! Likewise, if every black person in American gave a one-time donation of a thousand to this same fund, it would equal forty billion dollars. We all know forty billion dollars in donated black money could create black businesses, open black grocery store chains, black community banks, black schools as well as black housing developments, all across America in every in every urban major city that blacks reside.

"This would easily jumpstart us to black independence and ownership in America, causing a major difference in the future of our people. My brothers, the only thing stopping us is us. What's holding us is trust, fear and unity. Only when we overcome this, will we be able to advance as a people. It's a corrupt, vicious, hypocritical system that has castrated the minds of our black men, and the only way we can get back at it…is to strike it with unity, education, dedication and determination.

"Look around you, the person next to you has the same skin, same hair as you. we are brothers. Together, we are stronger. Put the Glocks down. Tap into your minds for ideas to gain wealth, health and happiness. We are a special group of people…And to stand still is to die. Thank you." Yayo concluded his speech and the crowd of convicts went crazy as the gym erupted in applause and whistles.

Kewann looked at Yayo and winked, knowing he had just captured the minds and heartless hearts of the men who had heard his words. Yayo wiped the bead of sweat from his brow, knowing he was getting closer and closer to accomplishing his mission. It would continue to be an uphill battle, but he was racing up the mountain at a tremendous speed in attempt to save his race. As long as he continued to drop knowledge and awaken his people from the dead of poverty misery and violence, his righteous journey would be worth the work he is committed to put in.

While Yayo and the Save Our Youth Campaign was at the Cook County Jail captivating the minds of the lost, Quavon was in midday traffic patrolling through different areas of the city, picking up money from his lieutenants off his drug blocks. Three nights prior, he had found out about the killings on Wolcott and heard from an inside source within the Chicago Police Department that feds were investigating the shooting and had locked up a few of the foot soldiers.

Knowing that the feds were out and about, Quavon made the decision to make his exit. He had already paid Castilino for the last bricks he owed for, now he was just making rounds picking up the last of his bread he had tied in the streets. Quavon told Crusha and Reggie G to do the same. He had purchased a ticket at O'Hare Airport and his flight to California was scheduled to leave in two days.

Quavon was going to go to Cali and get up with Rio, who had a personal real-estate agent on hand and had some beachfront property in the Venice Beach area. Once Quavon got the property, he was going to send for his men. Quavon made his way down Stony Island. He was in his cocaine white Bentley truck with the matching twenty-six-inch Forgiatos. He was on his way to Curt's Chicken spot on 86th and Cottage Grove to meet up with one of his lieutenants, who was going to give him three hundred and sixty thousand dollars of dope money.

He had been riding around the city for almost five hours and had collected close to three quarters of a million, and still had two more spots to drop by. Quavon turned the music up and let Jeezy's "Thug Motivation" pound from the subwoofers as he stopped at a red light on 87th and Stony Island…not noticing the tinted Jeep Trackhawk SRT two cars behind him.

"On my kids, Moe…ain't no way that's Quavon in that Bentley truck," Nardo said, shocked to see Quavon Bentley truck in traffic.

Duck Moe squinted his eyes, trying to get a clearer view of the vehicle. "On stone, that's buddy," Duck Moe retorted, his heart starting to beat fast. Nardo and Duck Moe was from 51st and Troop from the notorious MoeTown and was now a part of the Homicide crew.

"I'm about to follow this nigga."

"Nah, fuck that. I'm about to blow his ass down right here," Nardo said, grabbing the Sig Sauer from under the armrest.

"Man…naw Moe…it's too many witnesses," Duck Moe said, trying to talk Nardo out of doing what he was about to do, as it was broad daylight on a busy street. Nardo pulled his White Sox snap-back over his eyes and hopped out the car. The light turned green as Quavon was about to pull off, not noticing the person creeping on the driver's side of the truck. The rearview mirror shook from the bass of the music. Nardo reached the driver's side window, aimed and squeezed. *Boc…* The driver's side window shattered. Quavon felt something hit his cheek. *Boc, Boc, Boc…*

The loud gunshots from the 9mm were muffled from the traffic. Quavon went into complete darkness. Letting his feet off the brakes, the Bentley truck slowly coasted across the intersection and crashed into the side of a Dunkin Donuts. Quavon's head slumped on the steering wheel. A small crowd surrounded the vehicle while Nardo hopped back in the car and Duck Moe pulled off and made a left on Stony Island. An older man called 911 after witnessing the shooting.

Ten minutes later, police and paramedics were on the scene. Quavon was taken from the demolished SUV and loaded on a stretcher and put in an ambulance. The ambulance raced off, as the paramedic in the back put an oxygen mask over Quavon's face. His pulse was almost non nonexistent, but yet it was still a pulse. "Hold on, brother…just hold on, brother. You gone make it," the paramedic coached Quavon, trying to keep his will strong, but knew that Quavon's chances of living were slim to none.

Yayo, Kewann and Doc were in the parking lot walking back to the car as Kewann and Doc were congratulating him on the insightful speech.

"You know, nephew, that was some real powerful dialogue you gave to them brothers. You shocked me with that one," Doc said, patting Yayo on the back.

"Well, when I was in the pen, me and your family used to build a lot. Everything I learned, I learned from Mr. B. I need my old head out here with us, then we can really make an impact on the community and save some lives." Yayo replied, his iPhone vibrated on the clip on his Ferragamo belt. Looking at the caller ID. he saw it was his mother and answered.

"Hey Ma, what's up? What? When? Oh my God!" Yayo stopped in mid-stride while his mother sobbed on the other line. "Ok, Ma, just calm down. Everything will be ok, Ma. Oh my God." The chilling news his mother just gave him about Quavon getting shot caused him to lose his breath and his chest to tighten.

"You alright, brother?" What's up?" Kawann asked, seeing the look on Yayo's face.

"They just shot...Quavon. He in the hospital in critical condition. I got to get to my people, fam," Yayo said, a tear escaping from his eye.

Yayo sat in the backseat with his head laid back and his eyes closed, praying to Almighty Allah...while Kewann smashed the gas to get to Mt. Sinai Hospital. Yayo was praying...Praying that Quavon would make it through this tragedy, because if he didn't...Yayo knew he would be crushed.

Chapter 25

When Yayo, Kewann and Doc got to the hospital, they walked through the hospital lobby. Yayo noticed his old comrades, Crusha and Reggie G, their eyes swollen and red from the endless tears that poured from their eyes. Crusha looked up to see Yayo walking briskly toward them. He stood and hugged Yayo, almost crushing him from his embrace.

How my brother doing, Crusha?" Yayo asked, full of emotion. Crusha stepped back and looked Yayo in his eyes.

"Not good, family. He in surgery now. He was shot in the head, Yayo. These fuck niggas shot my lil mans in the head," Crusha said through his tears. Yayo put his head down.

"Who did this, Crusha? Who shot my people?" Yayo's angry emotions were starting to rise from the surface where he buried them.

"I don't know, fam...we been beefing with the whole city...it could have been anybody. Quavon was on his way to pick up some money. He was supposed to leave for California in a couple days. We was all leaving, Yayo...it was over," Crusha said.

"What you mean y'all beefing with the whole city? I thought G.B.C. was a peaceful organization. What happened to that, Crusha? That's what it was all about when we started it."

"Fam, it's a young cat we been at odds with for a few years. He started recruiting a lot of shooters from different organizations in the city...they rebelled against their own and sided with him. His name is Omega, and he started a gang called the Homicide Crew, a clique of rebellious killers. They want nothing but to rob and kill. They robbed one of our men for some work a couple years back. We found out who it was, and you already know how Choppa get down...He stepped up and handled that Nation Business. That's why Choppa got nailed...it was retaliation from the Homicide Crew for Choppa knocking one of their main members down," Crusha informed, giving Yayo a brief run down on what ignited the beef between the Get It Boy Clique and the Homicide Crew. Yayo listened intently.

"I understand all that, fam...All I want to know is who this Omega cat is and where I can find him."

"Yayo, it's not that easy...It's like this dude is a ghost, he using all his cronies to do all the killing, while he stays behind the scene, being the puppet master...it's complicated," Reggie G was explaining when Davon burst through the doors of the hospital lobby.

"Where is Quavon? How is he? Where is my fucking brother?" Davon bombarded Yayo with questions as he walked up on him frantically. He was traumatized after hearing the news about his twin brother. Yayo could do nothing but hug his brother as he released his tears in his chest, like the dam of the river had just broke.

"He gone be alright, lil bro...just be cool, everything gone work itself out," Yayo said, holding his brother.

"Them niggas gone pay, Yayo...I swear to God...I'm a kill the nigga who did this, I promise," Davon vowed. Yayo had never heard Davon speak like this, he knew Davon was hurting. His twin brother was lying in a hospital bed in critical condition, how could he not?

Three hours later, Karen and Darrell had made it to the hospital. They had booked a flight as soon as they were notified about her son being the victim of a shooting. Making her way across the lobby, Yayo could see the pain and worry stitched across his mother's face. She walked up and put her arms around his neck and broke down. She cried in his chest without saying a word. Mere words need not be explained about how she felt. Yayo just let his mother pour out her soul. Darrell came over to where they were standing. "How is my son doing?" he asked, with almost no emotion at all. As if on cue, the doctor came out of the surgery room, his scrubs soaked in fresh blood.

"Is there anyone here who is immediate family?" he asked, looking over the faces of the saddened family who was waiting to hear the news. Karen and Darrell walked over to the doctor who was standing in the corner of the room.

"We're his mother and father," Karen said, holding on to her husband. The doctor took off his glasses slowly, hating to have to speak the words he was about to speak.

"Ma'am, we have done all we could do to save your son. The gunshot wounds to his head and chest were too traumatic and there was too much blood loss...I'm sorry, ma'am." Karen fell to her knees, letting her tears stain the floor.

Yayo and Davon had heard the doctor clearly and knew at that moment their lives would never be the same after losing their brother. Crusha and Reggie G put their heads down in defeat. They just knew their boss would fight and make it through, he had been through so much and accomplished a lot in his young life...Quavon had died a boss.

Karen's screams of grief only intensified the feeling of his brother's death...Yayo broke down. The way he was hurting was unexplainable. He had no words, there was nothing like the situation he was going through at this moment... He didn't know how to take the blow fate had just bestowed upon him.

Later that night, Yayo sat in his furnished basement, a fifth of Demetris gin between his legs, with only a quarter of the bottle left. This was the first time since he had been home from prison that he had gotten completely drunk, but not even the strong alcohol could numb the pain in his chest. Yayo sat in the dark basement, drowning in guilt. He blamed himself for Quavon's death, feeling if he hadn't given Quavon the game to excel in the streets, Quavon would've probably chosen a different path and would be alive today, instead of in the morgue.

His tears flowed endlessly while his family was upstairs grieving over Quavon. The basement light came on, Yayo looked over to the steps, only to see Shamira's little legs descending down the basement steps. Shamira walked over to her father and stood there for a moment, before she grabbed the bottle of gin and sat it on the table. She climbed up on her father's lap and wrapped her arms around his neck.

"It's going to be okay, Daddy...Mommy said Uncle Quavon is in heaven with the angels and that he is going to look over us forever." Yayo looked in his daughter's beautiful brown eyes...amazed at how strong she was being for him, which only made him cry harder as he hugged her.

"Shamira, let me talk to Daddy, okay?" Shakira said...Neither Yayo or Shamira noticed that she had come downstairs and was standing behind them.

"I love you, Daddy...Everything will be alright," she said, then kissed her father on the cheek before going back upstairs, leaving her parents some privacy. Shakira came over and took a seat next to her king. She was displeased to see Yayo drunk but had empathy, as she knew what was going through his mind. She scooted her body close to his and softly guided his head to her chest, his tears wetting the front of her shirt. Shakira placed soft kisses over his bald head.

"Let it all out, baby...it's okay."

"As Allah as my witness...I'm a kill all of them, Shakira...All of them," Yayo slurred.

"No, baby...You have been through too much. You been doing so good...how can you preach one thing and do something else? No Yaton, you have to stay on the righteous path. This is Satan trying to test you, baby, be strong. Please, Yaton, it would kill this family if something happened to you." Yayo looked Shakira in her eyes. He shook his head.

"No, they have to die, I'm going to bury them like I have to bury my brother...they have to and will die," Yayo vowed. His murderous dialogue plus his bloodshot eyes caused Shakira to stiffen. Yayo looked like the devil as he spoke. She had to do something to get him out of this evil mood he was in before he did something crazy.

Shakira straddled his lap and put her warm tongue in his ear while she grinded on his dick. She then started to kiss him, she could feel him getting hard under her and slid off his lap, unbuckling his belt and pulled his pants and boxers down to his ankles. His ten inches stood like the Eiffel Tower. Shakira pulled her Polo sweats and thong off and got back on Yayo's lap...using her hand she guided his meat to her hot honey box, lowering herself on him. She could feel all of him in her stomach as she slowly rocked back and forth. Yayo gripped her ass cheeks, spreading them as he pushed upward in her.

"Baby, your family needs you. You are everything to us…I want you…Baby, we are getting married in two months…our future, Yaton…we are going to have more babies. She came all over his dick, and two humps and a pump later, Yayo exploded in four strong spurts inside of her. Shakira stayed sitting on his lap until he softened.

They cried and held each other for the rest of the night until they fell asleep in each other's arms. Today was a violent sad day. Quavon had lost his life to the streets of Chicago. Yayo was told a long time ago, "Yayo, never love the game…Because this game will never love you back."

Chapter 26

Yayo sat in the front row with his family and friends at Gatlings Funeral home. This was the fourth time he had been at Gatlings…when Shakira's mother Joyce was murdered, then Shakira's brother TJ when he was killed. Choppa a week ago and now his own flesh and blood…his brother, Quavon. Karen sat next to him, her Prada shades covering her swollen eyes, she had cried her last tear and now just sat in a daze listening to the preacher preach. His words fell on deaf ears.

Doc, Musane, Kewann and Muhamad stood in each corner of the funeral home on security dressed in all-black, dark shades over their eyes and semi-autos concealed under their suit jackets. Yayo had told them about the shooting at Choppa's funeral and that his mother and family was there, so safety precautions needed to be taken. The Save Our Youth Campaign was a peaceful movement, but all of them were from the streets, and knew the dangers the streets could bring.

They loved Yayo as he was their brother, so the pistols were there to protect him and his family. Shakira sat on Yayo's left side, with Shamira on his lap. Davon sat in the same row. For the past few days, Yayo had been quiet and distant from her, she couldn't read his emotions as she normally could. Which was starting to worry her. She knew he was hurting bad, she just prayed that Yayo wouldn't do nothing that would jeopardize his freedom or his life.

Crusha also attended the funeral, the loss of Quavon had impacted him greatly. He was lost. Revenge, regret, guilt and resentment filled his heart to its capacity. He regretted not getting Quavon to leave the game sooner. They had enough money to leave the game years ago. Crusha was the oldest of the G.B.C. Quavon looked up to him, Crusha felt he should've guided Quavon in the right direction, all he had to do was let his voice be heard.

The guilt he felt was the guilt of letting the money blind him, instead of moving with integrity and dignity. He should've given Quavon a boss mind frame instead of a gangsta's mind frame. He knew that all gangsters ended up in either the penitentiary or the graveyard. The revenge Crusha held in his heart for the opps was strong...He wanted blood.

Reggie G stood on the side of his Cadillac Escalade in the funeral home parking lot. He took a strong pull from the Backwood and let the smoke fill his lungs. Quavon was his boss...his brother, as well as his best friend. There was no way he could go in there and see Quavon laid in a casket. His grief and love for Quavon was so strong that he had even contemplated putting the Glock to his own head and blowing his brains out, so he could go with Quavon on his journey. Whether it be heaven and the golden gates...or the depths of hell, he just wanted to be with his mans.

Reggie G looked up at the gray cloudy sky...a lightning bolt traced across the sky, giving the sky an evil look, as the warm raindrops began to pour down over the venomous city of Chicago, washing the blood off the streets...the blood of young black men like Quavon, who lived their lives chasing the all-mighty dollar and living by the street code of respect me or die!

Inside the funeral home, the preacher finished his sermon, and the family and friends were able to view the body and see Quavon Anderson for the last and final time. Karen walked up to the casket only to see her son looking peaceful in an all-white Brunello Cucinelli lightweight Solaro suit, white Ferragamo square toe shoes adorned his feet, while his three-sixty waves seem to look like the waves in the Pacific Ocean. The mortician did a remarkable job with his gunshot wound to the head, making it look non-existent. The two, 1-carat diamonds resembled small glaciers, while his favorite watch, a two-hundred-and-fifty-thousand-dollar, diamond studded Richard Milli surrounded his left wrist. The watch was a gift to himself after he sold all of the three hundred thousand bricks of heroin that he robbed and killed Top Cat for. The watch was a symbol of status in the game and the ambition he had to attain it. Quavon looked how he lived, like the Don.

Karen tried her best to hold her composure while she stared down at her deceased son but couldn't...she broke down. Darrell had to pull her away from Quavon's casket as she screamed, "Wake up, baby...Wake up for your mama." He took her out of the funeral home, her heart was shattered, knowing her son would never open his eyes again.

"Quavon, why you always gotta be so damn clean? I know you gone have all the girls in heaven, just make sure you save some for me. I love you, bro…You my other half, and know I'm not going to rest until I get the one who caused this, I promise," Davon vowed, a tear running down his cheek. He bent down and kissed his twin brother's cheek before walking off, revenge evident in his heart.

Yayo stood over his brother's body staring at the savage he wished he didn't create. No more tears needed to be shed, the pool of tears had been drained and replaced with an insatiable thirst of retaliation and relentless revenge. Yayo had made Mr. B a promise. As a man, he had given him his word, as his word was his bond. But the circumstances had changed, and now his own flesh and blood was lying in a casket, about to be buried six feet deep in a cemetery. Justice had to be handed down and swiftly.

Yayo stared at his brother for the last time. "See you when I get there, Quavon," was all he said before he left out the funeral home.

Once Yayo made his way out, he was approached by four men who were all dressed in blood red suits. Yayo had noticed them inside the church but paid them no mind. He just figured Quavon knew them somehow and they came to pay their respects.

"Excuse me, Blood…You Yayo, Quavon's big brother?" the individual asked, walking up on Yayo with his men. Kewann walked up and stood next to Yayo, his hands inside his suit jacket on the handle of his 10mm.

Yeah, brother. That's my people, what's up, Ock?" The man extended his hand.

"My name Suge…I'm from Memphis, Blood Gang. I worked for Quavon. My condolences to you and your family…and murder to the niggas that did this."

"I appreciate that, fam," Yayo said, shaking Suge's hand.

"Listen Blood, I did good business with Q and the G.B.C. and my loyalty will remain with the squad. Put my number in your phone and when y'all ready to soak these streets, don't hesitate to get at me…Just know you got shooters in Memphis that's gone come at your beck and call. Again, my condolences." Suge gave Yayo his number and social media hook up before him and his Blood homies left.

It made Yayo slightly proud that his brother had genuine love from hustlers all over the U.S., as he'd always taught him the importance of networking.

The rain continued to pour down over the city while Quavon's casket was lowered six feet deep at the Burr Oaks Cemetery. Once the casket was lowered, everyone began to leave…leaving in tears, guilt and grief. The streets had lost the face of the Chicago underworld and there would be no one to ever exceed Quavon's street intellect and his passion for the game. He had set the bar and he died a hood legend.

Yayo was the last to leave. He grabbed the shovel and started putting dirt on his brother's casket. One thing he was certain of, Quavon wouldn't be the only one getting buried. He thought the demon that once succumbed him was nonexistent, but his thoughts were wrong…that demon had now resurfaced full force and as he threw dirt over his brother's casket, Yayo welcomed that savage demon back into his life.

Omega was at the Congress Hotel in downtown Chicago, his suite was on the 15th floor. He was high as a kite. A half a kilo of cocaine on a glass table sat in front of him. Automatic weapons were all across the room, the coke had him paranoid. He grabbed the rolled-up hundred-dollar bill and sniffed from the half brick of raw. Quavon's murder was all over the internet.

Two of the Stones Omega had put down from Moe-Town had took responsibility for the killing, which he had rewarded them for with fifty G's a piece and two bricks of soft. Omega had run through the G.B.C. with ease as he had set out to do. He had loyal killers on his team now and the Homicide Crew's name was starting to ring bells. The money was flowing. Omega knew that if he stayed getting money in Chicago, he would eventually die in Chicago or worse, get life in prison.

It was now time to start planning to leave the city. He knew Ace and K.I. was smiling down at him for taking care of that business and making sure all of their opps was dead. Now that his enemies were dead and gone, it was now about longevity. Omega had a cousin named Clip, who was a shot gun Crip from Minnesota but had moved to Miami. He had found through family that Clip was in Miami doing his things, plugged in with some Haitians on the work and having it his way in Florida. Omega figured he would holler at Clip and get a number on the birds, cop and make one more move in the Chi then bounce, where he would move to the south and live like a boss.

Omega's thoughts were interrupted when his cellphone vibrated on the glass table, looking at the caller ID. he saw the number was restricted. He sent the caller to voicemail and sat the phone down on the table as he didn't like answering private calls. He was about to take another sniff from the powder when the phone vibrated again. His curiosity got the best of him.

"Hello," he steered into the phone.

You have a collect call from ...Marcus, from the Stateville Correctional Facility. to accept this call press five, to refuse this call press seven, to block this call press nine. Omega looked at the phone confused. He hadn't heard from Marcus in over two years. *What the fuck this nigga want*? Omega thought. He pressed five. This call will be subject to monitoring."

"Hello?" Omega answered after the automated recorder ended.

"What's up?"

"Fuck you mean, what's up, nigga? You called me...And how you get my number anyway?" Omega asked nonchalantly.

"Fuck how I got your number...damn homie, it's like that? I been hearing in the inside how you out there flexing...I stuck to the G-Code and niggas gone just let me sit up in here to rot. Fuck me, huh?" Marcus fumed. He was doing a fifty-year sentence for a body he caught with his crew and still had to go to Tennessee to face the music for the gun store episode.

"Man, fam, come on with the bullshit. You only did what you was supposed to do. What you want, a hero cookie or some shit, for playing by the rules? I would have did the same shit...this shit come with the game, should have did your homework before you signed up," Omega said, being heartless as he sniffed another line of cocaine from the half brick.

"You know what, Omega, fuck you…You bitch ass nigga! You and Goon, y'all some hoe niggas…I'm a see you when I see you!" Marcus spat.

"When, in a hundred years? Get your stupid ass of here and go find something to do with your time, pussy," Omega said, then pressed "end" on his cellphone, leaving Marcus with the dial tone. He couldn't care less about Marcus, he always thought Marcus was a soft nigga anyway. He was Goon's partner and Goon was Ace's partner, they wasn't originally from 59th and Bishop like Ace and K.I. So, anybody outside of 59th was expendable.

It was Marcus's own fault he got booked. Had he not thrown up on the scene of the crime like a bitch, or got caught with a hammer used in a homicide, he wouldn't be in the predicament he was in. "Fuck Marcus," Omega said out loud and continued to fill his nose with coke. Tomorrow, he was going to get Clip's number to see what it was looking like in Miami. He had a vision and if everything worked out, it would flourish into something great.

Marcus slammed the receiver down on the pay phone on the wall inside the day room. Everybody looked in his direction. "Fuck y'all looking at?" Marcus said through clenched teeth, with his hand inside his khaki pants, clutching his shank. Marcus was heated from the conversation he just had with Omega and was ready to hurt somebody. The inmates continued to play dominoes, spades, watch TV or whatever they were doing. Everybody knew Marcus was a bug and was with the violence. He had already been to solitary confinement twice for stabbing, in one of those incidents an inmate had lost his eye. To say Marcus was feared in Stateville would be an understatement. Marcus walked back to his cell fuming. His celly was on the top bunk reading an urban novel called *Addicted to the Drama* by an author named Jamilla when he came in.

"This hoe ass nigga think shit sweet. On Rick grave if I ever get out this bitch, I'm a smash his ass. That's on me," Marcus said, flopping down on his bunk.

"What that nigga say, scud?" Tick said, putting the urban novel down and sitting up. Tick was from the south side of Chicago and fresh in on a twenty-five-year sentence for attempted murder. He was the one who told Marcus how Omega was out there moving and had shit on lock. He had even got Marcus Omega cellphone number from his cousin, Duck Moe. Marcus and Tick were cool, to say the least.

"Naw, this nigga just woofing…Basically said fuck me, dude a straight clown."

"That's messed up, fam…niggas like that all cap, them the type of cats don't even deserve to be on the streets. Straight up. Aye Marcus, didn't you say them people was gone knock your time down if you gave up your co-defendants?"

"Yeah, why?" Marcus asked, throwed off by the question he was just asked.

"I'm just saying, my nigga, it's apparent that dude don't fuck with you like you think he do, so why should your loyalty lie with him? Fuck that nigga, you got to think about you and your situation. Otherwise, you gone die in this bitch, straight up." What Tick had just suggested had just put a bad taste in Marcus's mouth and he now looked at Tick different. But at the same time, Omega didn't give a fuck about him…and he knew that was fact from the conversation he had with him on the phone. Marcus didn't want to die in prison, and the wheels in his mind began to spin.

Before he got sentenced, the district attorney was willing to lower his time if he gave up his co-defendants. They knew it was more people involved in the crimes and if they didn't get a conviction, then that meant the killers would still be on the streets terrorizing and doing what they do best…murder.

Tick had told Marcus his people said Omega was out there getting plenty of money and letting his hammer bang, which meant it was some bodies lying around the city with nobody incarcerated for them. If things was going to play out right, he had to get Tick to get his people on board to bring Omega a move that would be federal.

"You know what? Tick you might be on to something. Your cousin still fuck with that goofy?"

"I'm quite sure. Cuzzo just copped a Maserati on sixes, he getting money with dude and them," Tick replied.

"Alright this the business, this what I need you to do." Marcus and Tick sat up all night scheming and plotting on ways that they could come up on a get out of jail free card. In the end, Omega would regret not keeping it a hundred with the gang!

Chapter 27

Yayo pulled into the parking lot of the Glass House, a small bar on 79th and Halstead. He had called Crusha and said he wanted to meet with him and Reggie G, ASAP. Crusha told Yayo to meet him at the bar, which was owned by the Get It Boy Clique. Yayo had Musane, Doc and Muhamad follow him, while Kewann rode with him in the QX50.

After parking in the empty parking lot, Yayo sat and waited for Crusha and Reggie G. It was 3:00 in the morning, so the bar was closed. At 3:15, Crusha's S-class Benz pulled into the lot and parked next to Yayo's SUV. Yayo turned the ignition off and he and Kewann got out. Doc, Musane, and Muhamad followed suit and got out the Cadillac CT6.

Crusha and Reggie G got out, dressed in the color of their mood...black.

"What's the bizness, big homie?" Crusha said, walking up shaking hands with Yayo.

"Same ol shit, just wanted to speak with y'all face-to-face on some Nation Business." Crusha smiled wickedly, hearing Yayo say Nation Business gave him hopes that Yayo was about to jump back down.

"You know, Yayo...The Nation is the family...I see you brought company," Crusha said, nodding his head to The Save Our Youth Campaign workers.

"My fault, Ock, let me introduce y'all. This Kewann, Doc, Musane, and Muhamad and from this point on, they are family. And y'all, these my G.B.C. brothers, this Crusha and that's Reggie G."

"What's good?" Reggie G said, leaning up against the Benz.

"Now that we all acquainted, let's slide up in here," Crusha said and led them to a door on the side of the bar where he used the key to gain entry. Once inside, Crusha turned on the lights, went behind the bar and grabbed two bottles of Rémy Martin 1738 and some glasses. The men took a seat while Yayo remained standing. Crusha began to pour glasses of Rémy.

"This the business, my beloved ones. I just buried my little brother. My mother is grieving...my whole family is grieving. The brother that caused this must be properly dealt with...period. Whoever this Omega is, must die," Yayo said, walking around the table, the only thing in his mind was his brother laying in a casket.

"Yayo, like I told you. We would be at war with the entire city of Chicago. It's a lot of niggas siding with this nigga...he feeding them, fam," Reggie G said taking one of the glasses of Rémy from the table and downing it.

"Whoever sides with Omega will perish with him, that I'm standing on. It's not about numbers, Reggie, it's all about the mind-frame," Crusha intervened.

"Brother, a lot has changed since you have been gone. Money is the ruler of all evil. Money wins wars. Quavon was the one with the plugs, he just made sure our bellies were full. we need a steady flow of currency if we want ever a chance to war with these cats."

"Crusha, you not sounding familiar, all we need is our hearts. It's about having the beast ambition of a lion...these dudes are a bunch of hyenas looking for prey. We will tap into a cash flow."

"We can go holler at Castilino. He was the plug, but Quavon severed ties with him. But I'm sure we can holler at him. I got the line, fam," Reggie G said.

"No, fam...we will do this without poisoning the community. It's bad enough blood has to be shed. But Allah will forgive us for what we are about to do. What about guns...what does the armory look like?"

"Choppa was head of all that. We have some designated shooters that was under Choppa. They are the elite. We calling the Blackout Squad, they know more about the hammers than we do."

"Get them on it. We need arms immediately."

"I got a plug on guns in Seattle, we just gone have to make a trip, but it's official. MAC-90s AKs, ARs, vests, grenades, whatever our money can touch," Musane said, speaking up for the first time.

"Make it happen, Ock."

"Say no more," Musane retorted. The men continued to plot and strategize. It had been a major turn of events. Yayo and the Save Our Youth Campaign was out promoting positive change, and how to live a pro social lifestyle, but Quavon's death had reconstructed Yayo's thinking.

He was no longer that same person, he was now the Yayo that commanded the G.B.C. into a position of power. He was not the Yayo that was indicted into the feds and accepted his life sentence like a boss. He was now Yayo, Chief of the Get It Boy Clique and the love that Kewann, Musane, Doc and Muhamad had for him, made them want to ride shotgun with him on his journey of revenge and they were now Yayo's subordinates.

Two hours later and a bottle of 1738, the men left out the doors of the Glass House. It was 5:00 in the morning and the morning traffic was buzzing. Walking in the parking lot, they noticed a hooded person sitting on Crusha's Benz. Musane sensed danger and pulled his .45 and pointed at the hooded man. The man looked up and pulled the Marc Jella hoodie off his head.

"Wait, hold up...don't shoot!" Yayo said, grabbing Musane's arm after seeing his brother Davon.

"Davon, what are you doing here?" Yayo asked, staring at Davon's bloodshot eyes.

"I know y'all about to get those dudes back for killing our brother...I want in."

To Be Continued...
YAYO 5
Coming Soon

Submission Guideline

Submit the first three chapters of your completed manuscript to ldpsubmissions@gmail.com, subject line: Your book's title. The manuscript must be in a .doc file and sent as an attachment. Document should be in Times New Roman, double spaced and in size 12 font. Also, provide your synopsis and full contact information. If sending multiple submissions, they must each be in a separate email.

Have a story but no way to send it electronically? You can still submit to LDP/Ca$h Presents. Send in the first three chapters, written or typed, of your completed manuscript to:

LDP: Submissions Dept
Po Box 944
Stockbridge, Ga 30281

DO NOT send original manuscript. Must be a duplicate.

Provide your synopsis and a cover letter containing your full contact information.

Thanks for considering LDP and Ca$h Presents.

Coming Soon from Lock Down Publications/Ca$h Presents

BOW DOWN TO MY GANGSTA

By **Ca$h**

TORN BETWEEN TWO

By **Coffee**

THE STREETS STAINED MY SOUL **II**

By **Marcellus Allen**

BLOOD OF A BOSS **VI**

SHADOWS OF THE GAME II

By **Askari**

LOYAL TO THE GAME **IV**

By **T.J. & Jelissa**

IF LOVING YOU IS WRONG… **III**

By **Jelissa**

TRUE SAVAGE **VIII**

MIDNIGHT CARTEL III

DOPE BOY MAGIC IV

CITY OF KINGZ II

By **Chris Green**

BLAST FOR ME **III**

A SAVAGE DOPEBOY III

CUTTHROAT MAFIA III

DUFFLE BAG CARTEL VI

By **Ghost**

A HUSTLER'S DECEIT III

KILL ZONE **II**

BAE BELONGS TO ME III

A DOPE BOY'S QUEEN III

By **Aryanna**

S. ALLEN

COKE KINGS V

KING OF THE TRAP II

By **T.J. Edwards**

GORILLAZ IN THE BAY V

3X KRAZY II

De'Kari

THE STREETS ARE CALLING II

Duquie Wilson

KINGPIN KILLAZ IV

STREET KINGS III

PAID IN BLOOD III

CARTEL KILLAZ IV

DOPE GODS III

Hood Rich

SINS OF A HUSTLA II

ASAD

KINGZ OF THE GAME VI

Playa Ray

SLAUGHTER GANG IV

RUTHLESS HEART IV

By Willie Slaughter

THE HEART OF A SAVAGE III

By Jibril Williams

FUK SHYT II

By Blakk Diamond

TRAP QUEEN

By Troublesome

YAYO V

GHOST MOB

Stilloan Robinson

238

YAYO 4

KINGPIN DREAMS III
By Paper Boi Rari
CREAM II
By Yolanda Moore
SON OF A DOPE FIEND III
By Renta
FOREVER GANGSTA II
GLOCKS ON SATIN SHEETS III
By Adrian Dulan
LOYALTY AIN'T PROMISED III
By Keith Williams
THE PRICE YOU PAY FOR LOVE II
By Destiny Skai
CONFESSIONS OF A GANGSTA III
By Nicholas Lock
I'M NOTHING WITHOUT HIS LOVE II
SINS OF A THUG II
By Monet Dragun
LIFE OF A SAVAGE IV
MURDA SEASON IV
GANGLAND CARTEL III
CHI'RAQ GANGSTAS II
By **Romell Tukes**
QUIET MONEY IV
THUG LIFE II
EXTENDED CLIP II
By **Trai'Quan**
THE STREETS MADE ME III
By **Larry D. Wright**
IF YOU CROSS ME ONCE II

239

S. ALLEN

ANGEL III
By **Anthony Fields**
FRIEND OR FOE III
By **Mimi**
SAVAGE STORMS II
By **Meesha**
BLOOD ON THE MONEY III
By J-Blunt
THE STREETS WILL NEVER CLOSE II
By K'ajji
NIGHTMARES OF A HUSTLA III
By King Dream
THE WIFEY I USED TO BE II
By Nicole Goosby
IN THE ARM OF HIS BOSS
By Jamila
MONEY, MURDER & MEMORIES II
Malik D. Rice
CONCRETE KILLAZ II
By Kingpen

Available Now

RESTRAINING ORDER **I & II**
By **CA$H & Coffee**
LOVE KNOWS NO BOUNDARIES **I II & III**
By **Coffee**
RAISED AS A GOON I, II, III & IV
BRED BY THE SLUMS I, II, III

240

YAYO 4

BLAST FOR ME I & II

ROTTEN TO THE CORE I II III

A BRONX TALE I, II, III

DUFFLE BAG CARTEL I II III IV V

HEARTLESS GOON I II III IV

A SAVAGE DOPEBOY I II

HEARTLESS GOON I II III

DRUG LORDS I II III

CUTTHROAT MAFIA I II

By **Ghost**

LAY IT DOWN **I & II**

LAST OF A DYING BREED

BLOOD STAINS OF A SHOTTA I & II III

By **Jamaica**

LOYAL TO THE GAME I II III

LIFE OF SIN I, II III

By **TJ & Jelissa**

BLOODY COMMAS I & II

SKI MASK CARTEL I II & III

KING OF NEW YORK I II,III IV V

RISE TO POWER I II III

COKE KINGS I II III IV

BORN HEARTLESS I II III IV

KING OF THE TRAP

By **T.J. Edwards**

IF LOVING HIM IS WRONG…I & II

LOVE ME EVEN WHEN IT HURTS I II III

By **Jelissa**

WHEN THE STREETS CLAP BACK I & II III

THE HEART OF A SAVAGE I II

S. ALLEN

By **Jibril Williams**

A DISTINGUISHED THUG STOLE MY HEART I II & III

LOVE SHOULDN'T HURT I II III IV

RENEGADE BOYS I II III IV

PAID IN KARMA I II III

SAVAGE STORMS

By **Meesha**

A GANGSTER'S CODE I &, II III

A GANGSTER'S SYN I II III

THE SAVAGE LIFE I II III

CHAINED TO THE STREETS I II III

BLOOD ON THE MONEY I II

By **J-Blunt**

PUSH IT TO THE LIMIT

By **Bre' Hayes**

BLOOD OF A BOSS **I, II, III, IV, V**

SHADOWS OF THE GAME

By **Askari**

THE STREETS BLEED MURDER **I, II & III**

THE HEART OF A GANGSTA I II& III

By **Jerry Jackson**

CUM FOR ME I II III IV V VI

An **LDP Erotica Collaboration**

BRIDE OF A HUSTLA **I II & II**

THE FETTI GIRLS **I, II& III**

CORRUPTED BY A GANGSTA I, II III, IV

BLINDED BY HIS LOVE

THE PRICE YOU PAY FOR LOVE

DOPE GIRL MAGIC I II III

By **Destiny Skai**

242

YAYO 4

WHEN A GOOD GIRL GOES BAD
By **Adrienne**
THE COST OF LOYALTY I II III
By Kweli
A GANGSTER'S REVENGE **I II III & IV**
THE BOSS MAN'S DAUGHTERS I II III IV V
A SAVAGE LOVE **I & II**
BAE BELONGS TO ME I II
A HUSTLER'S DECEIT I, II, III
WHAT BAD BITCHES DO I, II, III
SOUL OF A MONSTER I II III
KILL ZONE
A DOPE BOY'S QUEEN I II
By **Aryanna**
A KINGPIN'S AMBITON
A KINGPIN'S AMBITION **II**
I MURDER FOR THE DOUGH
By **Ambitious**
TRUE SAVAGE I II III IV V VI VII
DOPE BOY MAGIC I, II, III
MIDNIGHT CARTEL I II
CITY OF KINGZ
By **Chris Green**
A DOPEBOY'S PRAYER
By **Eddie "Wolf" Lee**
THE KING CARTEL **I, II & III**
By **Frank Gresham**
THESE NIGGAS AIN'T LOYAL **I, II & III**
By **Nikki Tee**
GANGSTA SHYT **I II &III**

By **CATO**

THE ULTIMATE BETRAYAL

By **Phoenix**

BOSS'N UP **I , II & III**

By **Royal Nicole**

I LOVE YOU TO DEATH

By Destiny J

I RIDE FOR MY HITTA

I STILL RIDE FOR MY HITTA

By **Misty Holt**

LOVE & CHASIN' PAPER

By **Qay Crockett**

TO DIE IN VAIN

SINS OF A HUSTLA

By **ASAD**

BROOKLYN HUSTLAZ

By **Boogsy Morina**

BROOKLYN ON LOCK I & II

By **Sonovia**

GANGSTA CITY

By **Teddy Duke**

A DRUG KING AND HIS DIAMOND I & II III

A DOPEMAN'S RICHES

HER MAN, MINE'S TOO I, II

CASH MONEY HO'S

THE WIFEY I USED TO BE

By Nicole Goosby

TRAPHOUSE KING **I II & III**

KINGPIN KILLAZ I II III

STREET KINGS I II

YAYO 4

PAID IN BLOOD **I II**
CARTEL KILLAZ I II III
DOPE GODS I II
By **Hood Rich**
LIPSTICK KILLAH **I, II, III**
CRIME OF PASSION I II & III
FRIEND OR FOE I II
By **Mimi**
STEADY MOBBN' **I, II, III**
THE STREETS STAINED MY SOUL
By **Marcellus Allen**
WHO SHOT YA **I, II, III**
SON OF A DOPE FIEND I II
Renta
GORILLAZ IN THE BAY **I II III IV**
TEARS OF A GANGSTA I II
3X KRAZY
DE'KARI
TRIGGADALE I II III
Elijah R. Freeman
GOD BLESS THE TRAPPERS I, II, III
THESE SCANDALOUS STREETS I, II, III
FEAR MY GANGSTA I, II, III IV, V
THESE STREETS DON'T LOVE NOBODY I, II
BURY ME A G I, II, III, IV, V
A GANGSTA'S EMPIRE I, II, III, IV
THE DOPEMAN'S BODYGAURD I II
THE REALEST KILLAZ I II III
Tranay Adams
THE STREETS ARE CALLING

S. ALLEN

Duquie Wilson
MARRIED TO A BOSS… I II III
By Destiny Skai & Chris Green
KINGZ OF THE GAME I II III IV V
Playa Ray
SLAUGHTER GANG I II III
RUTHLESS HEART I II III
By Willie Slaughter
FUK SHYT
By Blakk Diamond
DON'T F#CK WITH MY HEART I II
By Linnea
ADDICTED TO THE DRAMA I II III
IN THE ARM OF HIS BOSS II
By Jamila
YAYO I II III IV
A SHOOTER'S AMBITION I II
By S. Allen
TRAP GOD I II III
By Troublesome
FOREVER GANGSTA
GLOCKS ON SATIN SHEETS I II
By Adrian Dulan
TOE TAGZ I II III
By Ah'Million
KINGPIN DREAMS I II
By Paper Boi Rari
CONFESSIONS OF A GANGSTA I II
By Nicholas Lock
I'M NOTHING WITHOUT HIS LOVE

YAYO 4

SINS OF A THUG
By Monet Dragun
CAUGHT UP IN THE LIFE I II III
By Robert Baptiste
NEW TO MONEY, MURDER & MEMORIES
THE GAME I II III
By **Malik D. Rice**
LIFE OF A SAVAGE I II III
A GANGSTA'S QUR'AN I II III
MURDA SEASON I II III
GANGLAND CARTEL I II
CHI'RAQ GANGSTAS
By **Romell Tukes**
LOYALTY AIN'T PROMISED I II
By Keith Williams
QUIET MONEY I II III
THUG LIFE
EXTENDED CLIP
By **Trai'Quan**
THE STREETS MADE ME I II
By **Larry D. Wright**
THE ULTIMATE SACRIFICE I, II, III, IV, V, VI
KHADIFI
IF YOU CROSS ME ONCE
ANGEL I II
By **Anthony Fields**
THE LIFE OF A HOOD STAR
By Ca$h & Rashia Wilson
THE STREETS WILL NEVER CLOSE
By K'ajji

S. ALLEN

CREAM
By Yolanda Moore
NIGHTMARES OF A HUSTLA I II
By King Dream
CONCRETE KILLAZ
By Kingpen

BOOKS BY LDP'S CEO, CA$H

TRUST IN NO MAN

TRUST IN NO MAN 2

TRUST IN NO MAN 3

BONDED BY BLOOD

SHORTY GOT A THUG

THUGS CRY

THUGS CRY 2

THUGS CRY 3

TRUST NO BITCH

TRUST NO BITCH 2

TRUST NO BITCH 3

TIL MY CASKET DROPS

RESTRAINING ORDER

RESTRAINING ORDER 2

IN LOVE WITH A CONVICT

LIFE OF A HOOD STAR

S. ALLEN